PRAISE FOR
AUDREY CARLAN

"FIVE STAR REVIEW! I recommend this book to anyone looking for a sweet, fierce love story. It takes a lot to write an original story that takes twists and turns you won't see coming."

~Abibliophobia Anonymous Book Reviews Blog

"Damn Audrey did it again! Made me smile, made me laugh & made me cry with her beautiful words! I am in love with these books."

~Hooks & Books Book Blog

"A sensual spiritual journey of two people meant for each other, heart and soul. Well-crafted and beautifully written."

~Carly Phillips, New York Times Bestselling Author

Divine Desire

A LOTUS HOUSE NOVEL: BOOK THREE

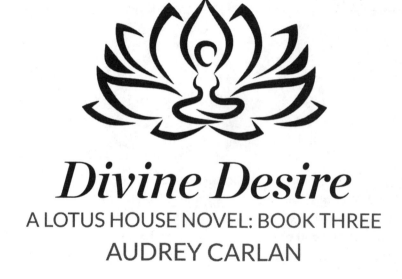

Divine Desire

A LOTUS HOUSE NOVEL: BOOK THREE

AUDREY CARLAN

WATERHOUSE PRESS

DEDICATION

To my sister Michele Moulyn.

*If there is anyone in this world
who knows the value of striving to achieve,
determination, and sacrificing
for those you love...it's you.
You've set an amazing example
of what it means to work hard.*

With gratitude and love, this one is for you.

NOTE TO THE READER

Everything in the Lotus House series has been gleaned from years of personal practice and the study of yoga. The yoga positions and chakra teachings were part of my official schooling with The Art of Yoga through Village Yoga Center in Northern California. Every chakra fact and position description has been personally written by me and comes from my perspective as a Registered Yoga Teacher following the guidelines set forth by the National Yoga Alliance and the Art of Yoga. The Tantric references are my personal understanding of the teachings through hours of research.

If you want to attempt any of the positions within this book or as detailed in any of the Lotus House novels, please consult a Registered Yoga Teacher.

I suggest everyone take a yoga class. Through my yoga schooling and teaching the gift of yoga to my students, I have learned that yoga is for everybody and every body. Be kind to yours, for you only get one in this lifetime.

Love and light,

Audrey

CHAPTER ONE

SOLAR PLEXUS
C H A K R A

The official Sanskrit name for the third chakra, or the solar plexus chakra, is called Manipura. It is located in the area of the abdomen and digestive system. Strengthening our body's energy balance, the third chakra centers our vitality and health.

M I L A

"Mila, my God, it's incredible!" Moe gasped and hovered one delicate hand over her full lips. "Lily will love it. Thank you for doing this."

I rolled my eyes. "Moe, stop thanking me. You're my best friend, and Lily is my niece by proxy. Of course Auntie Mimi is going to paint a beautiful mural on her wall. Who better?" I cocked a brow to let her know I meant business.

Moe, short for "Monet," was Chinese American and insanely beautiful. The woman was a dead ringer for Lucy Liu. She had long, black hair that cascaded down her back and trailed against the top edge of her white capri pants near her ass. She sat cross-legged on the floor and inspected my work.

A few more leaves in the far right corner and some additional work on the bridge, and my three-year-old quasi niece would have a secret garden fantasy mural covering an entire wall in her bedroom. Since Moe's nasty divorce, I'd spent more time over here than I should have, but when my best friend needed me, I made time. Besides, I knew she'd do anything for me. I'd spent years perfecting the skills to do just about anything I needed on my own. Working at Village Yoga Center as their core female Vinyasa Flow teacher paid well as long as I continued to teach ten plus classes a week. Of course, now that they'd hired that new male teacher, one who was "supposed to bring a fresh perspective" and a unique new class to the schedule, I had a bit more to ponder.

Should I start teaching at other places?
Branch out and open my own little studio?
Would that go against the goals I have set for my art?

I sighed and looked at the garden-inspired mural I'd painted on Lily's wall. I knew I was a solid artist. Better than most even, but talent wasn't what I lacked. It was time. Even my weekends were busy teaching the brunch painting class I'd coined "Monet & Mimosas" after my best friend. She thought that was clever. The side job definitely brought in the extra money I needed for art supplies and to keep the lights on in my studio apartment.

"What did La Luz Gallery in Oakland say about a showing?" Moe asked, her gaze still focused on the mural.

I took a slow breath and picked at the threads in the carpet. "They like my work. A lot actually."

She flung her hair over one shoulder and stared at me. I hated when her black eyes sparked with laser accuracy, as if she knew what I was going to say before I said it. Moe had always been intuitive. More so when it came to me.

I clucked my tongue and patted the wooden end of the paintbrush against my lips. The scent of paint was sharp enough to tingle the sensitive tissues in my nose. I sneezed into the back of my hand. "You know what they said, Moe. We've had this conversation before."

Her eyelids relaxed, covering her pupils while she glanced down and away. The gesture was enough to make me smash my lips together and consider all the reasons to avoid any more of this conversation.

"Mila. You have to set aside time to work on your art."

I groaned and flopped back onto the plush carpet. "They said I didn't have enough pieces to show. I need at least twenty-five, unless I wanted to show with another three artists. Ten a piece."

She pursed her lips. "Well, that's an option. I mean, in order to make some money, you need to sell some pieces. But I also know that's not your dream."

The weight of my "dream" felt like an anvil on my chest, crushing my sternum and pressing my rib cage into my heart. If I focused hard enough, I could imagine the subtle cracking of each bone as my dream destroyed me from the outside in.

"No, it's not. Then again, who says you have to have it all at once. Maybe dreams are meant to be something that you achieve bit by bit. Like climbing up a ladder. You can't just jump to the top. It takes effort and hard work. Right?"

Moe slouched before leaning one arm back and sliding to her side on the floor next to me. She rested her temple on her hand. "How long have we known each other, Mila?"

I rolled my eyes. "Uh, since high school. I was a freshman, you were a senior."

"So close to a decade then," she summarized.

I smiled. Moe the therapist was always so precise. I had a feeling she was going to start psychoanalyzing me the way she did her clients. Being best friends with a woman who could analyze every facet of your brain was not always ideal. Usually she kept her head shrinking to a minimum. I wasn't sure that today would be one of those days. "Moe..." I warned.

She waved her hand in front of her face. "No, no. Just hear me out."

"Okay, shoot, Dr. Holland. Bust out your psychobabble. Go ahead. Do your worst." I canted my head to the side.

Moe smirked. Oh man, was I in for a doozie.

"Seems to me that you've found any way possible to stay busy. All of which is doing things not related to creating additional paintings."

"Seriously?" I scoffed. "That's what you're going with? Moe, you know I have to work. I have a mouth to feed. Mine! And bills. Let's not forget about those pesky things that come on set days every month."

She sighed long and low. "You drive me crazy. I've invited you to move in here plenty of times. Since Kyle left..." Moe grimaced and swallowed before continuing. "Well, it's just me and Lily. You know she'd love having her Auntie Mimi around more often. And the three-car garage could work great for a painting space."

I grumbled low under my breath, "Moe, I'm not your charity case."

She sat up like a snake had sneaked under her and bitten her on the ass. "Don't you dare call yourself my charity case! You just spent three weekends in a row on your one day off painting Lily's room. I'm just asking to repay the favor."

I snorted through my laughter that time. "Yeah, right. A mural does not constitute a place to live, Moe. Maybe dinner and a movie but not a rent-free ride!"

Her lips compressed into a flat white line. Oh man, I'd pissed her off, which was not an uncommon occurrence. I had a habit of rubbing people the wrong way. Moe, though, would handle it with her usual respect and grace. Kindness like hers was innate, a personality trait that couldn't be taught. She was good right down to her core. That's probably why I loved her so much. She was everything I wasn't. Gave me something to work toward. Not that I didn't have enough on my plate.

"Be that as it may, I'd love to have you live here. The house is big enough for a family of six. You know that Kyle and I had planned on having a big family, but then, well, the rest is history."

"Yeah, it is. That reminds me. Where's that ax? Out back? I just remembered some chopping I have to do."

Moe caught me at the wrist. "I know you hate him. I do too, but violence is never the answer."

"Really? I'd feel better with some violence right about now." I gave her one of my big-cheeked smiles.

Moe laughed. "Just think about moving in with us, will you? I'll even let you pay rent. Say two hundred dollars."

I shook my head. "Room and board, plus utilities and a

workshop is worth way more than two hundred."

Her eyes narrowed into an expression of aggravation and frustration. She hated being tested and absolutely despised discussions of money. When her husband screwed her over in a way that could never ever be forgiven, he'd had the gall to go to the judge for spousal support. Bad idea all the way around. Moe had more friends in the county courthouse than strangers.

She not only had a very successful private practice as a psychologist and therapist, but also served as a court mediator. Every judge and most attorneys loved her and would never have allowed her to get taken for a ride by her scumbag ex. Aside from her own success, Moe was the sole heir to the Holland family fortune. As the only biological blood relation in the Holland family line, she'd gotten everything her grandparents had in their import and export business. To the tune of millions. Though most people in our lives would never have a clue she was worth that much. She didn't flaunt her money.

"You know money isn't an issue for me." Her tone was flat and agitated.

"I know, but what you need to understand is that it is...to me. Thank you, though." I stood up and prepped my tools for cleaning, wanting to drop the subject.

"Just promise me you'll think about it. I'd much rather you were here with us, keeping us company, not working your fingers to the bone. You need those fingers for your art."

"Moe, I love yoga; it's not too much."

She cocked her head to the side. "No, but ten classes a week, plus teaching painting to drunk lushes every weekend, along with trying to paint your own projects is. If you lived here, you wouldn't have to use your weekends for work but for art. Think about it. You know I'm not going to give up on this until you swear you will."

I walked over and wrapped my arms around her, pulling her into a hug. She smelled of fresh jasmine right off the vine. I think it was her lotion, but in all the years we'd been friends, I'd never asked. I'd always just enjoyed the familiarity of her scent.

"I promise. And take a video of Lily seeing her room for the first time, will you? I want that texted to me."

She grinned. "For sure. She's going to just die when she sees it. She's been obsessed with the book *The Secret Garden* and how the kids escape into a private world. I love that her little mind worked out that it was special. You doing this for her..." Moe sniffed, and her eyes turned glassy.

Oh no. She was going to cry. "No tears! Gah! No, don't even. If you cry, I'll cry." I shook my head and threaded my hands through my shoulder-length hair. "Just don't."

Moe sniffed and wiped her nose on a handkerchief she'd pulled out of her back pocket. Did all moms carry those things? Weird.

"I know, I know. After the divorce, though, and the fact that he doesn't want anything to do with Lily because she's not technically his biological child...I just..." A tear slipped down her cheek. I lifted my hand and wiped it away with my thumb.

"He's a real piece of work, Moe, and his karma is going to get him in the end. You know that. *Her* too." I didn't have to even say the name. We were both all too aware of who *she* was.

Moe nodded, wiped her eyes and nose once more with her handkerchief, and then shoved it in her back pocket. "Okay. So go on, get ready for class, I'm going to finish the room before I pick up Lily from playgroup. Wish me luck!"

I hauled my bag over my shoulder. "Luck is not necessary. Lily loves her mommy, and she's going to love the room. Dinner soon?" I said while heading to the front door.

" 'Course. To the moon and back?" she said.

"To the moon and back."

ATLAS

"You want to teach what?" Jewel asked, her facial features leaving nothing to the imagination.

"Tell us again how you think this would work, without us getting sued for sexual harassment or public indecency," Crystal, co-owner of the center and the more level headed of the two, stated calmly.

I paced back and forth along the length of the small administrative office of my new employer, Village Yoga Center. "I know it's a very radical and new concept that at first is hard to get your head around."

Crystal laughed. Jewel scoffed.

"Okay, clients would have to sign a waiver that would release the center from liability for sexual comments, lewd behavior, et cetera. I'd handle each waiver personally prior to them entering the class."

Jewel frowned. "I'm just not sure this is the way we want to go. I mean it's definitely out there, even for the yoga community, and we're probably the most open-minded if you compare physical and spiritual fitness centers against one another."

I pointed at Jewel. "I couldn't agree with you more. This class strips the client bare of any of their misgivings, allowing them to truly go inward in a way that is freeing and liberating, not only spiritually, but physically as well."

Crystal chuckled. "I'll say. And you've seen this type of class work before? In New York?"

I nodded and leaned against the bookcase that held yoga DVDs and meditation CDs for patrons to purchase. "I studied under a guru last summer. At first, the clientele is awkward about it, but the ones who make it through the first class are sold. The experience is beyond unique. Shedding all the layers that weigh you down is like finding your own personal salvation."

Jewel pursed her lips. "I don't know, Atlas. What do you think, Crystal? Is Lotus House ready for something this hip?"

Crystal took a deep breath. "What if we tried the class for a short time? Like a four-week plan. If people see it on the schedule, sign up, and love the new style, then we expand, adding more time slots. Fair?"

I wanted to jump over the desk and kiss her dead on the mouth. If she didn't have the all-of-her-staff-are-her-children-type nature, I would have.

"Eight weeks. I'd need at least eight weeks to get the class off the ground. Dash told me that his Tantric yoga workshops took months to catch on, and those are now sold out with a waiting list. I know this is just one class a week, but I need to build up the hype, get people interested. I was thinking of putting a flyer together that we could keep at the front desk. I could design the promo myself."

Jewel and Crystal sat silently, staring at me. They were polar opposites in coloring and features. Crystal looked like a modern-day angel with her long, golden hair, clear blue eyes, and one of the softest smiles I'd ever seen. Jewel had more waiflike features, with blazing red curly hair and skin as pale as a freshwater pearl. Her eye color was harder to determine through her ever-present black-rimmed glasses.

While waiting for them to speak, I swear I could hear the faint sounds of the yoga class down the hall. Heck, I could hear my own inhalations and exhalations as if they were blaring through a megaphone.

"I'm thinking six weeks," Crystal offered.

"Agreed. But you have to do all the leg work to get this concept off the ground," Jewel added.

I clapped my hands together. "You will not be sorry."

Both women looked at one another and smiled. "Don't let us be," Crystal said.

"So what's your plan?" Jewel placed her elbows on the desk and cocked her head to the side.

Now that I knew they were going to allow the new class for a minimum of six weeks before committing, I sat down in the loveseat. "Well, I'm going to start by asking each of the teachers here to commit to attending at least one class that I hold in the first couple weeks. My thought is that if the clientele know one of their regular teachers, someone they trust, is going to attend, then maybe they will. Plus, I was hoping the teachers would enjoy the experience and share the new concept in their classes."

Jewel frowned. "That's a lot to ask. As you know, we pay a flat twenty dollars per class to start, regardless of whether you have one or thirty people in your class. However, you know for every person after five in attendance, you get an additional two dollars per person. That means if that person is not going to their class, they are adding to your weekly income versus theirs."

I let out a long, hot breath. "I see. Makes sense, but still. I'd want to help get a friend off the ground in a new class. All the teachers here seem willing to help one another." As I said that, I immediately conjured an image of one wildcat hottie Mila Mercado, whose mere existence set my blood on fire in the best possible ways. But she'd be a tough sell for sure. "I hope to connect with them and offer the same shared promotion in my classes."

"Fair enough. Do your homework and preparation. I'll have my husband add the new class to the schedule," Crystal said. "We'll need a working description e-mailed to us by the end of the day. Also, make sure you rework one of our disclaimers and send that through for us to review and approve."

I made notes in my cell phone of everything they said. I didn't want to forget or let them down. Besides, I had a gig tonight. I'd need to knock out all of these things right after leaving so I could get over to the club for a sound check. And, first thing tomorrow morning, I had a heated Vin Flow to teach. The night would be long but worth the extra work if I could get this new concept off the ground.

"Thank you, ladies. Really. I know this is outside of the box, but I just feel it deep in my bones that the clientele at Lotus House will take this new concept and share the experience with their friends and colleagues, and hopefully, a horde of new clients! I'm certain this concept will go over smashingly with the college kids, and you're always looking for new ways to bring them in each year. This one...this is the golden egg!"

Crystal smiled, and Jewel stood and held out her hand. "We're counting on you."

I shook her hand, smiling like a loon. "Oh, I'll make it

happen. I have faith."

At that point, Crystal stood up, came around the desk and hugged me. "Faith is all anyone needs in life."

Boy, she was not wrong. I felt as though I'd spent all my twenty-eight years on this earth hoping and praying for things to happen. This was the first time I felt like I was using my creativity for something magical. Unfortunately, my music gig wasn't happening as I'd hoped, even after spending the last decade attempting to become a somebody in a sea of nobodies.

The music industry was beyond tough. I'd come so close to being signed I could now count them on both hands and feet. And that didn't include the drawer full of rejection letters I'd received from countless producers telling me that my voice worked, the lyrics were stellar, but the entire package was lacking. I still hadn't figured out what that "it" factor was, but I was driven by the desire to make my dreams come true. I'd never stop until one day my passion became my job. For now, yoga gave me an outlet not only to make money, but also to find myself. Yoga helped to bring it all inward to a place where things were simple, easy, balanced. Now I just needed to take that same Zen spot and merge it into my music.

One day at a time. That's what my buddy Dash told me all the time. He'd be the first person I would talk to about attending my class. Maybe he'd get Amber on board, and she could get her best friend, Genevieve, who teaches hatha and prenatal yoga, to come. Although she just had a baby. Then again, maybe that celebrity baseball-playing man of hers would come out and show support. Having him, in particular, come to this class would bring the ladies in droves.

Yeah. That was it. I made a mental note to talk to Dash and his wife about the idea and the special request to involve their friends. It was all coming together. I could do this. Then, once I got things settled and my income on solid ground, I'd work on figuring out what the "it" factor was that I needed to add to my repertoire. I tugged on the key that hung around my neck, a talisman I carried with me. The key was the very last thing my father gave me before he up and abandoned Mom and me twenty years ago. I still didn't know what it opened, but like all things, I figured one day the answer would present itself.

"Ladies, thank you. Thank you for giving me a chance. I'm going to work hard at making this successful. I promise."

I opened the door to exit the office and ran right into a pint-sized wildcat. "Hey, hotness." I glanced at the small Mexican American fireball from her medium brown shoulder-length hair to her perky breasts. She'd covered the girls in a tight black sports bra type top. Her midriff was bare, leaving a scandalizing swath of brown sugar-colored skin I'd like nothing more than to bend down and press my lips to. I just knew she would taste of the sweetest honey. Her knee-length black yoga pants dipped low, well below her navel, making my mouth water. The pants fit her like they were painted on, leaving absolutely nothing to the imagination. Thank the good Lord above for women's athletic attire.

"Curly," she addressed me flatly.

I ran a hand through my messy curls. Her caramel eyes watched in what I hoped was fascination. For a scant second, her mouth opened, and her pink tongue licked her bottom lip. The instant sexual tension that crackled and zipped between us was heart-stoppingly magnetic. If I were a lesser man, I'd have walked her backward until she was up against the wall opposite the office door and taken her mouth right here, right now. But I wouldn't. Not only could the action get me fired, but she also might actually backhand me. Not the best way to get in good with a girl, though I'd experienced worse during my late teens when I was wild and out of control.

She planted her hands on her rounded hips. "Did you get a good look?"

The woman had an insane body. Tiny but built. Her breasts were small, high, and enough to fit in the center of my palms. However, her perky tits were not her best feature. Hands down, it was the ass. Tight, shaped like a perfect heart, with enough bubble to it that I wanted to bite it. Hard. Mark it as my territory. Damn, I'd always been an ass man, and this woman could bring me to my knees to worship at the cheeks of her fleshy heaven.

I petted my bottom lip with just my thumb as I tilted my head and glanced at her finest attributes. "Maybe if you'd turn around."

"Pig," she mumbled and pushed past me.

For a sprite, she was strong as an ox. "Mmm...even better from the back. Not as much chin wagging either to distract from the view."

She huffed, flipped her hair, and lasered her gaze on mine. "You want to do this here?" She hooked a thumb over her shoulder at the two women who had mysteriously gone radio silent. Once I saw Mila, I'd pretty much forgotten my name, and the fact that I was standing in the admin office at Lotus House with my bosses in the background.

I responded without thinking. "I'd do you anywhere." Crass but true. She was my current walking wet dream.

"You disgust me," she growled, her teeth obviously clenching, providing a sharp contrast to her cheekbones.

"You love it."

"I do not!" Her huff was indignant, but her erect nipples, labored breathing, and dilated pupils said otherwise.

"No, but you will." I smirked and then jutted my chin toward Crystal and Jewel. "Thanks again. I'll be in touch this evening."

Crystal waved and Jewel crossed her arms. Crystal, I'd been told, was in love with love and probably enjoyed the show. Jewel, on the other hand, I had to watch out for. I didn't know enough about her to determine whether or not I was in trouble. Time would tell.

"Catch you later, wildcat," I quipped while closing the door and heading out, purposely not waiting for her retort. I'm sure whatever she'd have said would have been great.

Sparring with the feisty woman would be the highlight of any day. I needed to plan more time at the center to take her classes. Operation Hotness would commence this week.

I walked out of the center into the California sunshine with the *Mission: Impossible* theme running through my mind.

CHAPTER TWO

Lotus Pose with Arm Extended (Sanskrit: Padmasana)
There are a wide variety of modifications or variations on the
standard lotus pose in yoga. A teacher may have you raise
your arms from heart center while in prayer position to start
the gentle stretch of your back and spine. A great upper body
stretch is to extend the arms full and lean ever so slightly to
the right and hold, come back to center, and then lean slightly
to the left and hold. You can place a hand on the ground if you
feel unbalanced.

MILA

"Can you believe him?" I pointed at the closed door. My
entire body was alight with a heat that couldn't be tamed.
That man set everything within me aflame, and all I wanted

to do was put it out. Immediately. Too damn bad my traitorous body didn't agree. Every time I laid eyes on the tall hunk of studliness, I lost my ability to think straight. Probably why I defaulted to threats and sarcastic remarks. It felt like the only defense I had against the infuriating male.

Atlas Powers. *What kind of name is that anyway?* Sounded like a superhero. And he was *not* super. Not even close. At least that's what I kept telling myself. His six feet of pure male muscled perfection could lead an unsuspecting woman with a Barbie doll-sized IQ to believe he was heroic.

"Yes, I can. What I'm finding entertaining, however, is how much you let him get to you. I think, Ms. Mila, you're smitten with the new yogi. Am I wrong?" Crystal observed with a soft smile adorning her pretty face.

I scoffed. "*So* wrong. If smitten means string him up by his toes and toss water balloons at him until he cries uncle? Then yes. Otherwise, absolutely not. The smug, insanely—"

"Gorgeous," Crystal supplied.

"Yeah, that." I recalled the way his hair fell enticingly into his eyes. "Frustratingly egotistic—"

"Sexy," Crystal added.

"Uh-huh." So sexy. If I were a stupid woman, I'd climb him like a tree, build a nest, and stay awhile. A long while. "Downright overconfident and devastatingly—"

"Proportionate," she supplied once again rather unhelpfully.

I closed my eyes and remembered his body when he'd stood before me moments ago. His form was beautiful. The epitome of a fit, healthy male who was active and took supreme care of his body. He'd worn loose, black men's-style yoga pants that clung to a pair of thick muscled thighs. A black-and-white marble-esque painted tank top hung low enough in front that his defined pecs were clearly visible in all their sculpted glory. A mop of curly, dark brown hair flopped in ideal bunches along his head in that classic, lackadaisical, hot boy way women couldn't get enough of.

"Inviting," I whispered and then opened my eyes, realizing I was daydreaming in my boss's office. A sense of dread rippled up my spine and out my pores as I covered a gasp with my hand. "No, I mean I *despise* him!" I swallowed, straightened my spine, and locked my hands into fists.

Crystal chucked, and it sounded like church bells. "If by despise you mean crave in a way that any woman alive would, I understand. Sweetheart, there's nothing wrong with being interested in a fellow yogi."

"I am not interested in *anyone*." I compressed my lips together, wanting to keep my retort simple. *Do not allow my lack of restraint more recognition than it needs.*

Jewel stood up from her seat behind the desk. "Mila honey, we basically watched you both verbally and mentally caress one another. You're hot for Atlas Powers. Just admit it. There's no shame in being attracted to a man. Especially one that looks like a male fitness supermodel."

And he did. Look like a supermodel. He could easily grace the pages of any men's magazine and have the girls drooling. Just pretty enough to be photogenic and a heaping dose of rugged, raw male that made women stupid. I crossed my arms over my chest and glanced out the window. "I'll admit he's attractive. But he's smug..."

"Overconfident and egotistical. I know, you said as much." Crystal's blue eyes were as bright as a cloudless sunny day and sparkled with mirth.

"Well, it's true."

Crystal came over to me and took my hand. "Sweetheart, you've worked here for four years, and in all that time, I've never seen you date anyone. Any particular reason why you're holding your heart to yourself?"

"Dating is not my thing, Crystal. I don't have time for a man in my life." Which wasn't altogether true. What she didn't know, and what I'd never told anyone, even Moe, was that I was the queen of one-night stands.

Every few months I'd hit a bar in Oakland, find an attractive guy, and let him buy me a couple drinks, which would lead to me following him home. We'd have sex, and I'd be on my way. Like scratching an itch. We both got what we needed and went about our lives. Unattached. Simple. No complications. And through it all, I was the one in control. Always.

Crystal frowned and cupped my shoulder. "That's a very lonely way to look at life, my dear. Don't you want someone to come home to? A person to say good night to at the end of a long day?"

I tried to hold back the choked retort and failed. "I have more going on than the lack of a man. I'm perfectly capable of hooking a man if I wanted one. Really. You needn't worry about me."

Technically, I could probably score a man in my life. I hadn't tried in years, but it was easy enough to nail a hookup for a night. Didn't matter, though. A regular man would just cause more problems. They needed the one thing I didn't have to offer. Time. Surviving as a single woman in her mid-twenties without a college education and no support from family was hard enough. Adding a man into the mix, someone who would want me to give up my weekend activities, or the number of classes I taught, or prevent me from working on my paintings until well into the wee hours of the morning... Not an option.

God. I needed to paint. Running into Atlas, having this conversation with Crystal, the nagging of my best friend. It was all beginning to form a heaping pile of crap I didn't have the time or energy to deal with.

"Look, not to be rude, but I only came in here to confirm my schedule for the next two weeks. I didn't expect to get a life lesson." My words were clipped and short.

Crystal flattened her lips into a thin line. Ugh. I was such a weasel.

"I see. I apologize if I overstepped my bounds," she said flatly.

"No, no, it's fine. It's just everything is okay. Perfect. I mean it."

"And Atlas? Does he bother you with his comments? If you feel he's being inappropriate, I can have a talk with him," Jewel offered.

I shook my head. "No, really. I can handle him. He's nothing more than a pest." A ridiculously handsome pest. A man that I honestly loved battling, for no other reason than the entertainment value alone. He shook up the monotony of the day. Of course, I'd never breathe a word of it to a soul. It was better that everyone thought I couldn't stand him. Maybe if that was the case, I'd come to believe it, too.

"Then you wouldn't mind attending his new class for us and reporting back?" Crystal was smiling like her normal happy self. Briefly, I wondered if they sold pills that could make a person that happy.

Why me? I didn't want to take any of the sexy bastard's classes. It was better that we just ran into each other on occasion. "I guess, if you need me to. Were you expecting me to give you details on his methods for Vinyasa, the instruction, the overall flow?"

Crystal smirked and Jewel smiled before glancing away. There was something brewing between the two of them, but I had no idea what, only that it had to do with me and Atlas in what would likely be some cosmically twisted way. "Why do I get the feeling the two of you are setting me up?"

Jewel blinked and pursed her lips. Crystal's face didn't change. "Whatever would give you that impression? Have we ever had nefarious purposes for anything?"

"Well, no, but..."

"Then we'd appreciate one of our veteran yogis taking the new class that's offered and reporting back to us on the experience, instruction, class environment, how the clientele reacted. You've done this for us before. Remember when Genevieve started a couple years ago?"

I sighed. "Yes, but..."

Crystal shook her head and picked up a stack of papers. "No buts." She straightened the stack into place against the desk. "The first class will be held next week. It's going to be scheduled alongside Nicholas's aerial yoga class and Genevieve's evening hatha. Will that be a problem? Of course, we're happy to pay for you to attend."

I blew out a long breath. "Not a problem. I'll be there, and you don't have to pay me. I'll attend as a professional courtesy."

Crystal's delight bloomed across her face. "Thank you, sweetheart. I look forward to hearing your thoughts." She leaned over and wrote something in blue pen on the piece of paper sitting on the top of her stack. "And here's your schedule." She handed me the paper she'd written on. It had my name scrawled on the top. Farther down the page in her very descriptive penmanship she'd written, "Yoga with Atlas" on Wednesday evening. Guess I wouldn't be painting that night.

"Thank you, ladies. I'll be sure to follow up."

"I can't wait." Crystal tipped her head to the side and blinked amusingly.

I turned slowly and made my way out of the office and toward my room. An uneasy feeling followed me. *What were those two plotting?*

For a few minutes, I started yoga breathing, attempting to center my mind and overactive thoughts. I had to teach a class in the next twenty minutes, and I'd planned on grabbing my schedule and reviewing it over a cup of coffee at the bakery. Now, I didn't have time.

Time. The bane of my existence. And now I had even less of it since I had to go babysit Atlas Powers. Damn sexy yogi. Why couldn't he be a dog-faced man? I hadn't planned on sitting through any of his classes, mostly because keeping my eyes off his body was like asking an art student not to look at a Van Gogh or Picasso. A person needed to inspect the classics in order to know where it all began. And, oh goodness gracious, Atlas's body was something to behold. Now I'd have to stare at it through a ninety-minute class. Maybe I could skip out of it early?

I groaned and sat down on the riser where I'd set myself up to teach today's class. No, Jewel and Crystal were counting on me. They'd always been kind to me, and they'd been amazing bosses. The last thing I wanted was for them to think I was an ingrate. I could take the sexy man's class, tell them how it went, and move on with my life. Easy. No problem.

ATLAS

I felt her presence before I saw her. Somehow, the candlelit room brightened just a hair, as if the flickering light followed her essence through the rustle of air as she moved. Her eyes didn't meet mine when she laid out a mat in the front right corner of the classroom. A few other patrons near her set up their mats and continued to the back of the room. I'd closed the thick curtains over the window that separated the hallway and the class that allowed patrons to view the class from the hall. Usually, the owners wanted the curtains open unless it was a private session or one of Dash's Tantric couples' workshops. However, for today's class, privacy was of the utmost importance.

The entire room came alive with new clients, most of them women. I had to admit, going with Dash to walk the Berkeley campus and promote the class in person worked like a charm. We'd secured so many phone numbers through winks and smiles, I felt like I was carrying around a pocketful of confetti when the night was over, and I tossed them all into the circular waste bin. Amber, Dash's wife, had frowned when he told her about our day. Then she offered to take the class in support of her husband's friend.

At her suggestion, I'd laughed my ass off. I'd known Dash Alexander since high school, and the only time he'd lost his cool was over Amber. The woman had twisted him up with her innocence and intelligence. This time was much like when Amber had told him she was a virgin about six months ago. They were only dating then. Courting her had been the only time I'd seen him react like a lovesick fool. This time was different. He was worse. Positively rife with anger at the mere thought of his wife disrobing in front of a class full of people. In the end, he'd straight out forbidden her from taking my class.

I tried to act affronted, but I got it. Before him, his wife had been untouched. He owned her body, mind, and soul. Men like me could only dream of being so lucky. But with my daytime schedule and trying to make the music thing work at night, I barely had time for a quick roll in the hay with a willing groupie I'd met at the local bar, let alone a lifelong commitment. Amber, though, she'd been pissed. So upset, in fact, I had to leave in order for him to grovel in peace.

Walking around the class, I made sure that everything was set up just so. I'd met most of the clients outside so that they could sign the required forms, so the yoga center would not be liable for anything the client might deem inappropriate. From what I understood, none of the paperwork would hold up in court, but it helped to have something to deter legal action. Not that I expected anything to happen. At first everyone would look down, up at the ceiling, shyly glance at one another or only at themselves, and most often, they avoided all eye contact. Then they'd get into the poses, focus their attention within, and it would just be a regular yoga class.

Unfortunately for me, there was a divine cinnamon-colored, pint-sized goddess who currently held all my focus. I couldn't wait to drop the bomb on her. I wondered how long it would take her to roll up her mat and walk out of the class. That sass was hard to contain. My guess? Two point five seconds. Testing the theory was going to be a blast.

Out of the corner of my eye, I noticed people were starting

to disrobe. I checked the clock, went over to the door, made sure there weren't any stragglers chatting outside who needed to get in, and then shut and locked the door. Mila squinted and tilted her head, her gaze revealed the disapproval of the action.

I walked over to her and was about to welcome her when her scathing tone stopped me short.

"What are you doing locking the door? That's against the rules."

"Not when it locks from the inside. Any patron can easily unlock it and leave, not to mention the push doors for the fire exits. I don't want anyone else coming in mid-class. It would be inappropriate and incredibly disruptive."

Her head jerked back. "How so? You get paid for any additional latecomers."

I smiled. "You'll see."

Mila's caramel-colored eyes blazed an intense gold. Her high, wide cheekbones filled with a rosy hue. I'd have very much liked to feel those silky cheeks against my fingertips.

Wow. Irritation looked damn fine on her.

"Class, we're about to begin. You know what to do," I said loud enough for the room to hear.

She tapped her foot and squinted. "Is that how you start a class? You really should welcome them, introduce yourself."

Know-it-all.

I chuckled behind my hand. Boy, was she going to eat crow. "Oh, I have. Outside when I was having them sign their waivers."

Her mouth opened and her eyes widened. "Waiver for what?"

"So we don't get sued for sexual harassment, public indecency, or any of the other mumbo jumbo societal norms might consider inappropriate."

She pursed her lips. "I'm sorry, I'm not following."

I grinned, hooked my fingers into my loose tank top, and pulled it over my head.

Mila gasped and licked her lips when my chest came into full view. Oh yeah. The sexual tension between us was ripe, and I wanted so badly to bite into her, but the timing had to be just right.

"Mila, take off your clothes." My voice was thick with a desire I couldn't hide. Not from her. Not with her standing in front of me looking like God's gift to mankind.

"Excuse me." Her own tone was low and sultry.

"Look around." I held out my arms as if I was displaying a Thanksgiving feast, not a class full of yogis.

"Oh my God." Her hand went over her mouth as her eyes flicked from person to person. "What are you teaching?"

I looked into her brown eyes, grinned, and then pushed down my yoga pants and boxer briefs in one shove.

Her eyes didn't start at my feet and take me in slowly. No, her gaze went straight for the gusto landing right on my cock. I could almost feel the heat of her desire searing through me.

The gasp that came from her pretty mouth that time sounded more like a choked gurgle.

"Naked yoga."

If I could have, I would have paid to have someone capture the look on her face when I bared my body to the sexy wildcat for the first time. Her chest rose and fell far faster than was necessary for a person just standing there not moving a muscle. Her pupils were dilated, and her erect nipples poked through her flimsy sports bra. I had to think of my grandmother and the disgusting bathroom at the club I played to prevent an erection.

"You've got to be kidding me."

I cocked an eyebrow, lifted both hands to my head, and ran my fingers through my hair so that my naked body was on full display.

Her eyes blatantly raked my form from head toe.

"Jesus," she whispered and bit into her full bottom lip.

I grinned, took a calming breath, and opened my eyes.

"Yeah, that's what I think every day when I see you, and you're not even naked."

"Atlas..." she warned and glanced around.

The room was quiet except for the lilting, soothing sound of Enya I had playing softly in the background.

"Class, go ahead and start by sitting with your bum flat against the mat, legs crossed in front of you in lotus position. Press your hands, palms together, at your heart, close your eyes, and think about what you want to let go of today. You've already gotten rid of the physical parameters you entered with; now, let's work on the mental ones."

"I don't...I don't kn-know what to say," Mila stuttered, her voice filled with trepidation as much as curiosity.

I pressed my hands together in front of my chest. "There's nothing to say. Either remove all your clothes and get into lotus position or leave. Your indecision is disrupting my class."

A silent war of wills seemed to be fought in the few seconds that passed as I stood in front of her, naked as the day I was born, waiting for her decision.

Without preamble or a single uttered word, she reached her arms behind her back, and arched her chest delectably. Then she crossed her arms in front of her, grabbed the bottom edge of her sports bra, and lifted it above her head in one swoop. A pair of the most succulent, perky, small breasts came into view. My dick stirred from its sleepy place, wanting to rise up and greet the day.

Vomit on the floor mixed with torn pieces of pissed-on toilet paper.

Filmy mirrors.

Nasty phrases and women's phone numbers written on tile walls.

I rushed to think of anything disgusting so that I wouldn't embarrass myself.

Mila's loose brown curls fell back away from the front of her face and her eyes stayed on mine. Then she looped her fingers into her skintight yoga pants and pushed them down. Interestingly enough, this particular female yogi didn't wear panties. I'd have to ask Dash about it. He'd had more experience with yogis than I had. Though in that moment, when I took in all that was Mila Mercado's naked body, I swore on all things holy that this woman would be mine. I wanted to sample each golden-brown nipple until she begged for more. I wanted to taste the slickness between her thighs as if she was the finest delicacy.

I swallowed and stared. Just stared at her body.

"You gonna teach class or look at me naked all night?" Her eyebrow twitched, and her lips puckered.

A challenge. That was it. This woman absolutely had the power to break me. Sexy as hell, this fun-sized yogi could end me.

"Oh wildcat, I'd happily spend all night looking at your naked body. It's like fine art. You can never get enough. You have to see it over and over to appreciate all the little nuances. Which I intend to do. Another time. But I have a class to teach." I grinned and clapped my hands together signaling to the class that we were about to start.

I turned around, leaving Mila and her insanely gorgeous body in favor of starting class. The platform the yoga teachers used had track lighting shining directly on the riser, and there I stood in front of a class full of twenty-five naked people, and I only cared about one person's opinion of what she saw.

Much to my dismay, as I glanced around the room at the clients sitting in lotus pose, most of the bodies were young and in shape. Soon I'd get women and men of all shapes and sizes participating, and the experience would be even more profound. I preferred a more diverse audience in this class.

Mila hurriedly sat in position and closed her eyes.

"Now place your arms above your head and bring your palms together." I put myself into position and waited for the class to follow. Everywhere I looked, there were naked bodies. Large breasts, medium sized, small, flat male breasts, so many different nipple shapes it all became almost a game of connect the dots. No two alike.

When I was teaching a naked yoga class, my imagination turned all of their bodies into clay statues. They were no longer vulnerable naked forms; they were structures with which to create beautiful shapes through the art and practice of yoga.

"Breathe in and, on the exhale, bring the arms down and let it go. We're going to cross the knees over one another, lining them up. Take your arms and cross the elbows." Everyone followed suit, but I had trouble not focusing on the one woman who did not want the attention. "That's it," I said when everyone caught up. "This is cow face pose. Focus on the feeling between your shoulder blades, your hips, and breathe..."

I took them through sixty minutes of a beginning to intermediate class. Eventually, I wanted to offer naked yoga and have it be specific to the type of yoga, such as Vinyasa Flow, hatha, perhaps even some Yin yoga.

When I shifted the class to the side of the mat and had everyone stand in a wide legged downward facing dog pose, I instantly felt my mistake sizzle through my veins. Mila's ass came into perfect view. There was no one standing close enough behind her to block it. Jesus Christ, that ass. I tightened my hands into fists, the act preventing me from doing something stupid, like storming over to her, placing my palms on those succulent globes and squeezing to my heart's content.

Then she bent over. I groaned as her pink pussy became visible. As she flipped her upper body over at the waist, her small, perky breasts bounced and her head hung between her legs. She was naturally flexible and an advanced yogi. I wasn't surprised when she rested the crown of her head on the ground. She reached out both arms and grabbed her ankles. Her entire body was folded in half and open. So open. I could easily stand right behind her and impale her where she stood. And it would feel *so* good. I'd hold her hips and pound into her so that she had no way of escape, could feel every deep thrust intensely, stuck on my cock, only able to take what I gave. Over and over I'd bang her until she convulsed in orgasm. Her pussy milking me for everything I had to give.

That did it. My dick rose to attention, hard and proud. Mila's eyes opened and caught sight of my very big problem. She licked her lips and pressed against her thighs, lifting up her head, chest and then the rest of her body. When she stood, she looked over her shoulder coyly, perfect ass on display. My heart sped up, my dick hardened painfully as I glanced around to make sure no others eyes were on me. Just for her, I fisted my cock and stroked it once, so she could see exactly what she did to me. To my extreme surprise, she smirked, faced the wall, and moved back into position, ass in the air, pussy open and ready for the next instruction.

Truth be told, based on her response, I knew I had my work cut out for me. This woman was trouble. Beyond trouble. She was a damn lit stick of dynamite.

CHAPTER THREE

SOLAR PLEXUS
C H A K R A

Individuals who relate most with the solar plexus chakra tend to be worldly, extremely intelligent, possibly speak many languages, and take very good care of their bodies. They are interested in securing many material possessions and seek fame and fortune as a measure of their success. Prestige and power are driving forces in these individuals.

MILA

Atlas Powers was handsome. Fine as fuck and hung like a horse. His body was a tight mesh of sculpted muscles. The indentions of his abdominals were so cut I was certain I'd feel them like Braille under a blind person's fingers when dragging my tongue over them. And that's all I could think about.

My lips dragging over his hard muscles.

My tongue tasting wave after wave of his abdominal wall.

When he reached his hands behind his head and displayed his body like the Viking warrior I imagined him to be in that moment, with the mop of curls falling into his eyes, the rugged angle of his jaw dotted with a couple of days' growth of beard, I lost the ability to breathe. He seriously had no right to look that damn good.

A hot burst of arousal arrowed to my core, making my sex tender and needy. An ache built within my body. My nostrils flared at the musky male scent taunting me, hooking me with gossamer tendrils of male pheromones. Atlas watched me as I looked my fill, not even trying to hide the smug smile. The bastard knew how good he looked and had no problem flaunting it.

I had to give it to him. When he told me to remove my clothes before class started, I almost swallowed my tongue. The words "clothes" and "naked" had banged around in my head like a pinball machine until finally the ball sank home along with the meaning behind his lusty choices in syntax. He'd meant to shock and stupefy me with his request, and he'd won. That round. Until, of course, I'd lifted my arms over my head and removed my sports bra.

When the tables were turned on him, Atlas caved, and he caved for all to see. His eyes seemed to run up and down my body as if he was memorizing every inch of my small breasts when they bounced free of the Lycra confinement. The way he licked his lips indicated that he was not bothered by the small handful—rather, that if I was willing, he'd be grabbing those handfuls with fervor. Then I figuratively punched him right in the gut when, instead of cutting and running, I'd pushed my yoga pants down and smirked back. Smug son-of-a-gun.

My heart pounded a symphony in my chest waiting for

him to respond further, wanting to see that fat cock between his thighs raise up to make my acquaintance. Only that's not what happened. No, he turned on a heel and started class. I tried to take his abruptness as a compliment, that he was overwhelmed by my nakedness, but a quick glance around the class proved that theory was bogus. The entire class was filled with young, college-aged women stacked with breasts the size of cantaloupes, Barbie-sized waistlines, and legs that went on for days. Even if I could stand to spar with Atlas for more than ten minutes before losing my mind with anger, there was a sea of willing women with less bark and no bite to choose from.

Choosing to stay the course, I sat down and got into it. After about fifteen minutes, magically, I forgot I was naked. Moving through the twelve steps of the sun salutation, going from standing to bending, lunging, planking and circling back around always put my mind in a state of utter Zen. I often did the series in my classes. Once a student learned the twelve steps, they became confident and zoned out, which is what yoga was all about. Not only did the act of moving the body in an aerobic way tone and strengthen the physical form, but it also built a quiet place for the mind to rest and rejuvenate.

Toward the end of the class, he'd instructed us to face the side of our mats and go into a wide-legged forward bend. This put my best asset on display, along with opening me wide. I tried my best not to look through my legs. I didn't want to see who would be staring at the most vulnerable place on my body, and how that would make me feel, until a heated sizzling pricked against my neck. It was like the feeling a person gets when someone is following you. Almost as though I just knew someone was there, watching me.

I was right.

I opened my eyes quickly. The entire room was bent over facing the opposite direction. No skeevy young college dude was staring down my vagina. Then that prickling sensation hit again, and I glanced at Atlas. His eyes were zeroed in on mine. He stood, seemingly stunned. The fire in his eyes was scalding. My face and chest became heated at the carnal lust so clearly flowing off him in thunderous bolts of energy. Pressing into my thighs, I arched my back and came up before I fell over. I glanced over my bare shoulder and watched as his dick hardened right before my eyes.

Finally! Eureka!

My God, he was virile. His cock was long and thick, with a powerful root and a wide crown. His lower half was devoid of hair and completely smooth. Nothing guarded the proud stem from pushing up when he clasped his hand around the base, locked his gaze with mine, and gave one brisk tug.

Ribbons of desire poured through me so forcefully, it took everything I had to rein it in, smirk, and present him with my best asset by bending over back into the pose. I kept my eyes closed and the crown of my head resting on the ground. I needed the support.

Atlas called out a few more instructions that I followed to the T. Every chance I could, I'd sneak a peek at his body. Everything about him was perfection—with the exception of his curly hair, which hid his eyes more often than not. I'd give my left breast in order to paint him. He'd be the ideal nude model. Dark hair, high sculpted cheekbones, a chiseled nose, plump lips, and a body that could make angels weep. He'd be exactly what I needed to finalize my showing. A few nudes of this man and I'd sell out.

My fingers instinctively curled around a paintbrush that

wasn't there. I *needed* to paint. Finally, my muse had been stroked. The desire to craft and create rushed through me. If only we could stand one another long enough for me to paint him. Unfortunately, we hadn't been able to be in front of one another for longer than a couple minutes without verbally attacking one another.

"Okay, class, get settled into Corpse pose, which is just lying on your back, your feet and ankles resting outward, your arms down by your sides with your hands open to the ceiling. We want to bring the universe's energy inward through our deep relaxation or *savasana*, not push it into the earth by pressing our palms to the floor. I've placed a bolster near your mat. Push it under the meat of your thighs so your pelvis rests comfortably."

As I lay there listening to the gravelly timber of his voice, a white-hot fire slithered along the surface of my skin, making me antsy. A familiar tic started in my jaw, and my heart beat against my chest. I couldn't relax. I had to go.

Standing up, I kneeled behind my mat and rolled it up with a flourish. The sound of bare feet slapping against the hard wood floor got louder and louder until it stopped right behind me.

"What's wrong?" Atlas whispered, leaning down behind me. His naked body was so near, the scent of musk and spice swirled in the air around us, cloaking me in lustful images of sweaty, mind-blowing sex. It was something I hadn't had the pleasure of smelling in far too long. It had been months since my last hookup. My mouth watered at the desire to turn my head and lick along what was sure to be stubbly skin. In my mind, Atlas would groan and gasp when I bit down and marked the succulent column with my teeth.

God smack it. I had to go. *Now.*

I pushed up, and my body slammed backward into his. His arms came around my waist. My hands went to the thick trunks of his thighs, my nails digging in as much for balance as with need. The need to put my hands on his beautiful body. To feel it just once.

At first, he didn't move a muscle aside from his hardening length, the hammering of his heart, and slow inhalation. At full mast, his cock rested densely between the cushion of my ass cheeks, and for the love of God, it felt extraordinary. Atlas tensed his fingers against my belly, pressing my back further against his chest. His body was warm, encompassing, and safe. I hadn't felt safe and sound in a man's arms in a long time. Too long, because I responded instantly by rubbing my ass against the thick erection lying there.

He leaned his head against the crux of where my neck and shoulder met. "Keep that up, and I'll bend you over right here and now in front of an entire class. You test my patience as it is with your cinnamon skin and firm body," he growled low and purposeful, directly into my ear. The music was loud enough, and a quick glance around showed that everyone was well into their deep relaxation.

I arched, pressing into him again, wanting to test him, to make him feel how insane he made women just by existing.

"You're going to regret that, wildcat," he purred into my ear.

I closed my eyes and took a slow breath. "I doubt that very much."

And since I'd already lost my mind, I figured why not go for gold? Grabbing both his hands, I pulled them away from my waist, spun in his arms, flattened my breasts against his bare chest, curled an arm around his neck, and hauled myself up on my toes where I pressed my lips to his.

Within half a breath, his arm banded around my waist and hauled me up higher. The rigidness of his steely erection dragged perfectly along my pelvis. I prevented myself from moaning but just barely. He took that slight lip loosening as an invitation to plunge his tongue into my mouth. From the second our tongues touched, I was a goner.

His tongue licked into my mouth, flicked against my tongue, and swallowed me and my inhibitions whole. Atlas Powers kissed with his entire body. Hands kneading, lips nibbling, legs asserting, and arms embracing. There was nowhere to go, and no place I'd rather be than naked and smashed up against his powerful frame, lost in him.

Someone coughed and the bubble around us burst. I pushed away and scrambled to the clothes I had sitting next to my mat.

"Mila..." Atlas whispered, attempting to get my attention. No dice. My cheeks were aflame with shame and embarrassment.

I gritted my teeth and tugged on my pants. Then I yanked on my sports bra, fumbling more times than necessary. Atlas placed his hands on my raised arms, my breasts coming close to plastering against his chest once more. He curled his fingers around the twisted part of my clothing and slid it down easily. Slowly I watched while he feathered those talented digits over both of my breasts and put my sports bra back in place. I wish I could have said the same for my dignity.

Wanting to say something, anything, but knowing this was the absolute wrong place, I just stared into his blue, no brown...wait...

"You have one brown eye and one blue eye?" The question slipped from my lips as easily as my fingers around his neck moments ago.

"Very observant, hotness. Can we discuss at a later date?" He held his hands out to the people lying like the dead still lost to *savasana*. Lucky for them, deep relaxation was most people's favorite part. The ability to just let your mind wander, and the body completely melt, kind of like I did naked against...

I lifted a hand to my heated forehead and shook my head. "Insanity."

"I agree. You definitely have a few screws loose, but you're fine as hell, a phenomenal kisser, and I can't wait to hear you scream my name."

Anger sputtered to the surface, replacing all lusty thoughts with seeds of rage. I stepped forward standing on my tiptoes while he hunched forward, accommodating my smaller stature. In a scant breath, we were face-to-face, only now, the desire to kiss him was long gone and the need to punch him was firing on all cylinders.

"You think you can handle me?" I taunted.

"Oh, hotness, I can more than handle you."

"Doubtful."

"Name your terms."

Again, I took stock of the room. The bodies on the floor were lost to their Zen place. As much as I wanted to continue this conversation, because I felt more alive right now than I had in years, this was not the place to be verbally or physically attacking one another. I dug into my small purse and pulled out a pen. I grabbed his forearm and wrote my number on the inside.

"Text, don't call."

With a sway of my hips and a bounce to my step, I clutched my things to my chest, zigzagged on bare feet through the clients, and left. As quietly as possible, I unlocked the door and glanced over my shoulder. He stood ramrod straight, muscled arms crossed over his broad chest, legs apart in a wide stance, and his eyes on me.

His beauty was primitive and finely engraved with muscles that were a combination of God-given genetics and hard work.

He was everything I didn't need. A distraction of compelling proportions that would wreak havoc on my mind, bruise my heart, and break my soul. Taking in all that was him from head to toe, remembering his kiss, the power with which he held me to him...I didn't have the wherewithal to care.

ATLAS

Text, don't call.

That's what Mila said after scribbling her phone number on my arm and disappearing from class. Finishing up my first ever naked yoga with a hard-on had not been pleasant. I'd broken my one rule and pulled on my yoga pants and sat lotus-style on the riser before releasing everyone from their deep relaxation. If they were put off by my clothing, nobody said anything. However, I was excited to note how many thanked me for the experience and promised to come to next week's class. I requested they share the flyer with their friends.

A few more girls hung around trying to get my number. The strange thing? I had automatically answered by telling them I was seeing someone. Absolutely not true. Mila had entered my mind for a split second and, for no good reason that I could think of, I turned down the opportunity for meaningless sex with a willing, pretty female. All because she wasn't the female I wanted to bed.

Remembering my dick wedged between the cheeks of her fine ass took up all the space in my mind. I literally could not stop thinking about my wildcat. Although, for the life of me, I couldn't fathom why. Sure, she was God's gift to men. Small, fit, brown skin, hair long enough to grip and tug while fucking, perky tits. I bet I could fit an entire breast in my mouth. Bet she'd like that, too. Yeah. And that ass. Formed by master genetics. She could give Jennifer Lopez a run for her money. Smaller in size but even more bubblicious. I gripped my thighs and squeezed while I imagined digging my fingers into that ass. She'd love it, too. Little spitfire. As long as she kept her mouth shut, we'd be fine. Hell, I knew exactly where to put my dick to keep her quiet. Then again, I loved tossing barbs at her and getting them back. I never knew what flippant words were going to come out of her kissable mouth. All I knew was that I wanted to poke and prod her. Make her wildly angry and then gasp in pleasure.

Fight and fuck.

The perfect goal. I guess we'd come closer to reaching that target tonight. Seeing her ire when she realized the class was naked yoga had been priceless. Her eyes had glossed over, she'd bitten her plump bottom lip, and then she'd gasped. I wanted to see that look of surprise on her face but only when I was balls deep giving her the best orgasm of her life. I could imagine it so clearly.

I tossed my bag on the leather sectional and surveyed my pad. Technically, I rented a room. My buddy Clayton Hart owned the deluxe apartment in Oakland. He was a fitness instructor to the stars. He even worked with several of the Oakland Ports teammates, including Trent Fox, a friend of my buddy Dash's. I hadn't met the baseball player yet, but I had met his wife, Genevieve. She worked at Lotus House, but according to the grapevine, she wanted to scale back her teaching now that she had a salon to run and a small baby to care for. I crossed my fingers that I'd be able to take on some of her classes. The money I got from gigs was enough to keep paying my rent, but the yoga teaching helped feed and clothe me. I wasn't hurting for money, but I definitely didn't have a lot to spare. Of course, all that would change if I could just get a shot with a label willing to take a chance on me and my music.

Moving around the room, I slumped onto the couch and flicked on the stereo. Beck's quirky music filtered through the system, and I closed my eyes.

Text, don't call.

I dug my hand into my hoodie and pulled out my phone. I pushed up my sleeve and added Mila's number as a contact under the name "Wildcat."

Why did she want me to text her and not call? Fuck that. I hit her number and clicked the green button that would call her.

It rang several times and went straight to voice mail.

"You've reached Mila Mercado. Leave a message after the beep, and I'll get back to you. *Namaste.*"

"Hey, hotness, I'm calling. This is Atlas. Program my number." I huffed and hung up. Not more than a minute later, my phone buzzed in my hand.

From: Wildcat
To: Atlas Powers
Don't you listen? I said text not call.

I grinned, and my fingers flew across the keys.

From: Atlas Powers
To: Wildcat
Scared to hear my voice? Of what it will do to you...
Wildcat: *You're really that confident. And here I thought you could be nice.*
Atlas: *Oh, I can be nice. So nice. Let me show you.*
Wildcat: *Ha! Not a chance.*
Atlas: *You know you want to.*
Wildcat: *I know I want to throat punch you.*
Atlas: *You want to kiss me. Admit it.*
Wildcat: *No. Suck it.*
Atlas: *I'd be happy to. What? Your lips. Your tits. Your cunt.*
Wildcat: *You're sexting me?*
Atlas: *You can't possibly be this dumb.*
Wildcat: *Fuck you.*
Atlas: *Exactly! When?*
Wildcat: *You're driving me crazy.*
Atlas: *That's the point. I want you out of your mind for me.*
Wildcat: *Oh, I'm out of my mind all right. For even having this conversation. Go to bed.*
Atlas: *I'd be happy to go to bed with you.*
Wildcat: *Ugh...*
Atlas: *Joking aside. I want to see you. Outside of work.*

With that last text, my heart hammered and my mouth went dry. I waited. The display showed the message was delivered, which meant she'd seen it. Where was the response? The funny retort?

Finally, the message pinged and my stomach dropped.

Wildcat: *I want to see you, too. Naked.*

I grinned. She'd caved. Fuck yes! I shook my head and grinned. I hadn't expected her to admit her desire so completely. Could this night get any better?

Atlas: *I'm in. Time and place?*
Wildcat: *You promise. If I let you come over, you'll sit naked for me?*

Sit naked for me? Weird way of putting it, but whatever floated her boat.

Atlas: *I said I'm in. Time and place?*
Wildcat: *Tomorrow night. 7:00. My place.*

She then typed out her address. I didn't recognize it as anywhere I'd ever been. Didn't matter. With the promise of getting naked with her on the horizon, I'd drive anywhere.

Atlas: *See you then.*
Wildcat: *I'll see you then. Dress comfortably.*

CHAPTER FOUR

Chair Pose (Sanskrit: Utkatasana)

This pose is a basic strengthening pose that is used inside and outside the yoga studio. You may find this pose at a standard aerobics class or a trainer using it to build muscles in the thighs, calves, and core. In yoga, not only does it strengthen the body, but the balancing aspect also strengthens the mind and helps the yogi focus their attention inward. To do this pose, place the feet shoulder distance apart, lift arms up level with the floor and pretend to sit in a chair that's too far away. Make sure to tuck the tailbone.

MILA

My studio apartment was a nightmare. Paint supplies littered my large wooden table. It was the only table I had, so it doubled as a workspace and dining space. Since I ate while I painted most nights, it worked. The current canvases for the gallery showing I was working toward were all stacked in one corner, covered in painting cloths. Unfortunately, I also had yoga clothes strewn on every available surface. I ran around the apartment with my laundry basket dumping anything out of place into it and then shoving it in my closet. I'd organize it later. Once I'd picked up the mess and clutter, I made my bed. As annoying as Atlas was, I didn't want him to think I was a slob. Even if I was one. Some of the time anyway.

The studio I rented wasn't anything to write home about, but it's what I could afford. It worked for now. The apartment was a Cracker Jack box. My bed stood all of ten feet from my workspace, which was five feet from my small loveseat and TV. The tiny kitchenette had one long counter that shared a wall with the refrigerator and stove. I didn't even have an oven; however, I'd put a toaster oven on the tiny counter space. I'd also picked up one of those chopping blocks on wheels so that I had something to prep food on. Plus, it was mobile, and I could roll it in front of the fridge when I wasn't using it.

If my dad hadn't royally screwed up by embezzling money from his company, I'd have gone to college, gotten an art degree, and would be painting full time. Maybe even own my own gallery where I could display my art and that of others trying to live their dream through art. Unfortunately for me, my beloved dad was put behind bars when I was only fifteen.

Mom and I had tried to make it work, and Dad didn't fight the divorce when my mother had requested one after he'd been put away. We'd been doing well until one day she came home and introduced me to the new love of her life, Steve. I didn't find anything wrong with Steve other than the fact that he had two daughters he time-shared with his ex-wife. And he lived in New Jersey, which was three thousand miles away from California and my dad, who I visited regularly. I couldn't leave him. I was all he had left. I was the only person who didn't hate him.

Mom didn't understand. She wanted me to move to New Jersey, get to know Steve's daughters, and be part of their big happy family.

"Leave this disaster, that man, and what he did to us behind! Start over. A fresh go at a happy life," she'd said. Right then and there I lost her. Knew right down to my core that my mother had changed. What Dad did broke her in a way she'd never recover from. She wanted nothing to do with anything he'd touched. In the end, that included me, too.

So at seventeen, I filed for emancipation. Sure, it broke my mother's heart and put a knife so deep into our relationship I still didn't know how to fix it even nine years later. Our relationship now was one of obligation. She made the perfunctory calls on my birthday, Thanksgiving, and Christmas. I returned the effort by calling her on Mother's Day and her birthday. We weren't close. I hadn't spent a holiday with my mother since she left the land of fruit and nuts behind, and I doubted I ever would again. Sometimes I wondered what she'd think if I told her I was getting married or having a baby. She'd probably congratulate me and tell me all about how perfect her stepdaughters' lives were. Nothing I could ever say would matter. She'd had nine years to craft a new life with Steve. I was the one thing unsettled, but at least I lived a world away. She didn't have to think about me, worry, or even care how I was doing. Even though I thought about her all the time. Daily. When I saw Monet with her daughter, Lily, I thought back to when I had that with my mother. At three, my mother hung the moon, too. At twenty-six, I could barely remember what she looked like.

The doorbell dinged. I froze in place as icy chills ran up and down my back. Atlas was here. A slow grin slipped across my lips. I could not wait to use his words against him. When he told me to take my clothes off yesterday, I almost died of shock. Then I noticed all the other patrons disrobing and the realization hadn't quite hit me. It wasn't until he'd said the words "naked yoga" that all the pieces fell into place.

I did what any hot-blooded female with a fiery temper would do. I removed my clothes and took the class, pretending I wasn't at all affected, even though I was. Seeing his naked body made me feel perpetually wet. I wanted so badly to knock him down, hop on his cock, and ride him to the heavens. I even thought about picking up a man last night to relieve the ache, but I just couldn't. Something stopped me. If it wasn't Atlas, I didn't want sex.

This was a new thought process for me, because I always wanted sex. I just didn't always have the time to go out on the prowl. Plus, I'd convinced myself it was perfectly healthy to have a sum total of four to six sexual partners per year as a single twenty-six-year-old. I didn't know what the average number was for a woman, but I figured if I only had one guy every two or three months, then I wasn't technically a whore or even a slut.

The logic was made up to benefit me but hey, it worked when the guilt would seep in as I climbed out of a stranger's bed, put on my clothes, and silently scampered back to my home to crawl into my own bed. I didn't want any of my one-nighters to have my number or my name for that matter. To those men, I was simply *Chelsi*.

The bell rang again, breaking me out of my stupor. I looked at myself in the mirror hung over my bed. I wore a simple slip dress. Nothing impressive. It was what I painted in. Black, spaghetti straps, jersey cotton material with slits at both hips. That way I could straddle my stool and paint comfortably. I'd pulled my hair up into a messy bun. One stubborn curl kept falling out, so I pushed it behind my ear. I wore very little makeup usually since I taught sweaty yoga classes, and it would all melt off, but tonight, I'd put a bit more effort in. I'd lined my goldish-brown eyes with a soft plum, and I'd coated my lashes in midnight black, making them look a mile long. The room was warm, and my temperature was already high in anticipation of him arriving. I'd added a peach lip gloss that actually tasted like peaches, and I smacked my lips together. It would have to do.

I closed my eyes, took a breath, and opened the door. I was unprepared for the drop-dead sexiness that was Atlas Powers. He stood in my doorway, a bottle of red wine dangling from one hand, his keys in the other. He had on dark-wash jeans with a hole in the knee. A well-worn, apparently well-loved, Radiohead T-shirt stretched across his broad chest, the graphic on the front speckled from too many washings. Plus, the album it was from was older. Great band. At least we had that in common. Little else I assumed. Aside from the desire to bicker and bite one another.

"Hey, hotness." He looked me over from head to toe. His head leaned to the side, and he brushed the bottom of his lip with his thumb, a move I was starting to connect to him and him alone. Sexy and so hot, the simple hand gesture proved he was not unaffected by me, and I was licking my lips and yoga breathing to prevent myself from jumping him. Regardless of what he thought, sex was not why I'd invited him over here. Though I wondered how he'd react when he found out the real reason.

I didn't say anything, just watched him watch me.

"Can I come in?" He smiled, looking devastatingly handsome in his leather coat.

"If you must," I retorted snottily, keeping up with our standard banter.

He chuckled and walked in. The room became infinitely smaller with him in it. The hints of leather, earth, and wind coalesced in the air around him as he passed by. I sucked in a full deep breath of his essence and closed the door, leaning against the wooden surface mostly to hold myself up while the raw masculinity that he exuded dissipated and evened out. He stood with his legs in a wide A-shape as he casually took in my place. It didn't take long.

"You paint?" he said, turning in a circle around the room. There wasn't much to it. One three-sixty spin, and he'd be able to catalog it and commit it to memory.

I pushed off the door and went to my small kitchenette. "Yes. Would you like me to open that wine?" I held out my hand.

His gaze was stuck on the corner where my easel sat. "My dad was an artist." The words came out breathy and uncertain, almost as if he didn't mean to share that personal nugget about himself.

I decided to give him that and change the subject. "Cool. The wine?"

He shook his head and handed it to me. I opened it, poured a glass for us both, and then handed him one.

"Thank you for coming. You're really helping me out."

His eyebrows furrowed, and he sipped on the wine before a shadow zipped past his eyes briefly, and he gave me a dazzling smile. "Oh, it will be my pleasure," he said while glancing at my dress again.

I giggled, mostly because he had no idea what he'd inadvertently agreed to through text, and I had proof in the event he planned on bailing. Still, I wanted to enjoy the little verbal play on words a little longer.

"I take it you like my dress." I quirked an eyebrow up and took a sip of the wine. It was a lovely red blend with plum and cherry notes and the subtlest hints of currant. He'd done well.

He grinned, leering. "I'd like it better off you."

I hummed. "Would you?"

"Definitely."

This was going to be so much fun. I could hardly contain my laughter. It bubbled inside of me, dying to get out, but I had to hold off just a little longer. "You first."

He pouted and set his glass down on my wooden workspace. Then he removed the leather jacket and set it over my work stool. I'd have to move it when I sat down, but I wasn't about to miss this show.

"Keep going." I smiled and sipped my wine casually.

Atlas grinned, undid his belt buckle, the button on his jeans, and pulled his zipper down. Then he hooked his fingers around the hem of his kick-ass T-shirt and yanked it over his head.

My breath caught as his golden, muscled chest came into view. His body was ab-so-fucking-lutely perfect. Even that mop of crazy loose curls that reached the scruffy hair on his chin was beautiful. No. Adorable. He smiled, and I grabbed the desk to hold myself up. Those pearly whites, that honeyed chest with the rock-hard abs, the sexy V that dipped low where his pants were undone, all put together were going to be my undoing.

No. Mila. Get your shit together. You have work to do.

Yeah, like push him onto my bed and fuck his brains out. No, no. I shook my head, and he laughed.

"Talking to yourself, wildcat?"

"Um, no. Don't mind me. Continue."

He lifted his arms the same way he'd done in class, threading his fingers and clasping them behind his head. His biceps and forearms bulged with the effort. The musky hints of his cologne mixed with the leather and earth that must have made up his natural scent permeated the air like a trail of smoke from his body to mine. My mouth watered as his earthy male scent hit my nose and weakened my knees.

Get it together, Mila. Work. Think about how perfect he's going to be to work on.

"I'm thinking you have an unfair advantage. I'm half-undressed and you're still fully clothed."

"Ah, there's the rub. I never promised to get naked. You promised you would. Are you a man of your word?"

On that taunt, he curled his fingers into the tops of his jeans, kicked off his shoes, and dropped his pants and boxers to the floor. His cock stood at attention as if it, too, were greeting me. I licked my lips, and I swear to God, it bobbed right in front of my eyes.

"Fuck," I whispered.

Atlas growled, "Your turn." His voice was sand and rocks rubbing together when he spoke. That sound grated against the arousal coating my thighs.

I waved a finger in front of him. "Nuh-uh. Go over there

and sit on that stool."

He clenched his teeth, and in doing so his jaw squared, giving me exactly the delectable effect I wanted to capture on canvas. He was the perfect temptation, the ideal visual I hoped to recreate through my art. I watched him. He flared his nostrils and inhaled loudly. One of his eyes was white-hot blue and the other a deep melted chocolate brown. I could feel the intensity pumping off him in waves of energy as he moved to the chair. Like his eyes, Atlas was such a unique man.

He sat, bare ass on the stool, crossed his arms over his broad chest, and hooked one foot on the bottom rung. Dead sexy. His cock protruded from between his legs in a graphic display of his virility. "All right, wildcat. You've got me naked and sitting for you. What are you going to do with me?"

I grinned huge, picked up my paintbrush, my colors already laid out, and adjusted the canvas so I had the perfect view of his body. I moved his jacket to the loveseat and sat on my own stool, allowing the slits in each side of my dress to ride all the way up to my hips, exposing premium amount of leg. I gave myself a few moments to just look at him. God, he was beautiful.

"I'm going to paint you."

ATLAS

"Say what?"

She grinned one of those cat-that-ate-the-canary smiles and dipped her brush into a color, touched it to another, and swirled them together. "Are you deaf?"

"My hearing is just fine."

Mila hummed and put the brush to the canvas. I could see

her arm working in fluid strokes the full length of the canvas. Her gaze focused on mine, but I could tell from the glassiness of her gaze that she wasn't *seeing me*. My guess, she was seeing nothing but angles.

"You initiated the conversation by asking me to come over and get naked."

Her nose crinkled as she concentrated on the canvas and then on a spot below my waist. Her body was situated at an angle so that I could see all of her but very little of what she painted.

"I did."

"And you knew I thought you wanted to fuck."

That got me a chuckle and a smirk. "Yes."

"And yet all you wanted to do was paint me?"

Her eyebrow rose, and finally, her eyes met mine. "That's not *all* I want to do."

I went to stand up, and her head jerked. "Sit down. Exactly as you were. I have to get the outline and as much as I can. My memory is good but not that good."

Her panicked reply was enough to get me to sit back down. I shifted to make room for my dick. My slowly softening dick.

"Can't you stroke it or something? Having you hard in this one would be perfect."

"You want me hard?" I quipped so fast she gasped and looked down at my cock. Having her eyes there alone helped stir the beast to attention.

She nodded.

"Take your dress off. It's only fair that we're both naked. Otherwise, I'm going to get up and walk out."

She stood and put one hand to her hip. "But you promised!"

I rubbed at my chin. "No. I told you I'd sit naked for you. This is me, sitting naked. Now if you want to keep me here, you're going to remove your dress so that I can look at you and imagine wrapping your legs around my waist and lifting you up and down my cock."

"Jesus. Must you be so vulgar?"

"Look, wildcat, you got me into this. You want to keep me here, you need to give me incentive."

"Fine!" she roared. Her jerky movements and flattened lips did nothing to detract from her beauty. An angry Mila was just as smokin' hot as a calm one. Hell, maybe even more so as she dipped one shoulder, allowing the speck of a strap to fall off and then the other. In less than a second, she was bare before me. As in fully naked.

I grinned and licked my lips, wanting to lick her instead. "You seem to have a surprising lack of underwear."

Her head jerked back. "Are you complaining about me being naked when you just asked me to get naked?"

She sat back down on her stool, dipped her brush in her paint, and continued painting.

"Merely making an observation."

Without breaking stride, she painted and spoke, "If you must know, I hate underwear."

I laughed and ruffled my hair. She glared. "Sorry. It's just funny. What woman doesn't like underwear?"

She tilted her head and narrowed her gaze directly on my chest. "This one. They're uncomfortable. And they almost always show panty lines."

"Not a thong."

"A thong what?"

"A thong doesn't show panty lines."

"Thongs are uncomfortable. A strip of lace or cotton shoved up your ass crack?" She bit her lip and got really close to the canvas before eyeing me again. "No woman wants to wear thongs. She does it simply for a man or her girlfriends."

I lifted my head back and laughed hard. "A woman does not wear a thong for her girlfriends."

This time she turned to me, opening her legs wide as if she didn't realize she was bare-ass naked, and I could see right through to the heart of her. My cock hardened further, painfully even, seeing the lips of her cunt so pink and pretty. Ready to be licked, sucked, fucked.

"You're killing me." I groaned and fisted my dick.

Her eyes widened, and she looked down. Then she slammed her legs shut. "Shit! I'm sorry. Uh, uh, what we talking about? Oh yes, thongs. Girlfriends. Men don't realize how women actually dress for one another more so than for a man."

I hefted the base of my dick and held it tight while breathing through my nose. "Explain."

She continued to paint, arching her spine, that damn tendril of hair falling across her face. I wanted to wrap my finger around that curl, sniff it, and take in her essence.

"Well, women care more about what other women are wearing, how they look in it, even how they look naked. It's human nature. It's almost like we're checking out our competition for the male population so that we are secure in our place in the lineup to find a mate."

"That's ridiculous."

Mila shrugged, and the gesture made her small tits bounce delectably.

"I want to taste your tits."

When I said that, she turned her head and took a slow breath. Her pupils were dilated, and her chest heaved, making the very object of my extreme desire sway again. I groaned.

"Atlas."

"Tit. Mouth. Mine. Now. Or I'm out," I gritted through clenched teeth.

"We shouldn't."

"We are. Right now. Give me your tits. Just a taste and then you can go back and paint." Fuck. I could already imagine what they would taste like. Warm with a hint of salt.

She swallowed and bit the end of her paintbrush. "You don't know how bad I need to paint. My dream..."

"Tits. Mouth. Now. I won't say it again. Then I'll sit here all fucking night, but I need *something* sweet to get me through."

Mila nodded and then lifted off her chair. Her fingers trembled as she put down her supplies. Those hips I'd been salivating over swayed as she walked over.

When she was two feet away, I leaned forward, tagged an arm around her waist and lifted her up. She yelped and wrapped her legs around my waist. My cock rested just under her heat. Then I latched onto one quarter-sized brown nipple and sucked. And sucked. My cheeks hollowed out with the effort. Her fingers threaded through my hair, and she arched, pushing more of her breast into my mouth.

She tasted of cinnamon and smelled like roses. Keeping one hand around her lower back, I lifted the other small breast and tongued the tip. "Taste so fucking good. Like cinnamon gum."

"It's peppermint...uh, natural body wash. I buy it at the local...oh God."

I bit down on her erect tip and then lavished it with soft sucks to soothe the burn of the bite.

"Local farmers' market. It's edible." She sighed and let her head fall back, offering up her body on a silver platter.

I growled, opened my mouth, and pulled as much of her left breast into my mouth as I could. I was right. Fuck, yes. I could put most of it in my mouth.

She moaned and rubbed her lower half against me. I could feel her moisture wetting my pelvis as she ground against me.

I closed my eyes and released her tit. Definitely the last thing I wanted to do, *ever*, but something about the way she proclaimed that she had to paint stopped me from continuing.

My dream. She'd said those words. Two words that had the power to destroy me, almost as much as the world's hottest yoga teacher-slash-artist was doing right now.

Shifting her, I lifted her head and took her mouth. The kiss was brutal and hard, nowhere near gentle and definitely not sweet. I bit at her lips, sucked on her tongue, and took the kiss from her. With my eager lips, I impressed that this was not over. We'd take it there. Just not now. Then I pulled away on a huge breath, stood, lifted her along with me, walked the few paces to her stool, and set her back down. Her eyes were awash with lust and desire. At that moment, if I wanted to carry her to bed and fuck her, I could have. She'd have allowed it. But it didn't feel right.

"But..."

"Paint. Talk. Tell me your dreams."

CHAPTER FIVE

SOLAR PLEXUS
C H A K R A

Manipura is associated with the natural element fire and directly linked to one's sense of self. It is depicted as a golden bright yellow, like the sun. This energy center relates to self-esteem, personal identity and sense of purpose in life. Keeping this chakra open is necessary to keep one's self goal-oriented and focused on future dreams.

MILA

I swallowed back the instant prick of fear and anxiety that came with speaking about my true desires. The only person who knew my dreams was Monet. I'd never told a man anything of value about me. About what I wanted out of life. What I worked so hard for.

Atlas, hot as Hades, both fists gripped at his sides, as if physically preventing himself from grabbing me, turned, and walked back to the stool. He sat his ass in the seat, crossed his arms over his chest like he'd done before, and leaned back. His rock-hard cock stood tall and thick, ready to pillage and plunge. And right now, I was so on board with that plan. I shifted on the stool, feeling the arousal coating my thighs and looked down. My nipples were no longer a soft brown but a reddened plum color. Dots of broken capillaries speckled around the tips where Atlas had sucked like a Hoover. There was even a round bruise the size of a nickel spreading across the upper swell of one breast.

Damn sexy bastard had marked me. "A hickey!"

He smirked. "I can't control myself around you. I want to bite you as much as I want to fight you."

I sighed, picked up my painting supplies, and went back to work.

"Dreams?" he asked again.

"Tell me yours first." I was stalling.

Atlas cracked his neck from left to right, the pop audible on both sides.

"Ouch. Sounds like someone is tense."

He glared. "Perhaps because I'm sitting on a stool, less than ten feet away from the naked girl I want to fuck, and my dick is hard as stone. Ever heard of blue balls?"

I grinned. "Hey, moments ago you stopped what could have gone further."

He scowled. "Yeah, yeah, and then I'd get to be the douchenozzle keeping you from your dreams, which obviously has something to do with painting me or painting in general, because I doubt that you've had an ongoing desire to paint me since we haven't known each other that long."

"Very observant." I slathered a long blob of color down

the center of his chest where a shiny key hung. "Hey, can you remove the key? It's impeding the view."

He shook his head. "No. Paint me with or without it, but I'm not taking it off." His words were harsh all of a sudden, not even a hint of the playful edge we'd developed.

I let out a breath and focused my attention on him. "I'm sorry I asked. Is the key important to you?"

"Is painting important to you?"

"It's my life, my future."

He ran a hand through his messy hair. At least the hair I could paint how I wanted since it moved around so much. Those lengthy curls could go whichever way, and the painting would work just fine. "Yeah well, the key is my past. It stays with me. Always."

Huh. Interesting thing to say about an object. "What does it open?"

Atlas's nostrils flared. "If you're going to continue this line of questioning, I'm going to need to put my mouth on you again. Maybe my fingers too. Depends."

I stopped painting mid-stroke. Him even mentioning his mouth and my skin in the same sentence sent a fireball of lust roaring through my body. I gripped my paintbrush and clenched my teeth allowing a moment of calm to come over me so I could respond.

"Depends on what?" I asked.

His entire face went from grump to solicitous in a heartbeat. "On how you want to come, wildcat."

"God, you're such a filthy animal," I spoke through clenched teeth, pretending his words didn't turn me on.

He laughed. "Honey, this is nothing. I'm happy to show you filthy. Finish up what you need to, and I'll show you filthy."

I put my brush to canvas and outlined the features of his face. "Is this your normal way of picking up women? Talk dirty to them?"

"Do you always paint the men you want to fuck?"

"Never. You're the first."

"So you admit you want to fuck me." He waggled his eyebrows.

I snickered and outlined his brow on the canvas and then moved to his soulful eyes. I hadn't decided yet if I wanted to fill in this painting with color or do the entire thing in black and white. When I painted something in color, it came to life in a very "real" way, like the image could jump off the canvas at any moment. With black and white, everything seemed more abstract.

"Why do you always answer a question with a question?" I asked.

"Do I?"

I groaned, and he chuckled. All in all, I was getting a lot of painting done, my muse having been so stoked that I hardly noticed that I was sitting on my stool naked while I painted an insanely sexy man not ten feet away. A man who I wanted to pull off the stool and push onto my queen-sized bed and have my wicked way with. That in itself would be a first. Having sex on my bed. I'd never had sex in my apartment, because I didn't bring men here. I always went to their homes. Less mess involved and I could just get up and go. Be free.

"What's that on your face? A smile? Are you thinking about finding new ways to paint me?"

I smiled huge. "That's not hard. I've already imagined you in a hundred different settings naked and willing."

His eyes widened to the size of saucers, and he smiled big,

full teeth and all. "Really? Do tell."

"Ways to paint you, curly. Jeez. Do you always have sex on the brain?"

"With you in the room, yes. Normally, no. I've always got a tune in my head."

"Music?" I asked while filling in his arms crossed over his chest on the canvas.

He nodded. "Yeah, I play guitar, sing."

"Professionally?"

"I'd like to, but no. I play locally. Clubs, bars, that kind of thing. Write my own music, sometimes I write for others. Whatever it takes to get the bills paid, you know?"

I nodded. Now *that* I understood. I worked my ass to the bone in order to pay rent, utilities, and feed my muse in art supplies. "I get it."

He placed his hands on his thighs and leaned forward. His gaze seemed to dig right into my psyche, straight through to my soul. "You do, don't you?"

"Yeah. Whatever it takes to make it happen. Don't stop. If you want it, believe it. Be your strength."

"Be your strength. I like that. Something tells me you know a lot about being strong." He glanced around my room, focusing on one thing for a few moments and then moving to the next. "You only have two pictures in frames."

I tensed and hovered the brush right at his elbow on the canvas. "Again, very observant, curly. Do you want a medal for that?"

"No, I want to know why."

I shrugged. "Don't have a lot of pictures to put in frames."

He rolled his eyes. "Now that's a line of bull and you know it. An artist who doesn't have a lot of pictures? Try selling that ice to another Eskimo, because I'm not buying, hotness. What's the deal? You not from around here?"

"No, I am. I just don't have a lot of people in my life that I'd want to frame. My dad, my best friend, and her daughter, that's about it. I don't have time to build on relationships, so I cherish the few I have. Is that okay with you?"

He lifted his hands and waved them in front of him. "No harm, no foul. Sorry. Didn't mean to piss you off. This time..." He grinned, and the tension that emanated between us momentarily disappeared.

"So your dream is to make it big in music, I gather?"

He grabbed the key around his neck and pulled it along the beaded strand. The sound of each bead ticking against the metal of the key clicked like a zipper being pulled, only he kept doing it. Over and over like a nervous tic. "Yeah, or something. And you want to paint."

"Or something."

ATLAS

"Done yet?" I was tired, hungry, and horny. Three things that did not make me a happy man.

Mila ignored my question, her concentration on the job. She had her lip firmly between her teeth, her brows were pinched together, and her eyes were lasered on a point on the canvas. Her face was mere inches from the painting.

I hadn't seen any of it yet. For all I knew, she could have been drawing naughty stick figures for the last two hours. What I did know was that my ass hurt, my dick had long since gone soft, and I had a cramp in between my shoulder blades from holding my arms across my chest. Every time I tried to move them, she'd ask me to put them back. Something about holding the integrity of the pose. Whatever.

While she did her thing on the painting, I got up, grabbed my jeans, and tugged them on. I shook out my shirt, turned it right-side out, and jerked it over my head. Still, her focus never left the tiny strokes she was making, her hand barely moving. As quiet as a mouse, I planted myself behind her and stood as still as I could and watched her, really *watched* her.

Mila Mercado was beyond beautiful, a blind man could see that. Her skin glowed like the sun glinting off the smooth waters of Lake Tahoe in the dead of summer. Wisps of soft, honeyed curls caressed her nape. Her back was long for such a petite woman and devoid of any birthmarks or even freckles for that matter. The tiny pebbles of her spine dotted down her back, and the stirring of something bigger than my dick came to life. A song...

Everything I didn't need...
Bring a man to his knees...

Cinnamon lips so hot and fresh...
Wait until I steal your breath...

Curls that twirl and tangle...
Don't let this lust dangle

Fill me up with your spicy heat
With you, I'll trust the deep

It wasn't great but definitely a start to something, and for that, I was grateful. I hadn't written a word in months. One night sitting naked for a hellion artist with a sassy mouth and an ass I could bite a hundred times and never get enough of, and my muse was stoked. I ran a hand over the hefty bulge between my thighs. Looked like something else was stoked, too.

I tiptoed on bare feet until I was right behind Mila. Her head tilted to the side as if she was assessing her work. I took the opportunity to place my lips on that open space on her neck and wrap my arms around her. She gasped but leaned back into me, arching her chest. Invite accepted, I gripped the small globes of her breasts and rolled each nipple between thumb and forefinger, elongating them until she mewled in pure ecstasy.

That's when I opened my eyes and looked at what she'd been working on. My hands froze over her tits. Hell, my entire body froze. There I was. Me. In stark black and white with bits of random colors layered to highlight the shadows.

"Holy fuck, Mila," I croaked in awe. Complete and utter awe.

She groaned. "You don't like it. It's not done." She hurried to add, "I have hours of work to put into it."

"Like it." I swallowed the golf-ball sized lump that clogged my throat.

Everything I didn't need
Bring a man to his knees
Fill me up with your spicy heat
With you, I'll trust the deep

With you, I'll trust the deep. The line ran a marathon as I took in every harsh slash of paint, each smooth ripple of muscle as she saw it.

"Is this how you see me?" My voice was so filled with emotion I could have cried. Fucking dropped to my knees and wept. Shit. Fuck. What was this wildcat bringing out in me?

Her hands gripped mine at her waist where I'd pulled her into a hug. A hug. Not a grope where I'd been headed before. No, a god's honest tight embrace. One I was nowhere near willing to let go of until I'd gotten my shit under control.

Her naked body trembled in my arms. "Well...yeah. To me, this is how you look. But it's art, you know. It's..." She tried to say something more, but I couldn't hear it. Didn't want her mouth to get in the way of what was honestly the most beautiful thing I'd ever witnessed in my life. I put my hand over her lips.

"Shush. Don't try to explain it, wildcat."

Another quiver ran through her, and I removed my hand from her mouth. Thank God she kept quiet while my eyes hoarded their fill of her work. Of me.

I shook my head and focused on every little nuance I could take in. "You're magnificent."

She tried to push off me, but I held her tight and wrapped my arms fully around her so she couldn't move away.

"Mila, you made me look like a god."

She guffawed. "Narcissistic much?"

This was no joke. The painting was definitely me, mostly in stark black and white, but with the added sweeps of rainbow colors in the hidden spaces, it was as if I could come alive. And in the painting, I was cut, strong, beautiful. She saw me as more than I was. My chest puffed up in pride.

"You see me this way?" My tone sounded scratchy and as raw as I felt.

I held onto her but walked around the stool. "When you

look at me, this is what you see?" I hooked a thumb over my shoulder at her art.

Her eyes wrinkled at the edges, and her mouth opened and closed. Then an expression of resolve came over her face, and she lifted her chin and looked me in the eye. "I don't have to explain my art. Just like you don't have to explain your songs."

I grinned. "No, you don't. But you know what this means."

"No, what?"

"Means you think I'm hot."

She scowled.

"You think I'm sexy." I grinned and leered at her tits.

"Puh-leeze," she muttered and looked off into the distance.

"Admit it. You want me to get all up in your sweetness."

She tipped her head back and laughed. "Oh, I'll admit I want to let you in. The problem is...will I be able to get you right back out?"

Her words, those caramel-brown eyes, the stiffness to her chin spoke volumes about what she wanted.

I ran a hand up her arm and curled it around her nape. "What, not the cuddling and spooning type?"

Mila smirked and pressed both of her hands under my T-shirt to caress and fondle my abdomen. Her fingers were freezing cold, and I jerked when she laid them flat.

"I'm more the hit it and quit it type," she deadpanned.

Now that surprised me. However, I figured if I wanted to get anywhere with the wildcat, I needed to play her game.

"And what about me makes you think I have anything more than an interest in making you scream? All. Night. Long."

She harrumphed and tugged my neck until our foreheads pressed together. "Then why are you dressed?"

"Because someone was neglecting me while I sat for hours being an artistic god."

Mila groaned. "Oh, poor little baby." She shook her head. "Now you've ruined it. The mood is broken. Why are you such a pain in my ass?"

I wrapped both of my hands around her neck and lifted her chin with my thumbs. "Oh, I plan on being a very big pain in your ass. And soon." I ground my pelvis against her leg so she would be reminded of just how big of a pain I'd be. Her gasp was music to my ears. "Besides, it would be a far improvement over that sassy mouth, though I have the cure for that as well." Another pelvis roll had her straightening, trying to get closer.

"But first..." I caressed her nose with mine and kissed my way to her ear.

She craned her neck, giving me more room. "Yeah?"

I grinned against her buttery soft skin and whispered, "Food. I'm starving."

Her fingernails dug into my biceps as she pushed me off and away from her. "You're a bastard, you know that?"

I laughed hard and kept laughing as she grabbed her dress, pulled it over her head, and hid her insanely beautiful body from my gaze. Good move, because I was having a hard time choosing between fucking her and feeding her. The digital clock on the microwave across the room displayed a glaring green ten p.m. We both needed to eat. I wouldn't last in the sack on an empty stomach, and after all this buildup, I wanted hours to tame my wildcat. Hours.

Her entire body stiffened as I looped an arm around her shoulders. "Come on, hotness. Let me feed you. Then I'll fuck you. All night long. Promise."

She tried to shove away from me but I held firm. "You think you're getting me in bed now? You're delusional."

"No, I'm hungry and horny. In that order. You are, too. If I went down on my knees right now, you'd be wet. And I'm sorry I'm not taking care of that, but you lost that time when you wanted to paint me. Now come on. How do you feel about sandwiches?"

"Hate them," she growled.

"Pizza?"

"Not happening." She flipped her hair, supposedly disinterested.

"Thai?"

"Fuck you. Let me go."

I steered her to the door where our shoes were. I let her go long enough to put my shoes on and tossed her flip-flops in front of her. She was leaning against her tiny kitchen counter.

"I'm not going with you."

"Yes, you are."

Her eyes went from that chocolaty brownish gold to blazing with anger. "I said no."

"What's it going to take to get you to go have dinner with me?"

"Hell freezing over," she grated.

I chuckled. "Aside from that. Name your price."

She looked over my shoulder and then slowly an expression that mimicked a woman scorned filtered to the surface. Unfortunately, I knew that look well. Women who wanted more from me romantically regularly gave me that look when I blew them off for a gig, a last-minute open mic night, or some other reason.

"Let me paint you again. Naked."

"Deal," I agreed too quickly. My ass was still feeling the ache from the hard stool.

"That easy?" She slipped her small feet into her flip-flops and grabbed a cardigan that hung on the tree by the door.

"Yep."

"I'll bet that's what all the girls say." Her tone was matter-of-fact with a dose of snide bitch. I loved it.

"Ouch!" I clutched at my chest. "You wound me so," I joked, opened the door, and then slapped her bubble butt hard enough to leave my imprint as she walked through.

"Dammit, curly! That hurt!" she yelled and rubbed at her sore cheek.

"Now *that* is what all the girlies say." I winked and led her down the hall.

CHAPTER SIX

Seated Forward Bend (Sanskrit: Paschimottanasana)
Keeping the front torso long and straight, lean forward from the hip joints, not the waist. Flex the feet and breathe as you lengthen the tailbone away from the back of the pelvis. If possible, take the sides of the feet with the hands, thumbs on the soles, elbows fully extended. If not, rest the hands on the calves, ankles or whatever you can reach besides the knees. You do not want to put unwanted pressure on the knees. Breathing rhythmically in and out will help you move further into the pose. Eventually you will be able to touch your heels and rest your entire body alongside your legs.

ATLAS

Turned out, Mila was not a picky eater. I'd never seen someone of her size put away so many slices of pizza. And this wasn't the thin cut, no crust stuff. I had a friend who owned the local Fat Slice Pizza place bring a couple pies over on his way home. I owed him a song sung in honor of his girlfriend's birthday this weekend, but that was a small price to pay to see Mila chowing down. The woman was a beast. Half a pizza gone, and she was picking up her fourth slice. And these slices were more like twofers.

"Hungry?"

She nodded while shoveling in a gargantuan bite. "Haven't eaten since the banana I had for breakfast." Mila chewed and shimmied from side to side while sitting on my apartment floor in front of the glass-top table. I sat on the couch across from her. I wanted to look at her gorgeous face while she ate, or in this case...binged.

After my third slice, I sat back with my hand to my gut and loafed on the couch.

"Tell me about you. What makes Mila tick?"

She glanced up and then blinked slowly while wiping her mouth with a napkin. "Aside from irritating, overconfident musician yogis with messy hair?"

I grinned. "You love my hair. I see you staring at it constantly."

"No, I really want to chop off those pieces that fall into your eyes. Do you realize how often you run your hand through it? At first, I thought it was because you were trying to show off your bulging biceps, but now, after spending two hours looking at nothing but you, it's annoying." She took another huge bite, taking half of the veggies on the slice with it.

Ouch, that potshot burned. I glared at her, wanting to toss her a barb after that callous hair comment. A woman should never, ever, comment on a man's hair like that. Before I knew it, I was nailing her on her eating. "Who eats like you do and stays fit?"

She pursed her lips, licked each finger on the hand that had held the slice, and leaned her elbows on the table. "I teach no less than ten ninety-minute classes a week. I stay up for hours painting and I work every weekend. This"—she gestured to her seated form—"is constantly in a calorie deficit. I'm lucky if I catch lunch. Why do you care?"

I chuckled and leaned forward. "Honey, I don't. I like a woman who can eat, so eat up."

"I will!" she declared before taking a big bite of her now fifth slice, her perfect teeth sinking into the doughy crust and breaking off with a gorilla-sized gash left in its wake.

"You're something else, you know that?"

She nodded. "Yeah, probably why I don't have a lot of friends." She grabbed the cold beer I'd served and sucked back a few swallows. "That's not what I mean. Obviously, I have friends."

I narrowed my gaze. "You live alone, work all the time, and have two pictures up in your home. There's not much in the way of girlie shit at your place, basically implying that you don't have a lot of people buying you presents or giving you worthless totems that just clutter up your home. So my money is on you having very few friends. Why is that?"

She licked her lips and leaned back so that her elbows rested on the carpet. Her nipples were visible through the thin cotton of her dress since she'd taken off the cardigan earlier.

Such perfect brown tips. I could easily recall the taste of her on my tongue even hours later.

I watched as she inhaled and tilted her head to the side. "I don't have time to build relationships. As you said, I have a crazy work schedule. Monet, one of the people in the pictures, is my best friend. I see her when I have a break or need to commune with a female."

"And your dad? Does he live close?"

Instantly Mila's expression tightened, and the fingers of both hands dug into the carpet until her knuckles turned white. "You could say that." Her words were flat and cold all of a sudden.

"I asked that. Where does he live?"

"San Quentin," she mumbled.

I sat up straight. "Wait. San Quentin as in the state penitentiary?"

She peered at the beer bottle sitting on the table as if it held all the answers to the universe. "Yeah."

"When?"

"Ten years now. I was sixteen."

Not wanting to grill her, but still wanting to know, I had to ask. "What'd he do?"

She turned her body around and lay sideways on the ground, resting her elbow on the carpet and placing her head into her hand. "Embezzlement."

I cringed. "Ouch. Isn't that kind of small potatoes, though?"

She ran her hand along the carpet. "It would have been if he'd taken thousands. He embezzled millions from his own company and was caught for insider trading."

"Damn, how long?"

"Twenty years." She sighed as if admitting her father's sins added a heaping dose of weight onto her very small shoulders. In that moment, I wanted to take some of that weight and carry it for her, at least for a little while. Give her what I'd bet would have been a much-needed break.

It all didn't make sense. That was such a long sentence. "That long for stealing his own money?"

Mila groaned and shook her head. "It's more than that. The charges were doubled because of the two offenses, but since he had three investors, it was considered stealing from three different people. In California, you get five years for every person that you steal over a hundred grand from. Add the trading and boom." She snapped her fingers. "My dad, in the clink, three sentences to serve consecutively, so twenty years. His whole life over."

"Shit, Mila. I'm sorry. That had to rock your world."

"Yeah, at the time, it did. Still does."

"Where's your mom in all this?" I wanted to keep her talking. She was opening up to me, and for the first time in the long line of women before Mila, I actually cared. No, more than that. I wanted to know about her. This woman was feisty, sassy, had a body that could make men weep, and a talent so raw and untamed I found I wanted to know more about her. It wouldn't be enough until I knew *everything*.

Fuck. That thought hit me like a herd of wild stallions plowing into me at every direction.

Mila let out a long, strained breath while a lock of her hair fell into her face. She lifted it and twirled it with one finger before lying back completely flat on the floor to stare at the ceiling.

"She met a guy right away. Got married. Except he already

had a family, too. In New Jersey. She wanted me to uproot my life and move with them."

"Since you live in Oakland, I'm assuming that didn't happen, unless it was short-term and you came back," I pushed.

"No. I didn't go. I couldn't leave him, you know?" She glanced at me quickly and then looked away.

"I do know. Too well, I'm afraid. It sucks when one parent up and leaves no matter what the circumstances."

Her head turned my direction, and her voice lowered to one of curiosity and concern. "Sounds like you know from experience."

I half laughed, half groaned. "Yeah. I do. My father left when I was eight. I came home from school one day, and he'd rushed into the house from one of his many escapades. He was really excited. Too excited. Mom admitted he was probably high on meth or LSD. My father was the ultimate hippie artist. Painted, whittled wood, sculpted, created art from nothing. Truly amazing pieces, too, all of them. I used to be so proud of what he'd been able to make with his own hands."

"And that day he left?" she asked, bringing me right back to the very day.

★ ★ ★

"Atlas my boy! I'm off on a big adventure. Big. Huge. Life-changing." My father was a whirlwind as he jumped around, tossing clothes and cassette tapes into a large, tattered green duffle bag.

"Where are you going?" I followed him around like I always did. Mom had joked that I was Kenneth Powers's shadow.

Dad whizzed by me and grabbed the foot-tall plastic pipe thing. It was rainbow-colored and had a spot where Dad sucked through the top and another spot where he placed a lit lighter. He'd use it to make smoke. He said it helped him think. Helped him create his art. When he wasn't home, I looked at the plastic thing. Sniffed it and gagged. It smelled like sour gunk that I couldn't imagine breathing into, but one day I vowed to have Dad teach me about how it helped him make art, because I, too, was going to create. I just didn't know what.

"Dad, where are you going?" I asked again.

His movements were jerky and his breathing fast. "Doesn't matter. But I'll be back. Eventually. It's going to be a long trip."

I started to cry. "Take me with you," I pleaded and tugged on his shirt from behind.

Dad whirled around and got down on his knees. He took off a key he'd carried around his neck for as long as I could remember. He put the key around my neck and placed his hand over it. "This will change your life. More than I ever could or will."

"But I want to be with you."

He kissed my forehead and pressed his hand over the key. "And you always will be. I love you, son. Be good to your mama. She's going to need you."

"When will you come back?" I screamed and followed him out our tiny shoebox-sized duplex. I hated the neighbors because they had four kids, and they were always mean and dirty. Also, they kept their house filthy, which made us get those nasty roaches in our house. Mom spent so much time battling those big black bugs, all because the neighbors didn't clean up their house.

My father opened the door of a powder blue VW Bus with a white top. A bunch of his friends were piled in there; one of the women hooked an arm around his neck and kissed him there.

"I don't know, my boy. Maybe never, probably someday."

★ ★ ★

"You and your mom were abandoned?" Mila sat up quickly, her tone horrified.

I rubbed a hand over my face. "Yeah. That was the last time I saw him. Still don't know where he is."

"Did you ever try to look for him?" she asked.

I shrugged. "A bit. When I was old enough and smart about the Internet. I typed in his name, did some searching but never found anything concrete. It's hard to find a man who's been gone twenty years. The odds are he's probably dead."

Even the words sent a knife to my heart and a tightness so fierce to my gut, the desire to hurl the pizza I'd just eaten was strong. Imagining my father dead...brutal. I shook my head trying to dispel the vile image.

Mila sighed. "Well, aren't we a pair?"

I laughed. "You know what? I think we just might be."

MILA

Even though Atlas and I had enough desire zipping through our systems to light up a football stadium, we'd ended last evening thoughtful and far more melancholy than a raucous night in the sack could have conjured. After pizza, we drank one more beer, talked a bit more about our families, or lack thereof, and just hung out. As much as I hated to admit it, the evening overall was nice. Comfortable. The man was still one of the most infuriatingly annoying people I'd ever known, and I knew for a fact that he felt the same about me. Then again, maybe that was the way these things worked. Maybe we were just meant to be friends.

Friends.

Could I be friends with Atlas? Was it normal to want to have dirty, sweaty sex with your friend? I didn't think so, and unfortunately, I didn't have enough of those to ask.

My thoughts were all over the place as I made my way through the hallway of Lotus House to prep for my first Vinyasa class of the day. When I got to my room, fellow yoga instructor Dash Alexander was leaning against the wall.

"Hey, Dash. How goes it?"

He casually leaned one hand against the wall, putting his weight into it. "You tell me." He grinned.

I stopped at the door and used my key to unlock it, since I was the first to arrive for the day. Dash followed me in, his mat curled under his arm.

"I'm not sure I'm following."

Dash unrolled his mat not far from the front of the stage. He was in incredible shape, and had he been interested in the past, I would have taken him six ways from Sunday. Besides the kissing on the mouth that he did with everyone, he'd never so much as hinted that he was interested. No long, lusty glances, no checking out my assets. Nada. Zip. Zilch. I just figured he wasn't into Latinas.

"Saw you leave Atlas's apartment last night. At *midnight*." He lifted his eyebrows, putting his amber-colored gaze on full display.

"That's right. You live in that warehouse across the street from him." I nodded and ignored his subtle dig for info and laid out my mat.

He snickered. "Yes, ma'am."

"Whatever. So you're assuming I was banging your friend?" I let out a tired, frustrated breath. I had not had enough sleep last night to start a conversation like this. I'd spent the entire night dreaming about screwing the man in question, which had led to a lot of tossing, turning, and finally a round with my vibrator.

He walked closer to the riser where I was taking off my hoodie and shimmying out of my track pants. I wore a black sports bra and tight Lycra shorts for heated Vin Flow; that's what I was teaching this morning.

"Are you saying you didn't?" His tone was playfully accusatory.

"We didn't," I said, not all together a lie. Technically, we didn't have sex, and aside from a long kiss at the door and the fun we'd had earlier in the evening at my pad, there was nothing more to tell.

He lifted a hand and scrubbed at his jaw. "But when I crossed over to have a few words with Atlas, he was so relaxed and..."

"And?" I blinked, waiting for him to hit me with another bogus attempt at calling me out.

"...happy," he finished.

I laughed. "Okay. I admit we had an interesting evening, but mostly we hung out."

"Was that before or after you painted him...naked?" His eyes were ablaze with excitement.

I pursed my lips and put a hand on one hip. "He told you that, huh? You know I'm an artist. I'm doing a show soon, and I need more subjects. I'd love to paint you, if you're interested." I threw out the request; I'd have been damned honored to paint Dash. His body, his essence, exuded confidence but not in a skeezy way. People flocked to Dash because, at the heart of him, he was a good guy, a solid, caring human being.

He chuckled and stretched out one arm across his chest and then repeated the move with the other. "I would, but my wife would probably not be too pleased."

Wife. Male and female. Together.

I sucked in a huge breath and lifted my hands to my chest in a prayer gesture. "Would you and your wife ever consider posing together?" The nervous twitch I got in my hands when I was feeling the need to paint tingled at my knuckles.

Dash curled his hand around his neck. "I don't know if I could get Amber to agree to that. Maybe. Would people know who the subjects were?"

I waved my hands in front of us. "No, no. We could keep it totally anonymous. And...I can do you one better. If you both would agree to pose together, nude, I'll gift you the painting after the show."

He sighed. "Doesn't that defeat the purpose of selling your art?"

Without realizing it, I shifted my weight from foot to foot, getting more excited about the concept with every second that passed. "Yes and no. I need a full show with many facets of my art and canvases on display, but not all of them have to be available for sale."

"I don't know; can I talk to Amber?"

"Of course, of course! And the only one who would be seeing you would be me. Private session." I crossed my heart.

"Now that you've just floored me with an opportunity I would normally jump at...because well, I think being part of someone's art is an incredible experience...you have to give me something in return."

I frowned. "But I already told you I'd give you the painting."

He laughed. "Yes, that, too. Right now, though, I'm curious about what's going on with you and my buddy Atlas."

Never let it be said that women are the only gossips in the world. The more time I actually spent getting to know my fellow yogis, a lot of which I hadn't made a priority in the few years I'd been here, the more I found that they were all intertwined in one another's lives.

Take Dash for example. He was friends with Genevieve and got punched out by Trent for kissing her on the mouth, which I found out from Dara Jackson, our resident meditation specialist and local baker. And now Dash was married to Genevieve's best friend, Amber, and he and Trent were friends. He was also best friends with Atlas, who I was now entangled with.

"Right now, nothing's going on with Atlas. I mean, he annoys the heck out of me. He's good-looking. We made out, I painted him, then we sat around his coffee table, chatting, eating pizza and drinking beer, and then I went home. End of story."

Throughout my diatribe, Dash's eyes widened and his mouth dropped open.

"You better close your mouth, or you might catch flies."

He shook his head quickly. "I'm sorry. You spent all night together, made out, and talked?"

"Yes. Talked. Like we are now. Ever heard of it? I'm sure you do it all the time with your wife, your friends, people you work with."

He smiled wide. "This is big. Huge," he said with a dramatic flourish rubbing his hands together like he had a secret.

"What is?"

"Atlas Powers didn't seal the deal. Hmm."

I leaned closer into his personal space. "Are you referring to me as a score?"

He moved lightning fast, waving his arms like a crazy person. "No, you misunderstood. It's just Atlas doesn't have female friends, aside from my wife. If he's with a woman, he's *with* a woman."

I rolled my eyes. "I get your drift. Then again, I'm not like all women."

He looked me over from head to toe, his gaze lingering on all my sexy bits. I definitely did not expect that response since he'd never before given me the time of day. Dash Alexander was officially checking me out. For the first time ever. But why?

"No, you are not. Spunky and spicy seems to fit the bill. You are definitely his type. Are you going to see him again?"

"For sure. He promised me another painting session. He gave his word."

Dash crossed his arms and lifted one hand to his mouth where he bit down on his thumb. "I meant romantically, Mila."

"What are you, Dr. Phil? I don't know. Yes. No. Maybe. I don't plan my sexual escapades in advance."

"Sexual escapades. My, my, you are one hot tamale."

I shook my head and turned to finish setting up, clearly indicating that this conversation was over. "Shut up."

"Hot tamale!" were his parting words as he sat down to stretch for class.

Me? I had to spend ninety minutes teaching and sweating while thinking about Atlas Powers and his all-encompassing kisses, his mouth on my breasts, working me into submission, his hand on my ass. All of that, and the fact that I'd soon have his delectable, masculine, fit body on display again had me all twitchy with desire. What would I do with him? My sex clenched, and my clit throbbed.

Sexual escapades sounded pretty frickin' nice right about now.

CHAPTER SEVEN

SOLAR PLEXUS
C H A K R A

Men and women driven by the manipura are naturally competitive. They may actively participate in sports, projects, and hobbies where they excel and rate their accomplishments on whether or not they are better than the ones around them. It comes very naturally to them to be leaders. You'll find a lot of manipura driven individuals in high-level management positions, running their own businesses.

ATLAS

"Now splay your fingers and toes out in a morning stretch, slowly waking the mind, body, and the spirit. Ease onto your right side in the fetal position for a few more moments. Enjoy the last minute of your deep relaxation." I waited five full breaths before continuing. "Now press into your hand, coming into a seated position facing the teacher."

Once everyone got into place, I pressed my hands to the center of my breastbone or heart center. "We're going to do three community oms. The om has many different sacred and spiritual meanings. Primarily found in Hinduism and Buddhism, the om is much like a prayer, an incantation made before and during the recitation of spiritual texts." I glanced around the room, ensuring each student was following along. "In yoga, it is often used as the root mantra and the beginning in the act of chanting. For yogis, though, the humming and reverberating sound is grounding and forces the person to connect with the earth's magnetic energy. The om is often said to be that of all things, the universe, and the way we can access the essence of our very own self."

I started the first one, opening my mouth wide into a circular shape, pressing my heart, chest high, and letting out the first syllable. "Ooooooommmmmmmm," I called out, loving the moment when the rest of the class joined in. The first om was always soft and then built in volume when the voices of the rest of the students in attendance joined in.

In class, the second om was always full and resonated deeply within a person's heart and settled into their rib cage and gut.

The third. Now that was where the beauty lay. By the third community om, the class was secure in their ability to chant as one. The entire room lit up with the combined energy and freedom of so many filling their souls with a communal essence, one that would take them through their day feeling a sense of joy and peace unlike any other.

I closed my eyes and bowed. "Namaste," I said, silently wishing them happiness and love before sitting back up and opening my eyes.

Naked bodies everywhere. Each person bare and free. God, I loved teaching naked yoga. When clothes—symbolizing the walls and masks we all hide behind and the physical parameters—were stripped away, what was left was honest and pure.

I felt like the luckiest guy around.

Taking my time, I turned and shut off the music, grabbed my pants, and stood.

A few giggles behind me caught my attention. Two women were standing completely bare, waiting at the riser, while their young, bouncing tits were fully on display.

"Hi, Atlas," the brunette with the bigger breasts said. "I'm Jenifer with one N, and this is my friend, Kallie." She pointed to her blond friend standing next to her. The girl's entire face was pink with what I assumed was embarrassment. She didn't say anything as her long straight hair hung down over her smaller tits. Her pink, erect nipples poked through the strands of her golden locks enticingly. Usually, that alone would have my mini-me standing at attention gratefully, but for some reason, nothing. Not even a prickle of excitement.

"Ladies, how can I help you?" I said and held my bundled-up pants over my cock.

After-class chatting while naked did not appeal to me. I wasn't ashamed of my body, and I absolutely loved women in all shapes and sizes, but regular chitchat while naked didn't seem right. It took me out of the Zen moment I'd accomplished through the ninety-minute class.

Jenifer held a lock of her hair and twirled it around her finger, pushing out her large breasts for premium viewing. As if I could miss them. They were huge and fake. I'd seen and felt enough fake breasts to know I preferred the real deal. Nothing wrong with a woman enhancing what the good Lord gave her, but I preferred a nice round, bubblicious ass—*like Mila's*—to a huge pair of jugs. Damn, her ass was firm, round, with just enough bounce to jiggle when she walked. No amount of yoga would take away that ass. I should send her mother a thank-you card for her luscious genetics.

"Um, my friend and I were wondering if you wanted to grab a cup of coffee or a sandwich at Rainy Day Café with us. You know, maybe we could talk about whatever comes up?" She blatantly glanced down to where I'd held my pants.

I smiled and shook my head. Before I could respond, I was startled by the sound of a heavy yoga mat hitting wood flooring. I jerked around and was greeted to the view of the very fine ass I had been thinking about moments ago. Now *that* got my dick's attention.

Bouncy brunette cleared her throat and tapped my shoulder. "You were saying? About going out with us?" she supplied rather unhelpfully.

Mila grumbled something under her breath from behind me.

"As I was saying..." I backed up a step, purposefully bumping my bare ass into Mila. Her hands came up and held my hips.

Sha-wing! Mini-me was now at full attention.

Mila leaned her front against my back. "Watch where you're sticking that thing." She pushed off, forcing me to fumble, losing the grip on my yoga pants.

My hard dick was now hanging out in the open, my balls drawn up tight, all for the wildcat behind me, though the girls in front wouldn't assume that. Jesus. Just seeing her ass and I was horny as a toad.

The brunette Jenifer moved forward to help me balance. Her eyes went straight to my cock, and a look of pure feminine pride swept across her features as she licked her lips and openly gestured to my manhood. "Oh, sorry about that." She giggled and flirted. "So that's a yes then?" She jutted her chin toward my aching manhood.

Behind me, Mila was making a ton of noise. Flicking through the CDs so they made the optimum amount of clacking against one another. She also turned up her music, likely in a failed attempt to drown out the conversation in front of her. I chuckled under my breath when she organized the yoga blocks, dropping the yoga straps to the bare floor so the plastic clasps clunked noisily. Her obvious groans were not missed either.

"Hotness, do you mind?" I said over my shoulder.

"Mind? No, carry on with your setup for a ménage. Don't mind me," she spoke through her teeth.

I chuckled, turned around, tagged her at the waist, and then pulled her body in front of mine. I wrapped one arm around her chest, used that hand to cup her chin and lift her face toward mine, and planted a loud, messy kiss on her glossy lips. "Mmm, peach this time." I licked my lips and then kissed her again. She sighed and then blinked as if just realizing what I'd done.

"Sorry, ladies, not today. I've got plans with my girl later." Which was a total and complete lie, but it worked for Jenifer because she promptly frowned and crinkled her nose as if someone had just farted in her air space. The meek blonde, Kallie, turned without a word and bustled over to her clothes where she dressed in record time.

Jenifer, however, was undaunted. She took in my very

possessive hold on Mila, who, surprisingly, was holding her tongue for once. Jenifer placed her hands on her hips. "If that"—she gestured with one finger up and down Mila's body—"ever gets boring, feel free to hit me up."

"For real?" Mila growled. "His hands are all over me. He just put his mouth on mine and you're going to blatantly hit on him. While I'm standing right here?" Her voice rose along with her ire.

Brunette-fake-tits made a face that looked more like a duck than a flirty pout and shrugged. "He's fucking hot."

"I know! That's why I'm the one he's fucking," Mila snapped while her entire body tightened. Her anger sizzled all over her skin, making it warm to the touch, and a fine mist of sweat moistened the areas where I held her close. "Move it. He's not interested."

I ran my hands down to Mila's rounded hips and dug my fingers in. I couldn't help pressing my hard shaft against the roundness of her ass. The temptation was far too much to bear. "Yeah, sorry, Jenifer. I've got all the woman I can handle." I grinned and nuzzled into Mila's neck, placing a line of wet, lingering kisses until Jenifer stormed off.

Once the women were both out the door, Mila yanked her body from mine. "What the hell was that?"

I laughed and slipped into my yoga pants and covered my still *very hard* dick. "I could ask you the same thing."

She ran a hand through her hair. "You just publicly claimed me."

I looked at her sideways. "Wildcat, again, I could say the very same thing about you."

Mila groaned and moved around me, putting several feet of space between us. "I have to teach a class."

"That you do. We'll talk about this later."

She huffed. "No. We won't. There will be no later."

Slowly I leaned down, picked up my tank, and tugged it on. "There's a later. I want you to come to my show tonight."

"Did you not hear me? No later."

"Yes, later." I tugged her by the wrist, yanked her against my chest, and curled a hand around her neck and the other at her waist, locking her to me. Before she could get away, I lifted her chin up and slanted my lips over hers.

MILA

Why did the sexy bastard have to kiss like he'd won a medal in it? Atlas's lips were warm and soft, pressing hard and then pulling back slow. So sweet. He tasted of mint and man, a hint of salt where his top and bottom lip met skin. He growled when I opened my mouth, allowing him to delve deep. His tongue tangled with mine, over and over as though he couldn't get enough. I swear he wanted to swallow me whole, and for the life of me, I let him. My entire body became spaghetti in his arms. Nothing but loose limbs, soft curves, and long sighs as we drank from one another. Just when I'd start to kiss harder, he'd hold me tighter. When it turned silky again, he'd hold me like I was made of glass. Breakable. Valuable.

One of his hands scaled down my back, tickling my spine with the barest of caresses. It was like he had a direct remote to my clit. Every time he trailed those callused fingers down my spine, my hot bundle of nerves hardened, throbbed for those fingers to press into the part of me that ached for his touch.

I'd never before felt sex starved, until I was wrapped up in Atlas Power's embrace. He had some kind of voodoo spell over me. The second those lips touched mine, I was practically begging for it. Ready to lie down and let him have me any way he wanted, as long as he dealt with the fire he started.

Atlas licked deep, ran his tongue across my teeth, then circled my bottom lip, and then my top lip with the very tip. He gave me a last smacking kiss before releasing me so we could breathe and then pressed his forehead against mine.

"Tonight I'm playing at Harmony Jack's in downtown Frisco. Come see me play. Have a couple drinks on me," he said.

I sucked in a much-needed full breath, trying to calm the raging hurricane he'd built within my body. "Why?" I was still breathless. "You're just going to be swooned over by a bunch of groupies."

He chuckled and ran his hand through the loose locks of hair falling into our tiny haven. The entire world could have been in the yoga room with us, but we wouldn't have known. When we were face-to-face, it was just us. Everything else melted away. The calm before the storm.

"You're the only groupie I want swooning."

"I'm not your groupie. I haven't even heard your music. How do you know I'll like it?"

"Come and find out." He nipped at my bottom lip, tugging the swollen flesh until it smacked back in place.

I sighed and looped both of my forearms on his shoulders so I could put both hands into his unruly hair. I ran my fingers through his silky locks, using my nails to scratch along his scalp.

He moaned, and his hips jerked.

"Oh. Looks like I found an erogenous zone. You like having your head scratched?" I did it again, until he groaned and nipped at my lips with more intent.

"By you? Fuck yes. I'd prefer if it were in more of a private setting, though."

Private setting.

Shit. Our little bubble burst, and the sounds of the room filtered in. Soft voices whispering. My music playing into the third track already. Giggles and male grunts.

I slowly turned and looked over Atlas's shoulder. My class was full. Not like there were five or ten bodies set up. Nope. Closer to forty were lined up like usual, ready for their lunchtime burn. "Crap," I whispered and pulled away.

"Uh, sorry, guys," I addressed the class. "I was just..." With one hand I gestured to Atlas. "Just, uh..."

"Kissing her boyfriend good-bye," he supplied.

"Yeah. Kissing my boyfriend. Wait, what?" I found myself questioning his words more than any other.

He waggled his brows and winked. "I'll see you tonight, hotness." He curled a hand at my nape and then kissed my forehead. He grabbed his yoga mat and hoodie before padding off the riser. "Nine o'clock," he said while meandering through the various students sitting on their mats waiting patiently for their instructor to get a clue.

I looked at the class, a burning heat scalding my cheeks and neck. "I'm sorry, everyone. For the very inappropriate delay, I'll go easy on you."

A joyous round of "Yeahs!" and "All rights!" burst through the room.

"Okay, okay. Back to work. For giving me a hard time, we're starting with five rounds of *surya namaskara* B or sun salutation B for those of you less familiar with the *Sanskrit* terms. And...because I'm feeling generous, only a ten-second hold in the *chatarunga,* plank push-up transition. Start in Mountain Pose. Let's go. Everyone up to their feet."

I took the class through a very rigorous Vin Flow. Since I'd been screwing around and started a full ten minutes late, I gave them an extra five minutes of deep relaxation. I only hoped that the diehards weren't upset that they didn't get their full seventy-five minutes of pushing their bodies, followed by a fifteen minutes savasana.

When they left, I didn't get any complaints except one. The person I hadn't seen until midway through the class. My best friend. Moe.

Moe rolled up her mat and tucked it under her arm.

"I thought your lunch was sacred. Didn't you say that to me? *'Mila, I don't take your lunch class because my lunch is scared. Unlike you, I need food three times a day like a normal person,'* " I mimicked, trying to sound like her and failing miserably.

Moe smirked and stood silently.

"Saw that there, uh, with Atlas did you?" I said, avoiding her eyes. Black pools of honesty those eyes.

She still didn't speak. Crap. The silent stare. Not good.

"It's not anything. That part about him being my boyfriend." I laughed and knotted my fingers together, so I'd have something to do with my hands. "Total bullshit. He was trying to get my goat. I haven't even known him long enough to call him my boyfriend."

Moe tilted her head. That's all she did. Tilt her head. Her black eyes turned to ebony daggers designed to pierce the truth right out of her victims.

"Okay!" I threw up my hands in the air. "We fight. We kiss. We're probably going to fuck." I lifted my head to the swirls

I'd painted on all the ceilings. They'd been a nice addition for the patrons to have something beautiful to look at. "God, I hope we're going to fuck. I mean, we've been leading up to it all week."

I glanced at her and then away. "I'm sorry I kept it from you. It wasn't intentional. I swear. You know me. No rest for the wicked. I've been working my butt off and painting. I'm painting again. A new piece," I added excitedly. "One that's really coming along."

Still nothing. Moe licked her lips and let out a slow exhale.

"I would have told you about him. Honestly. I didn't know where it was going. Please, don't be mad. You know I can't stand it if you're mad. I'll do anything. Paint another room in your house? Go to the movies."

Nothing. Moe blinked innocently and tapped her manicured nails against the rolled up mat in her arm.

"Fine. I'll move in with you. Okay. I'll move in. End of the month. Just please stop with the silent treatment. I can't stand it."

Moe smiled wide. "Wow. You sure dug yourself a hole, scratched your way to the surface, and came out on top."

"I can't have you mad at me." I meant those words with my entire being. She was all I had in life. Moe and her daughter, Lily, were the only family I could claim.

Moe tapped her teeth with her fingernail. "I wasn't mad. Surprised, but not mad. That boyfriend thing threw me for a loop, but more so the way you responded to his touch was a sight to see."

"Ugh. Don't remind me. Every time he touches me, I turn to jelly. I lose all my faculties. It's stupid. A stupid, silly girl crush."

She frowned. "Having feelings for a man is not stupid, Mila. Being in a relationship has its advantages."

I scoffed. "I am not in a relationship with Atlas Powers. We're just having fun. We fight like crazy. He drives me absolutely bonkers!"

"Bonkers? I do not believe that is a clinical description for the insane. And there's nothing wrong with being in a relationship with a man."

"Moe..." I warned. "Don't you start..."

"There isn't."

I took that moment to gather my things, turn off the music, and head toward the door. "I don't do relationships."

She followed me through the Lotus House facility. We waved at the other teachers and clients that had taken my classes before.

"Just because you haven't done them before, doesn't mean you can't do them now."

"Do what? A hot guy? I definitely plan on doing Atlas Powers. Many, many, many times even," I said lustfully.

"Not that. Relationships. Don't change the subject."

We exited onto the sunny Berkeley street. The scent of cinnamon and coffee wafted through the air from the bakery. Briefly, I wondered if Dara was working today. Probably. The girl always ran the counter if she wasn't at work or teaching a class. Family businesses were tough, I'd imagine. A steady commitment.

"I don't think I'm the relationship type. It's not like I have anything to offer."

Moe's black eyes seemed like endless midnight pools as she focused on me. "You have so much more to offer than you're aware of, Mila. Love, friendship, honesty, that's all a good relationship needs to thrive and...survive." Her voice cracked when she said the last word.

"And you'd know about that because yours was so perfect?" I winced the second it was out of my mouth. Monet did not deserve what that jerk had done to her. Throwing away years of marriage and a family for a two-bit home-wrecking whore. "Moe, I'm sorry..."

She held her hand up. "No. No, you're right to some extent, but so am I. My relationship with Kyle wasn't honest, and in the end, it didn't survive. Still, I'd give anything to have a man in my life. A man who loved me for me and wanted to commit to a future with me and my daughter. One day, I hope to find it."

I gripped her hands in mine and then brought them up to my lips. I kissed her fingers. She was the only person besides her daughter who I was super affectionate with. Probably because we were more than just best friends. We were soul sisters. "And you will, Moe. That perfect guy is out there. I know it."

"Then why do you not think the same for yourself?" She whispered the question through her emotions.

I swallowed down the lump of unease. "Because I'm not as good as you. I'm not a prize. You are. Any man would thank his lucky stars to score you for life. Me...not so much."

"Mila," she gasped. "You can't possibly believe that." Her voice shattered and tears filled her eyes.

I shook my head, dusting off the emotion and focusing on the day. "What I believe is that you need to eat three square meals a day. And you haven't told me why you were at my lunch class. So let's get something good at Rainy Day, and you can continue trying to make me believe that everyone has their perfect better half out there for them."

She groaned, lifted her head to the sky, and spoke. "God. You gave me the most stubborn best friend in the universe. Thanks!" she finished dryly.

"Come on." I looped my elbow through hers. "You'll like me a whole lot more when I feed you."

"True. Besides, I want to know more about the hot yoga guy."

CHAPTER EIGHT

Modified Warrior 1 (Sanskrit: Virabhadrasana I)
*Warrior 1 in yoga can be difficult for individuals with very
stiff hips. Women who have given birth may have a harder
time moving into the full pose right away. I personally like
to offer variations on the traditional Warrior 1 in my classes
as shown in the image. In this picture, the woman's feet are
about half a leg distance apart, both facing forward and
spread away from the body about shoulder width. Instead of
moving her arms up straight and turning the hips perfectly
forward, her arms are held in a moon shape. Warrior 1 is a
balance and strengthening pose that often looks like a dance
move.*

ATLAS

The bar was hopping the moment I arrived. Harmony Jack's was one of the better venues I frequented. They treated me well, gave the talent free beer, and paid in cash. Nothing to report to Uncle Sam meant the three hundred I'd make tonight would go directly toward making a new demo mix. The last scout I'd talked to wanted a high-quality recording. All I had to offer was something lower class that I'd made in my room through a series playing to my computer. Stupidly, my theory was once these studio execs saw me live, they'd want to sign me straight off. That had not happened, and the potential for it was a candle right down to the last inch of wax. If I didn't score something in the next year or two, I'd be out. I'd given myself until thirty to make my dream of being a full-time musician come true. At twenty-eight, my prospects were nil. I couldn't continue to work night and day on something that wasn't bearing any fruit.

My mother had been suggesting I go back to school, get a bachelor's, and then teaching credentials. That way I could teach music and, in her mind, enjoy the best of both worlds— music and a steady paycheck. The option was solid but not what I wanted to do with my life. I'd much rather be behind the mic or at the very least, behind the artist, writing song lyrics and the accompanying music. Only I had to find a way to stand out.

I surveyed the room. Patrons danced in a corner. Opposite that was a set of four pool tables and a shuffleboard table where four scantily glad women were bent over, giggling and carrying on. Pink and blue flashing lights blinked over the long wooden bar, clearly stating Harmony Jack's was open for business. Every stool had a butt in the seat, which was good for me. On top of the three hundred, the owner, Jacqueline, who everyone simply called Jack for obvious reasons, allowed me to have my guitar case open for extra tips. Sometimes it made me feel like a peddler, but most of the time, I sucked it up. At the end of a good night, I've had an additional hundred or two to pocket.

I hopped up on to the stage and set out my equipment. The stage was dark, so moving around didn't draw much attention. A jukebox played R.E.M.'s "Losing my Religion," a classic if I'd ever heard one. After setting up, I headed down to the busy bar. Off to the side, I noted a head of spiky blond hair.

Using my shoulder, I rammed my buddy's bulk into the bar top. He turned with a grimace on his pretty boy face until he realized who it was. "What are you doing here, man?"

Clayton Hart, my friend and roomie, smiled wide, showing off his pristine pearly whites. His sky-blue eyes assessed me, and he curled an arm around my shoulder for a man-hug, which included a smack to my back so hard I coughed.

"Jesus, lay off the steroids!" I joked.

He chuckled. "You know this is all hard work. You want to look like this?" He gestured down his massive chest. There was not a lick of fat on the guy. "You let me know. I'll have you twice the size by winter." Funny thing about Clay, he did not lie. Every client he had seemed to be bigger than the last. Except for the celebrity females he trained. Those he tended to keep lean and fit yet still with some softness to keep Hollywood calling.

"Overachiever," I grumbled. "Seriously, though, did you have a client cancel? Usually you're home on Wednesdays."

That's when I realized he was not sitting alone. By his side was none other than baseball's finest, Trent Fox.

Clay gestured to his right. "Fox, you met my roommate, Atlas? He works at Lotus House with your wife."

"Wife. I wish. That fireball of mine does not yet have my ring on her finger. Soon though. Me and the little one are wearing her down." He grinned and then held out a hand to me. "Trent Fox. Good to meet ya," the man said, his voice a deep growl.

"Pleasure to meet ya, man. I love the Ports, and you've had a killer year so far."

He nodded. "Yep. Only downside is leaving the family."

"That's right, you just had a kid, yeah?"

He nodded. "Ten months old. William. Kid's huge. Wears double the size he's supposed to. Pisses his mother off something fierce how often she's got to switch out his clothes. Me, I laugh my ass off. My kid will not be picked on."

Jack made it over to the bar, a fine sway to her curvy hips. Her hair was cut into a pixie style and spiked every which way. It suited her. She wiped off the bar in front of the three of us, an arm full of tinkling bracelets clacking against the bar with each movement. "What are you having, Atlas?"

"Beer. Whatever's cold and on tap is fine."

"Gentlemen? A refill?"

"Gin and tonic for me. Beer for my buddy," Clay said.

Trent turned his barstool around so he could assess me fully. "So you're the talent I'm here to see tonight."

I glanced at Clay. He pretended to find the woman who'd been eye-fucking him since I walked up, all of a sudden interesting.

I rubbed my hands together. "That would be me."

"You any good?" Trent asked.

I shrugged. "You'll have to tell me."

"Fair enough."

"Hey, Atlas, what's the deal with you and that chick from the studio?"

Trent's body went stiff right in front of me. "Petite blonde?" He growled the question.

I shook my head. "No, man. I know Genevieve is your girl. Dash is my best friend and gave me the heads-up. Believe me. Every man alive knows you've claimed that woman."

"Damn straight!" He grimaced.

I laughed. Protective much? Jesus. I'd never been in a position to feel that old-fashioned sense of ownership over a woman before. Probably because the longest relationship I'd had was a month or two. Nah, probably more like six weeks.

Clay chuckled and shook his head. "Man, that little thing has you twisted up in knots."

"If she'd fuckin' marry me already, we wouldn't be having this conversation. As it is, I don't want to be having this conversation. Back to you." He pointed to me. "Who are you hot for at the studio? I know them all now. Let me guess...Luna or Dara?"

I grinned and thought about Luna. The redhead daughter of one of the owners was very pretty in a porcelain classic beauty type way and not at all my type. Dara, I'd bang the hell outta, but honestly, she didn't put off the vibe that she was interested in me or anyone for that matter. Girl was always in her head. Likely why she taught meditation.

"Nah, man. Mila."

Trent's eyebrows rose nearly to his hairline. "That girl. Damn, dude. She's a pistol. Hot as fuck but never gives anyone the time of day. Hard nut to crack for sure."

Clay nodded. "I've taken her classes a few times. Talented for sure. Agree on the hot as fuck. But I don't know, there's something about her that's..."

"Unapproachable?" I offered.

Both men nodded, and Clay pointed a trigger finger at me. "Nailed it. Exactly. But Dash mentioned he saw her leaving our apartment the other day."

Fucking Dash. "Dude needs to keep his trap shut. Jesus. What is he? The new Gossip Girl of Lotus House?" Shit. I'd need to talk to him. Last thing I needed was the gossip mill running at my new job. I liked working there, and I loved being close to where Mila taught. Gave me more cause to run into her fine ass in the halls and give her a hard time.

Clay laughed heartily.

"Mila, I don't know what it is about the wildcat. She just gets under my skin," I admitted.

Clay took a sip of his G & T while Trent pursed his lips and focused on me. "You into her?"

I shrugged. "I'd like to get into her." I waggled my brows.

Both men bust a gut laughing, and then Trent patted me on the shoulder. "Show her you want in."

"Oh, she knows it. And I'm pretty sure she's game. Asked her to come tonight. We'll see if she shows."

"That's a good test. Invite her to come watch you doing something you love, and if she shows and stays for more than just the cold beer and music, then you know she's into you," Clay offered and leaned his elbows on the bar behind him.

"Good point. I don't know though, man, there's something about her. Can't quite put my finger on it."

Trent leaned forward. "Felt that about my Genevieve.

Couldn't get the woman off my mind. Thought it was because I wanted her on my dick. Turned out, I wanted her in my bed and in my life for the long haul. Never had better, man. Your girl a game changer like mine?"

Was Mila a game changer? So far, she'd definitely had me bending over backward to chase her. "Remains to be seen, my man." I clapped Trent on the shoulder.

"If she is, or the score starts rising in her favor, don't fuck around. We're not getting any younger."

No truer words were ever spoken. I most definitely was not getting any younger, especially in the business I was in.

The lights around the stage started flashing yellow, signaling to me and the crowd that the live music would be starting soon.

"That's my cue, dudes. Thanks for showing up tonight. 'Preciate it." I shook Trent's hand before clasping Clay and giving him the bump-pound hug. They'd probably leave before I finished my first set. Clay didn't stay out late because he typically met clients at their house or the gym before the sun even rose. Trent had a new family. Didn't imagine Genevieve would be keen on him being out too late if they had a little one at home.

"Good luck, man." Trent jerked his chin to the stage. "And with the fireball."

I grinned. "Thanks. Enjoy the show," I said before making my way through the crowd, up the stairs for the stage where I hung my guitar over my shoulder. I picked up the stool Jack left for me and dragged it to the front. The spotlight came up and shone down on me when I sat in front of the audience. The night DJ already had my prerecorded drums and other instrumentals for the background for the songs I didn't do solo acoustic.

"How you all doin'? Tonight, I'm going to start off with a ballad called 'Creep' by a little known band called Radiohead."

MILA

When I arrived at Harmony Jack's at ten p.m., not nine as Atlas had requested, the place was already in full swing. Wednesday nights were hopping in a cool place like this. The room was one big, giant square on a lower level of a high-rise. During the day, the windows looked normal, but at night, they opened outward so that the passersby could see how much fun everyone was having inside. It also allowed for maximum airflow to travel through, making it seem more open. The place, however, was packed, including the crowd of women standing at the edge of the stage gyrating their hips to Atlas's voice.

Slowly, I made my way through the crush of bodies to the bar and ordered a shot of tequila and a beer. The bartender was a woman, dressed punk-rocker chic. She was small, like me, with smaller curves and a wicked cool edge. Her hair was black as night and shone a hazy blue when she walked under the track lighting that brightened certain sections behind the bar. All along the walls were hundreds of dollar bills with what looked like phone numbers in a man's uneven scrawl written on them.

I leaned over the bar to get closer to her when she placed my tequila and shot in front of me. "Those phone numbers?" I jerked my chin to all the dollars stapled to the wall.

She grinned wide, and I swear it took her from beyond

pretty to downright gorgeous. "Yeah, when a guy asks for my number, I tell him to write theirs on a bill. Then right in front of him, I slap it on the wall. Dumb asses haven't figured out I'm into women, they need their reminder up close and personal." She winked and turned to help another customer.

I laughed, twirled around on the barstool, slammed back the shot, and sipped my beer. I set my gaze right on the reason for my presence. Atlas was sitting on a stool on the stage looking ultracool. One knee was at a right angle, foot hiked up on the bottom rung of the chair. His eyes were closed as he sang a song I'd not heard before.

Belief is a bitter pill to swallow...
You said you'd be back...
Tomorrow...

I pretend the emptiness isn't stacked...
Yet I keep hoping every way that...

Maybe never...probably someday.
Is today.

Today...today...today...

I've learned there is no home...
In maybe never, probably someday.

Atlas's voice filtered through my body, sending a feverish chill in every direction. Maybe never, probably someday. Who was that song about? A woman. A flicker of jealousy scuttled down my spine, and I straightened and clenched my teeth. Did it matter? He wasn't mine. He could be singing to anyone.

Then why would he ask you to come? Relax, Mila.

I was getting worked up over nothing. And that was exactly what was between me and Atlas. Nothing. Just a bit of fun. It would be wise for me to remember just that.

Atlas leaned into the microphone, his brown, messy curls falling into his strikingly handsome face. From here, I could see his eyes and could tell they were smiling. He sat in his element. The spotlight on him, the bevy of willing beauties crowing in front of him, and his voice. From the little I knew of Atlas, music was his passion. And it showed in the way he sang, tilted forward as if he needed to get out every last inch of emotion before moving to the next word, and the way he closed his eyes, letting his mind go and his talent spill out. Breathtaking.

Every word he sang made me hot and aroused. The growl his voice took on when he got into a lyric made me think of hard-core fucking. The soft whisper of a melody was like a sexy caress across naked skin. A jolt of want rippled through me, settling between my thighs where I throbbed with every tap of his foot. Jesus Christ, I wanted him.

No longer capable of sitting back, I slid off my stool and walked slowly through the throng of beautiful women. I didn't push or tackle. No, I eased toward the front. Made sure that I stood in one of the spots where the light would hit as it flickered around the dance floor.

Atlas sang, and I swayed my hips. He lifted his neck and belted out a phrase to the sky. I lifted my arms in honor, taken with his song. The music moved through me like I was swimming in open water, flowing with the current, taking me to a new height. Nothing but peace, lust, and heat surrounded me as I focused on allowing his music to take me where I wanted to go. Home with him.

I opened my eyes and was caught in the snare of one blue and one brown eye instantly. Atlas had found me in the crowd; I knew he would. He continued to sing, only now he sang to me. Only me. His eyes didn't close, and they never strayed away. I moved with each lyric, offering up my body on a pedestal to this crazy music man who somehow pushed every last one of my buttons.

He grinned and finished his song. Then he stood and spoke into the microphone. "I'll be back for one more set after I refresh the palate. So hit up the bar, your waiters and waitresses, for a refill and get your drink on because there's more to come," he said with a goofy smile. Then, instead of taking the stairs on stage right, he jumped down the four feet, prowling right for me.

I didn't move. Not an inch. When he got to me, he curled his hand around my neck and slammed his lips to mine. My surprised gasp gave him just the advantage he needed to lick deep where our tongues tangled and danced. His other hand came around my body, splayed low on my back, and then went even lower griping a handful of ass cheek. I squirmed and then moaned when he kept up the massage, feeling the hardening ridge of his cock swell under his jeans against my belly.

After he'd spent long minutes kissing me as if this were our last day on earth, Atlas ripped his mouth away and rested his forehead against mine. I'd never had a man do that to me before. It felt bizarrely intimate, breathing in one another's breath, third eye chakras touching. I found I liked it more than I would have expected to, not having spent much time connecting to a man physically in that manner in the past.

Usually I just went straight for the cock. Holding one another never lasted long in my nighttime excursions. Then again, the point was to get off. With Atlas, I didn't know what the hell the point was. All I knew was that I enjoyed being in his presence. Enjoyed verbally battling with him. And most of all, I enjoyed the way he made me feel. Like a wanted, desirable, beautiful woman. I had no idea how long that would last, because once we hit the sheets, the odds were it would all be over.

Atlas inhaled sharply. "Seeing you there, shaking your ass for me, all for me..." He clenched harder on his handful of booty.

"Ouch," I said before putting an arm around his body and getting my own fill of man-buns. And, of course, his ass was firm and rounded to perfection.

"Christ. I want in. All in, wildcat. With your legs wrapped around me, I'd be so deep in you I'd never want to leave."

"Be careful what you wish for, curly. You just might get it," I taunted.

"Oh, I'm getting it. Taking it. Living and breathing it in until we're too exhausted to give it anymore."

A trail of excitement slid all along the surface of my skin. Every word was more tantalizing than the next. "You talk a good game for a man who still has another set to sing and a horde of hotties to play with." I nodded at the girls standing in the circle around us, their surreptitious eyes glaring at me while simultaneously lusting after him almost laughable.

"There's only one girl I'm interested in playing with tonight. And tomorrow night. And the night after that..."

I snickered. "Mmm hmm. I guess we'll see, won't we?"

His eyes sparkled under the bouncing lights, and one lock of hair fell into his face. I pushed the strand back, scratching along his scalp in the process. He jerked his hips against my pelvis, and I grinned.

"You are so bad," he growled and nipped at my lips.

"I can be better." I kissed him softly and tugged on the roots of his hair.

He groaned into my mouth and dipped his tongue to twirl with mine. He tasted like beer and oranges. Probably a citrus beer. Same as I was drinking.

"Stay till the end?" He traced the side of my face with two fingers. Hope and desire filled his gaze, drowning me with anticipation.

"Okay."

He smiled. "Okay. I want to introduce you to my roommate and his friend. I think you may know him already."

We walked over to the side of the bar where two giants teetered on stools that looked doll-sized in comparison.

"Mila, this is Clayton Hart, my roommate, and his friend..."

I smiled and held out my hand. "Trent Fox. You're Genevieve's man."

"Guilty as charged." His smile was warm and friendly.

"Where is she?" I glanced around, looking for the curvy blonde. The girl was my size, only the exact opposite. She was light everywhere I was dark. And her personality exuded kind, calm, and collected. Mine...well, mine did not.

"With our son and the rest of the fam. Guys night out."

"Cool."

Atlas put his arm around my shoulders, pressing me close to his side. A claiming move if I'd ever felt one. Being squished up against his bulk definitely spoke possession even if he causally caressed the ball of my shoulder with his thumb, sipped on the beer the bartender passed him, and joked with his friends. While he seemed completely at ease, I felt every muscle in my body locking down. I didn't know how to act in this type of scenario, had no clue what was expected of me. Was I supposed to just stand here and be quiet? Could I even do that? Most definitely not something that came naturally but for Atlas, could I?

"Hey, Mila, Atlas said you're an artist?" Clay said. "What kind of art do you do?"

Art. Okay. Whew. Now that I could talk about. Endlessly really. It also gave me a grand opportunity to mess with Atlas, something I enjoyed almost as much as my passion for painting.

"I'm working on an exhibition. All paintings. Right now, I'm painting nudes."

CHAPTER NINE

SOLAR PLEXUS
C H A K R A

The solar plexus chakra is influenced by the sun. Its earthly element is fire, and alongside the masculine nature of this chakra, it encourages individuals under its influence to find their appropriate place in society.

ATLAS

Music was my life. I loved playing. Only right now, it was the bane of my damned existence. Watching Mila down in the crowd shaking her ass for every Tom, Dick, and Harry had me semi-hard all through my set. I only had one more song, and then I was going to grab my feisty Latina, carry her over my shoulder if I had to, and take her to her place. I would have taken her to mine, but I wasn't planning on a quiet fuck. On tonight's menu was some doggy style, bucking bronco, maybe some sixty-nine, and all the oral delights she could handle.

I wanted her limping when she walked into that studio tomorrow, preferably with my stink still all over her.

I gritted my teeth and growled the next verse. It worked because I was grounding out a little "Sunshower" by Chris Cornell who, on a good day, sounded like he'd swallowed a handful of razors. Mila was unaware of the power she exuded over me. A silent seductress, lost in her own world, she danced like she'd been doing so for years. Moved her hips and arms to each vowel as if I was singing just for her. Every so often her eyes would open, and the pure, unadulterated lust in them shone right through me, to the point where I'd burn if I didn't get through this set, get my money, and get her under me. I felt like a lunatic caveman, wanting to drag her out of here by her hair, while thumping any man with my homemade tree trunk club who dared to set his eyes on her.

Maddening.

Insanity.

Everything about Mila Mercado screamed sensuality and sexuality, with a hint of spirituality. There were so many facets of her I wanted to tap into, the first one being her sensual side. I watched her dance to my songs, loving every one so much she'd closed her eyes and let the music rule her, trusting in the music to keep her standing. And it did. Boy, did it ever. I'd sing to her forever if I didn't have the need to put my mouth and hands all over her. We'd have eternity to sing and dance. Now was the time for our bodies to dance in a hedonistic way that led to sweat, sore limbs, a pleased woman, and one sated cock. Mine.

I belted out the last verse of "Sunshower" while standing. The crowd roared as I stood there. Normally, I'd smile, wave, and thank them for coming. Right then my eyes were set on one thing—a pint-sized wildcat who I fully intended on taming the second I jumped off this stage. I put my guitar into the case right over the cash the grateful patrons had tossed inside. I'd settle that up later. Way later.

Mila came up to the stage at the same time that Jack did, pile of cash in hand. I grinned at Jack and put my arm around Mila. "Want to get you out of here and get you naked. Now."

"Um, check please," she joked as I licked the entire column of her moist neck, tasting her in a carnal, animalistic move.

"Fuck. You taste so good. Working your body to my music. Like that, hotness. Like that a lot."

"Mmm," she mumbled as I kissed my way up her neck.

Jack cleared her throat. I ignored her, too intent on tasting this sexy wildcat.

"Whatever!" I heard her groan, and the back of my pants jerked as a tiny hand went in my ass pocket and back out of it, lightning quick. "There, you've got your money. See you next week. Now take that somewhere else!" she ordered as I pulled away from Mila.

"I don't think she wants you groping me here," Mila said rather shyly, a contrast to her normal abrasive nature.

I chuckled. "No, I don't think she does. We're not her type of show."

"Oh?" Her inflection proved she already knew that. "Is there a dollar bill with your number on it, too?" She grinned wide.

Her hand tagged around my waist as I gripped my guitar in one hand and her shoulder in the other. I scoffed, "No way."

She giggled. "I'd bet there is."

"You'd bet wrong."

Her eyes were slits as she tilted her head up toward mine. "I'd take that bet."

Little minx. We hadn't exchanged phone numbers verbally, so she'd have to look hard to find it on that wall, though my name was pretty unique.

I chuckled and leaned closer to her as we made our way toward the exit. "You'd be right," I whispered into her ear, rubbing my nose along the sensitive cartilage.

Her grin set my heart pounding. And then she was totally Mila. She pulled back and shoved me. "I knew it!" She laughed. "I so knew it! You hit on Jack, the lesbian bartender. Manwhore!" she said before falling into a fit of tipsy giggles against my side. The look, the laughter was so pretty on her. Mila smiled, sure. Just not a lot. Guarding her emotions and affections toward others tended to be her standard MO. Something I found absolutely fascinating about the sassy brat.

"Excuse me, Atlas Powers," a deep voice said at the same time a hand cupping my shoulder stopped our forward momentum.

I groaned and turned around, trying not to scowl. If a fan prevented me from scoring with Mila, I couldn't be responsible for my actions. Wound up didn't begin to cover the twitchy, anticipatory need to fuck the woman that clung to my side. Her hand splayed at my chest, rubbing leisurely, the thumb of her other hand was looped through the back of my jeans. She was in for the plan tonight, that much was blatantly obvious. My intent to blast out of here was also obvious to anyone in sight.

"I'm kind of busy." I jerked my head to the hottie I had a lock on.

The dark man smirked. I couldn't be sure in the light, but

he looked like he could be African American. His hair was cropped right to his dome in a way a soldier often sported. His eyes were light, too light to tell what color they were, but his teeth glowed a bright neon purple with the black lights shining over us.

The stranger clapped his hands together. "I only need a few minutes of your time."

"Who are you?" I asked, nonplussed, ready to hightail it out of there and get where I was headed, between the toned thighs of the woman to my right.

"I'm Silas McKnight of Knight & Day Productions." He held out a hand, and I looked at it. Just looked at it, unmoving.

Holy. Fucking. Shit.

I blinked, and all the sounds around me went dead silent. Every nerve within my body tingled and zapped as if I was being electrocuted over and over by a low level shock wave. Mila smacked my chest hard, breaking me out of my shocked stupor.

"Rudeness, shake the man's hand!" she urged.

Mr. McKnight chuckled while I grasped his hand and squeezed. Probably too hard. "I'm sorry... I just... You kind of, uh, surprised me there. I didn't expect to see someone like you here."

He rubbed his hands together and gestured over to an empty table not five feet from us. "Would you be interested in sitting?" he offered.

Both Mila and I went to the table. She followed without saying a word. I ran my hand down her arm and gripped her hand in mine so tight she hopefully understood what this meant—I wasn't blowing her off, but that this was a big deal. She seemed to instinctively understand if her rubbing the top of my hand with her thumb was any indication. Having her close, her hand in mine, soothed the instant anxiety that rippled through every ounce of my being. This was it. My moment. My one chance.

Don't fuck it up.

"So you, uh, wanted to talk to me?" I prompted, nervously running my other hand and sweaty palm over my jeans.

Mr. McKnight leaned both his elbows onto the tabletop. "I did. I heard your act. Stayed for the entire thing actually."

Holy hell. That was huge. I'd read somewhere that most music industry professionals were not the type to sit back and enjoy an evening listening to someone they didn't think had any potential. Please, God, let him think I have potential.

"And?" I left the question hanging out there for him to answer at his leisure.

He grinned. "Man, you were awesome. You do not lack talent, that's for sure. Those three originals, those were stellar. Do you have any more of those tucked into your head?"

Talent. He said I had talent. "Plenty more."

He canted his head to the side. "Now that's what I want to hear. I'm looking for a new guy."

"Mr. McKnight, I'm him! I'm that guy," I said, smacking the table with more confidence than I should have. It's just this was it. The moment. I had to give it my all. Put myself out there and bleed so he'd see I was worthy of a chance.

He chuckled. "Silas, please. I think we have a lot to talk about, but mostly I need to know...you against writing a song for other people to sing?"

My heart sank a little. Not much, but a little.

"No. If it's music and I can put my stamp on it, I'm in."

"Good to hear, man." He stood, put his hand in his blazer,

and pulled out a card. "I'm going out of town for two weeks, but when I get back, I want a meeting. You up for that?"

I smiled huge. "Absolutely. Thank you."

"We'll talk more about music, writing songs, and what I'm looking for. But you're special. Of that, you can be certain."

"Thank you. That means a lot, man." I held out my hand, and he shook it.

"Call that number and schedule a meeting with my receptionist for when I'm back. Two weeks."

I nodded. "Two weeks."

Silas clapped me on the back. "Looking forward to it." He made his way out of the bar. I watched like a lovelorn sap the entire way as he left.

Mila fitted her body to my side and looked up. I glanced down and drowned in her chocolaty gaze.

"That was big, right? For your music career?" she whispered as if she was afraid to put words to it. Hell, I was afraid to as well.

"Yes. Huge." I leaned down and kissed her lips softly. "You know what else is huge?"

"What?"

"My dick. Come on, hotness. My night just got even better. Let's make it the best night of our lives."

She laughed and followed me out the door and into the taxi, which took us right to her place.

MILA

The second I opened the door, Atlas pushed me forward gently, a firm hand to my lower back. His guitar case hit the wood floor of my apartment while I bolted the lock in place. I didn't live in the worst neighborhood in Oakland, but certainly not the best. Just as I put the slap lock in place, securing us in for the night, I was twirled around and lifted into a fireman's carry.

I laughed and pounded against his hard ass. "Let me down, you brute!"

"Never!" he joked before swinging me around until I slid down his muscular form, inch by perfect inch.

Once my forearms hit his shoulders, I practically dangled, my feet far from touching the ground. Atlas shifted and used his hands to grip my ass and bump me up until I wrapped my legs around his waist. We were face-to-face in this position, his multicolored eyes searing into mine, telling a tale of lust and desire I could drown in.

"Hi," I replied rather meekly, not usually staring into the face of the man I was about to have sex with. Honestly, I didn't usually spend much time kissing them, either. For me and my one-nighters, it was all about getting off. Kissing, looking someone in the face, sharing air space, these things were personal, private...intimate.

Atlas smiled softly. "Hi. Are you ready for this?" He nuzzled my nose affectionately.

The total opposite move of what I wanted. I enjoyed my men wild and out of control. I planned on bringing out his beastly side and fast. With Atlas, the best way to do that seemed to be sparring. So that's exactly where I went.

"Because your cock is so big it's going to wound me?" I teased and narrowed my gaze. "I've seen what you're packing. I'm not the slightest bit worried about fit."

His eyes filled with barely concealed fury, and his jaw clenched. A little muscle in the side of his cheek clicked out a beat while I watched. Fascinating.

"You're asking for it," he growled, biting into the space where my neck met my shoulder. God, I hoped he left a mark.

I moaned. "Asking?"

"Aching for it." He leaned closer.

A sound between air being let out of a balloon and choking spilled from my mouth letting him know exactly where I stood on his accusation.

"Positively begging for *it*." His tongue flicked at his bottom lip on the inflection of the T.

"Did you somehow secretly smoke crack from the time we got into the taxi and here?"

"Couldn't have. My hands were too busy groping you." His gaze was scorching hot, and his hands roamed up and down my back. I wasn't sure if it was to soothe or set aflame, but either way it worked for me.

What he said was not a lie either. In the taxi, his hands had been all over me, stroking my breasts through my tight top, palming my ass, and cupping my sex.

"Mmm...I remember that. Do it again," I whispered before nipping on his ear.

He chuckled, put a knee to the bed, and I went down flat on my back with him between my thighs. In that position, he felt so large, all encompassing.

One of his hands curled around my nape as he put his lips to mine. We kissed for long minutes. I wasn't keeping track. Each drugging kiss was more intense than the last, more meaningful than the first. I gasped when he pulled away.

He straddled me as he sat up, a knee to each hip. I appreciated the opportunity to take things up a notch and get this show on the road by tugging on my slinky tank and yanking it over my head. Foreplay was foreplay, but frankly,

I wanted to get off, preferably with that thick cock embedded deeply within me. I'd thought about nothing else since I painted him. The man was packing a seriously sexy weapon of mass pleasure. I could only hope he knew exactly how to use it.

I went to grab his shirt, and he stopped me with a firm hand right at the center of my breastbone. He held me to the mattress. "Stop, babe, let me look at you. Wild eyes. Hair fanned out. Breasts heaving." He traced the upper swell of each breast with the tips of his fingers. "You're so damned beautiful, and you don't even know it."

"Oh, I know it." I pumped my hips to get his attention, or at the very least, get the attention of a certain part of him.

He shook his head. "No, no, you don't. You hide all that is you. But sometimes, for me, your guard slips and the real you shines through. Like now. You're bare, wildcat. I see you."

Something about the way he said, "I see you," brought a prickling of tears to my eyes. I swallowed and firmed my chin.

"And what do you see?"

"I see strength. An unwilling survivor. You've had to manage a lot on your own. Your dad going away to jail, your mom gallivanted off into the sunset with another family. Who was looking out for you?" His words were but a whisper as he caressed my entire upper half. His fingers trailed between my breasts down to my navel where he leaned forward and circled the tiny slit with his tongue before dipping in.

Shivers racked my frame alongside a heaping dose of arousal.

"Can we stop talking and fuck? You're getting all deep, and really, curly, I just want you to get deep elsewhere."

Atlas grinned and placed endless kisses along my

abdomen. He moved his hands to encase each rib, fingers tapping one bone at a time as if he was tickling a set of ivories on a piano. I groaned and squirmed, wanting more.

"Please..." I begged.

Atlas inhaled sharply, slid his mouth up to my black lace bra, and shoved down each cup. His mouth latched onto a hardened tip instantly, sucking mercilessly.

"Fuck yes!" I called out, holding his head to my breast as I arched up, giving him more.

His other hand plucked and rubbed around my areola, flicking the tightened nub as it firmed and elongated under his ministrations.

Atlas pulled up and yanked off his shirt. Like a high-class bitch weak over a pair of Louis Vuittons, my hands splayed all over his firm body. Atlas was not classically buff like the meatheads who lifted weights and were all about giant muscles, but he had a cut body that showed how much effort he put into it in the gym and in his yoga practice. There wasn't much soft on him, but what he lacked in size, he made up for in mouthwatering hardness.

With a foot to the floor, Atlas pushed off me. I watched while he unbuttoned his jeans and shoved them and his underwear down. His cock was long, thick, and hard when it rose up toward his navel. I might have joked earlier about his size, but the man definitely had it going on. With absolutely no hair to speak of, his cock seemed even larger, protruding out in a graphic depiction of a mating call. I loved looking at a man when he was hot for me. Nothing like it in the world. Knowing I had that power over them, to make something on their body positively strain to worship me. Beautiful.

"You're incredible, but you already know that."

He grinned and leaned a knee on the bed as he crawled over me. "Always good to hear a positive accolade from the woman you're jonesing for."

I giggled as he unbuttoned my pants and tugged them down and off. "No underwear. I like that..." He leaned down and pressed a fiery, wet kiss against the slip of skin just below my navel and right above the tiny landing strip I rocked down below. "So much." He ran his tongue all over the space, teasing me, getting close to where I wanted him most and then backing away.

Making my intentions known, I gripped his hair and none too gently pushed him toward my aching center.

He chuckled against my upper thigh. "Want something, hotness?" He sank his teeth into my flesh, biting, marking me in a carnal way that sent a rush of arousal to slicken my pussy further.

Atlas breathed, nipping at the flesh all around my sex but never touching.

"I may kill you for this."

He sucked on the spot he'd claimed a moment ago. "For what? Foreplay?"

"You call this foreplay? I call this torture."

CHAPTER TEN

Half Wide-Legged Boat Pose
(Sanskrit: Paripurna Navasana)

Sometimes in yoga, your body isn't immediately able to move into more advanced asanas. When that occurs, there are endless modifications that can be practiced to strengthen and welcome additional flexibility. Full wide-legged boat pose has the spine straight, both legs out in front using the entire strength of the core to hold the legs up and out. Advanced yogis will even implement a yogi toe-hole by looping their first finger around their big toes to aid in the maximum stretch. However, starting with one leg is absolutely appropriate. Tuck one leg under or out in front of you, and use your arm to stretch and lengthen the leg. Keep the spine and head straight.

ATLAS

Her body squirmed around like a kitten trying to find its way out from under a heavy comforter. Hovering over her lower half, so close to the heat of her, I wallowed in the scent of her arousal, wanting her dripping with desire.

"Come on," she groaned and then did something I hadn't seen a woman do in a long time.

Mila opened her legs wide, my face scant inches from her heat. The fragrance of a misty morning in San Fran assaulted my senses making my mouth water. I wanted to lick her all over, suck her dry until she begged me to stop. But she was not in control here. Giving her what she wanted, right now, on this first run in bed together was only going to set up the rules for our next encounter. I couldn't have that. In the bedroom, I liked control, and I'd fight to get it. Hell, that was half the fun, especially when the urge to fight and fuck was so strong with my wildcat.

"That's it!" I roared before clamping her thighs together, running one arm under them, putting a heavy lockdown. To solidify my plan, I lay over her legs from knees to feet, pinning her securely. Just the way I wanted. My balls ached with intent, feeling full and needy for release.

"No!" she yelled. "I want to move. I *need* to move!" she groaned.

I shook my head and then laid my mouth over her little pink clit, poking out from its hood. Her hands flew to my hair as I sucked on that wicked bundle of nerves. She jolted around, but I held her strong as her musky flavor hit my tongue. A tingling set up in the base of my spine, and I closed my eyes to imprint this moment, the first time I tasted Mila Mercado.

"You're going to feel every lick." I flattened my tongue against her hot button. "Every suck." I wrapped my lips around the tight knot. "Every fucking taste...and there's nothing"—*lick*—"you can do about it." *Lick*. "So take it." *Lick*. "Let me own your pleasure, baby." *Lick*. "Just for tonight."

On that last word, I fluttered the tip of my tongue hard against her and locked her down even tighter. She screamed out, "Atlas!" and gripped my hair, the pain quickly turning into pleasure as she tried relentlessly to buck up against my face, attempting and failing to control her pleasure. What she hadn't realized yet was that it was mine to control.

Just when she was starting to come down, I let the lock go, pushed her legs wide, and covered her juicy slit with my mouth. Her flavor was far richer, like a hoppy beer, the deeper I pressed my tongue, flicking against her walls, tasting every inch I could reach. Fucking amazing. So wet, so succulent. She started to quicken again, her hips pumping with each lick. That little mewl she made as I moved faster, pushed her harder, went straight to my dick. Prickles of excitement roared through my muscles making them feel larger, tighter, ready to pound and plunge into this sexy woman.

"Fuck, fuck you're good at this," she admitted on a heated sigh. Her body was strung tight, focused on every flick of my tongue. Those fine hips of hers fucked my face as I went to town on her.

When she was close again, I held her thighs open wide and pulled back the petals of her lower lips. I allowed myself one mercy-filled second to catch my breath and tamp down the need to take my own pleasure. Once I'd take a couple breaths, her musky scent making my mouth water, I rammed my tongue as far as it would go, wanting to drink as deeply as possible from the sheer heart of her. Her fingernails dug into the roots of my hair and tugged. I winced as that prick of pain moved in a direct line to my cock.

While I ate her, I mindlessly rubbed my dick all over her legs, the tip leaking pre-cum. Knowing that my pre-cum coated her legs made me even harder. I gritted my teeth and forced myself to imagine dirty socks, the stink of the men's locker room at the gym, anything to prevent me from blowing my load too soon.

Using two fingers, I slipped inside, hooking my finger up the front wall of her pussy to rub against that bumpy patch that would make her lose it. The second I found it, I didn't let go. I tickled and massaged that spot and sucked on her clit, my cheeks hollowing out with the effort. Every last one of her sexy sounds was like a personal triumph, so much so that as I ground my cock against her legs, I reveled in my ability to make Mila insane with lust.

"Oh my God! I'm coming again. Fuck!" she howled.

I kept at her. That second orgasm turned to a third rapidly. Hearing her cry out my name, call for God above only urged me on. My dick was ready to pound sand, dig for gold, anything to assuage the lust rippling through my system ready to soak me in pleasure. When she was barely coming down from her third orgasm, I sat up, wiped my mouth on my forearm, and leaned over, grappling for my jeans. My fingers shook with unfulfilled need as I grabbed the condom I kept in my wallet, ripped the foil, and rolled it on.

Mila lay panting, her hair a wild mess of curls, her lips swollen from our earlier kisses, her cheeks pink, and her small tits jiggling. Pride swelled in my chest, putting a shit-eating grin on my face as I looked down at the mess I'd made of my girl.

"So fucking pretty," I growled, wedging myself between her thighs. I hitched one of her legs out and up my rib cage. "You ready, wildcat?" Even if she wasn't, there was no turning back. I'd long since lost any ability to go slow. My dick needed to plunder her tight, wet, heat. I was mindless with it, couldn't think about anything but getting in her. Right. Now.

"Give it to me," she demanded before slamming her mouth over mine. That was the first time I could recall her actually initiating a kiss besides the very first one. Pleasure zipped from my mouth down my chest to settle between my thighs in a powerful erection that absolutely needed relief, or I'd lose my fucking mind.

Our tongues tangled, our teeth gnashed, and at the same time, I lined up my cock with her wet heat and surged forward.

Holy fucking bliss. Her sex clenched around my cock like a too-tight fist. She strangled my dick in the best possible way. I lost my breath, my vision went black, and I clung to her small form so hard it was as if my life depended on it. There might even be bruises left in the wake of this fucking, I didn't know, and right then, I didn't fucking care. All I cared about was moving, fast and hard.

Her body arched at the invasion, and she moaned long and triumphantly. It was the sound of a well-satisfied woman. I had to hear it again. Each moan was like lyrical harmony in my ears. I retreated all the way to the tip, sucking in a huge bout of air at the intensity of her walls clinging to my rock-hard shaft before I plowed forward.

I clenched my teeth, trying my damnedest not to blow my load in two strokes. Jesus, this woman could have me blowing off like a thirteen-year-old twenty-second wonder.

She squeaked. Actually squeaked like one of those bath toys. "Holy fuck you're so deep!" She gripped my hair by the roots and forced my mouth to hers. I gave in, tasting her sweetness on my tongue, sharing the taste of her pussy with her had me growling into the kiss.

Jesus. I was root deep in her heat, my mouth full of the taste of her, her tits rubbing against my chest like a perfect caress, those firm, toned thighs high on my rib cage holding me close....*Jesus.*

"I could die a happy man. Right here, right now." No more words could be said. Instead, my mind went to that happy place that was all carnal fucking and rutting like an animal. Nothing but hot, wet, sensation as we groped and ground against one another. All I knew was that I was fucking my woman. I had no idea if she'd stay my woman, she definitely had attachment and commitment issues galore, but with each hard drive into her body, she became more mine than not. With every delicious kiss, I owned a little bit more of her, and I intended to keep it that way.

"More," she moaned into my mouth, our lips barely touching.

"You sure?" I asked again. I'd already been fucking her pretty hard for such a tiny thing but definitely had more in me. "I don't want to break you." I laughed and kissed her, breathing through our kisses so that I could catch a moment to focus on not coming.

"You couldn't. I was made for you to fuck." Her eyes were glassy, and pleasure rose and fell in her gaze. She had no idea what she said, but in that moment, something clicked. Something deeper than I'd experienced with any other woman, sexually or emotionally. I actually wanted more of her. I wanted everything she had to give. Wanted to make her mine for good.

I pressed her right leg up and toward her armpit. Being a yogi, she was naturally flexible, and her body opened easily. Using that advantage, my dick as firm as steel and ready to go, I powered into her. With my forearm pressed strategically on the bed, I dug my toes into the mattress, held her ass where I wanted it, and locked my cock in place. Her center squeezed the sensitive tip of my cockhead to the point that I saw stars, physical stars blinking all around her, but even that didn't stop me. No, she needed to feel exactly what I was feeling right then. This was the woman I was meant to be with. Meant to make love to.

"Fuck." I pulled my hips back, groaning at the suction her body had on my manhood, and hammered into her, over and over. The sensation was too much. Just too fucking much. My balls pulled up tight, my groin and abdominal muscles locked into place, and my entire body became stiff. The base of my cock began to tighten with pleasure, making me dizzy, signifying that I was ready to release, and it was going to rip my dick in half.

"Gonna come. Want you with me," I growled, not recognizing my own voice.

"It's okay, just come," she gasped, her own body clenching down sending me into a spiral of satisfaction.

I shook my head and clenched my teeth. A fine mist of sweat had built up on both of us. Aerobic sex. Jesus, she didn't realize how easily she could own me. Everything inside my mind and body was a ball of white-hot fire ready to explode.

"Want. You. With. Me," I grunted before pressing up her other leg, splitting her wide for each brutal lunge. I put my all into taking her, driving so deep her body moved up the bed with each thrust, and I lost hold of what little control I had.

"Oh my, God. Atlas...Atlas...Atlas..." she chanted over and over with each plunge until her body spasmed under me, and her pussy locked down around my cock so tight I could have passed out. Instead, I breathed through it, taking what was mine.

"So tight!" I roared, my hips pumping furiously. That was all it took, and my dick convulsed, and my seed shot from my balls straight up the column of my cock and into the waiting condom like a lightning bolt striking the ground. I held my eyes open, watching as her eyes closed tight, her mouth opened in a silent cry, and her body arched, those perfect tits pointing up as if being offered to me all over again.

I wrapped my hand around her neck gently, a possessive as fuck move, but I didn't care. My inner caveman was about to take charge as, with every thrust, a bit more ejaculate poured into the condom. I cupped her chin with my thumb and forefinger, leaned my head down, and smashed my lips over hers, forcing my tongue deep, mimicking our lower halves. I kept moving, wringing out every drop, letting her tight cunt milk me dry. I gripped the mattress as my body shook and trembled in gluttonous delight.

Eventually, Mila's body went lax, and she settled heavily against the mattress, her breath coming in labored puffs of air. The heat of her breath warmed my chest as the sweat started to chill on my skin. I buried my face against her neck and kissed every inch of skin I could find, needing her to feel how thankful I was that she'd let me in her body and hopefully would allow me to go there again. Shit, I'd just fucked the daylights out her, wrung my dick until there was nothing left, and I was already plotting out when I could take her again.

I was a dirty scoundrel, but right then, I didn't care. I'd pretty much sell my right arm for another round in the sack with my wildcat.

My thoughts were all over the place, remembering everything we did, all that I still wanted to do while she lay limp, and I shifted us to the side. Some twisted and controlling side of me wanted to stay inside her as long as possible. Caress her silky skin with the tips of my fingers and feel her all around me. Her bra was still pushed under her tits expelling them up and over the cups. I nuzzled one breast licking and sucking the nub and playing with the other one. She sighed and mumbled her pleasure as my dick throbbed inside her.

I ran my hands over her back, her skull, what I could reach, massaging away any tension that might have been left. I'd taken her hard and worked her over pretty good even though my hellion was a true soldier in the sack, ready for anything that I threw at her. Mila let me do what I felt like doing, while just lying there, allowing me to pet her.

"You good?" I whispered in her ear while trailing a line of kisses down her neck to her clavicle.

"So good. Let's do that again sometime," she purred sleepily and yawned.

Secretly I wanted to jump up and down on the bed, lift my hands to the ceiling in a touchdown dance move, but instead, I chuckled under my breath, not wanting to rouse her. I pulled out and she moaned and winced. Fuck, I loved that sound. A moan followed by a wince meant I did my job. Score one for me and my johnson.

"You okay?" A trickle of worry knotted my brow. What if I'd hurt her?

She nodded. "Just liked you there," she mumbled before snuggling into my chest.

Thank God!

With one hand, I eased off the condom then tied it off, losing her warmth in the process. A huge sense of relief racked my lower half as the last physical barrier of our mating hit me with a small shiver. There was a box of tissues within arm's reach, so I wadded it up in a tissue and then chucked it the few feet to the wastebasket, thrilled when it made it in. Score!

I grinned, thinking that was the second time I'd scored tonight. Only the first was far, far better. While I was messing with the condom, she'd turned over facing away from me. Something about that hit me sideways like a tiny fist to the gut. *Relax, man.* She was probably used to sleeping alone but not tonight. I'd had my fair share of one-nighters, not too many, a solid couple handfuls over the last few years, but tonight was the first time I'd ever wanted to actually *sleep* next to a woman. Usually, I'd share the bed because I didn't want to up and leave like an asshole, but I rarely *wanted* to sleep there. Right then, I curled my body around Mila's much smaller one, her warmth invading my senses. I tagged her waist to make sure she was flush against me and planted my face right into her cinnamon flowery scent at the crux of her neck. Christ almighty, I could get lost in her scent, especially when it was mixed with the notes of sex still simmering in the air. I gripped the comforter and tugged it over both our bodies. Right there, tucked up tight into the most unlikely woman I'd ever known, I fell asleep, my arm never losing hold of the small beauty in front of me.

MILA

I woke to the smells of coffee brewing and bacon cooking. Not exactly an occurrence that had ever happened in my apartment before, unless Moe was visiting.

Speak of the devil, my phone buzzed on the counter where I'd dropped my purse. The only person who ever called this early was Moe. Atlas's curly head popped into view behind the bar of my kitchen. Without even asking, the bastard opened the phone and answered.

"Yello, Mila's phone. How can I be of service to you this fine Thursday morning?" he answered, chipper as hell.

I groaned and pulled the comforter up and over my head, and I started counting.

Ten...nine...

He laughed. "Atlas Powers."

Eight...seven...

"Yeah, she's here." His gravel-thick voice responded to whomever was on the phone.

Six...five...

"I think she's still asleep."

Kill me now. Four...three...

"Uh, I'm not sure that's any of your business. Who is this?"

Fuck my life. Two...

"Looks like she's awake and hiding under the covers. Hold on."

One.

With both arms, I slapped the comforter down to my waist and sat up. "You"—I pointed an accusatory finger—"don't answer my phone!" I grated through my teeth.

He ignored my outburst. Of course he did. He was a total sexy hot bastard. Especially right then, standing in a pair of boxers and his T-shirt looking absolutely delicious and edible. Screw the food; I'd rather eat him. Again.

"Jesus, you're just as pretty in the morning." He tossed the phone across the room to land on the bed about a foot from me. "Soup's on in five." He bit into a piece of bacon he must have just cooked and then turned back to the kitchen.

I could hear the popping and sizzling across the room along with a gentle noise. What the hell was it? I strained to hear. Humming. The bastard was humming a tune while he cooked. Did he have to be so flippin' cute? Cooking and humming. Oh hell. That had to be a cliché. Right out of one of those chick flicks Moe made me watch.

Moe.

A trickle of dread rippled against the tiny hairs at the back of my neck. I shoved my hand through the knotted mass of curls falling into my face, pushed them back, and grabbed my phone. "Hello?" I waited for the shit to hit the fan.

"Good morning, sunshine. Or did you even sleep?"

I made a girlie type whine and flopped back to bed. "Did you have to call? Today? I mean, come on. Even bad teenagers skate by once or twice, Mom."

"Someone's been bad." Moe laughed heartily, loving every second of my embarrassment.

"Don't you have a job? People's heads to shrink, a case to mediate. Where's my niece? Where's Lily?"

"At preschool, as you well know. Now dish. Atlas answered your phone, and I hear the distinct sounds of breakfast being prepared in the background. You were still in bed, so I'm taking that to assume he spent the night."

"He spent the night." I ripped off the Band-Aid as quickly and painlessly as I could.

Her voice came softly when she continued her grilling. "And will he be staying more often?"

"Ugh." I turned over onto my side and stared out the window, the phone pressed to my ear. The sky was gray and overcast, unlike someone's mood in this apartment. Mine, I didn't know yet. "Yes. No. I don't know. Is that a good enough answer?"

I heard the ecstatic sound of clapping through the phone. "I can't believe it. I prayed for this day."

"You prayed for me to have sex?" I shot back quickly.

"No, brat! For you to find someone worthy of even a full night's sleepover. Don't think I'm not aware of your preference for one-nighters."

A cold chill ran through my entire body. "Moe..." My voice was uncertain with anxiety. I never wanted my best friend to know how loose I'd been in the past. "I can explain."

"Hey, everyone needs to take care of business once in a while."

Once in a while. She thought I had them once in a while, not a couple times a month for the last few years. Okay, that's fine. Let her think I was a ho only some of the time.

"Yeah," I said noncommittally.

"It's okay. Besides, I'd never judge you. You're a grown woman, but I do worry about you. I want you to have someone and maybe this Atlas—"

"Don't start, Moe. I don't yet know what's going on, so give me a little time to figure that out," I whispered quickly into the phone and glanced over my shoulder.

Mr. Hum had turned into Mr. Whistle, completely

oblivious to my conversation. Thank God for small favors.

"Look, Atlas and I are just having a bit of fun for now. Okay?"

"But he spent the night. Have you ever had a man spend the night before? All night?"

I didn't want to admit that I'd never even had sex in my bed before last night, let alone allowed a man to fuck me and sleep with me and now cook me breakfast. "No. There's a first for everything." I sighed. "Can we talk later? As in never?" I groaned.

She laughed again. "All right. I just wanted to remind you about this weekend. You promised to start moving in."

Stop the presses. "Excuse me?"

"The other day you said you'd move in. I'm holding you to it."

"Moe, you were mad. Giving me the silent treatment. I had to say something."

She sighed. "I've already told Lily. She's expecting you. She wants to discuss what color she thinks you should paint on your walls. And get this...you're gonna love it." The tone she used made it very clear I was not, in fact, going to love it.

"If you say a frozen landscape, I'll puke. Straight out blow chunks. Can't you burn that *Frozen* DVD? Every time she wants to watch it, I want to say...let it go...let it gooooooo. And toss the damn thing in the trash. You're her mother; you can make things disappear."

"She loves it!"

"And I love pizza, doesn't mean that I'm going to eat it every day and talk about it incessantly."

Moe laughed again. "You'll understand when you have children."

Fat chance. If I had a child, it would be an evil demon spawn with two heads and a tail. Not happening.

"All righty then, I'll let her offer her suggestion directly. When shall I expect you?"

"I don't know. I'll text you later."

"Breakfast, wildcat!" Atlas called.

Fuck.

"Wildcat? Is that a direct reference to your abilities and talents in the bedroom?" Moe did not miss a beat. Not even one. If I didn't love her so much, I'd hate her guts.

"Hanging up now..."

"Joking, joking. Wildcat!" she quipped and then hung up first.

Atlas strutted over with a steaming cup of coffee in his hand. "I didn't know what you liked, but since I found French vanilla creamer in the fridge but no sugar to speak of in your cupboards, I figured you preferred just the cream."

He handed me heaven in a cup, and for a brief moment, I thought I could get used to this. Someone bringing me coffee in bed and making me breakfast after a night of some pretty stellar fucking. Yeah, I could get very used to this.

"Thank you."

Atlas caged my body by placing one fist on each side of my hips. He dipped his head and rubbed his nose against mine before kissing me softly. He tasted of bacon and coffee, and I wanted to gobble him up for breakfast instead of whatever he'd made.

"Time to eat. Then I'd like to shower with you, but then I've got to hit my house and get ready for class. I believe you do, too."

I nodded, not sure what to say. Seriously, he'd stunned

me with the simple gesture of making me coffee, acting like nothing between us was strange, planning out my morning unabashedly, and telling me his schedule. Why did I care what he had to do today? Then again, the showering together did not sound unappealing. Having all his sexiness slick and wet? Yep. Not a bad idea at all.

"Okay," I found myself answering.

"I'll lay out the plates on the bar." He smiled, kissed me once more and then set about plating the food.

What the hell had I gotten myself into? This scenario positively reeked of domesticity.

I spent a moment sucking back more blessings from the coffee gods before finding a pair of panties and a tank top and tugging them on. As much as it would be fun to walk into the kitchen naked, I was hungry, and I didn't think I'd last long if I poked the beast. Besides, I wanted the beast poking me.

When I reached the bar and perched my bum on a stool, he set down a huge plate. Three fried eggs, four pieces of bacon, and two slices of toast.

"Were you planning on sharing?" I looked down at all the food.

He came over to me with a plate of his own, a frown in place. "No, why?"

I laughed. "This is a ton of food!"

He put down his plate, and I practically fell off my chair. He had five eggs, at least double the amount of bacon, and three pieces of toast. "You think so?"

"Uh, yeah. Do you always eat like that?"

He shifted to my side and kissed the ball of my shoulder. "After a night like last night, yes. Now eat up. I plan on burning off a lot of those calories with you before I teach today. And I recall you demolishing over half a pizza on your own."

"You're insane," I grumbled, knowing he was right.

"Why? Because I bedded you? I know. I'll probably get shit for it from all the other guys at Lotus House," he deadpanned.

A white-hot poker couldn't have wounded me more. I held my fork in the air, unmoving, staring into his eyes trying to find the man I'd gone to bed with last night. The man I'd willingly given my body and evening to.

He bumped me playfully with his shoulder. "Relax. Kidding, babe, I'm kidding. Wow, you need to lighten up. What happened to my snarky, sassy wildcat? The girl that didn't let anything get past her?"

A basketful of hand weights left my shoulders, and I scowled at him before biting into a piece of bacon. "Bastard," I got out before the flavor of maple, thick-cut bacon hit my taste buds. *Oh hell yes.* I moaned.

Atlas watched, seemingly fascinated by my response. "Now you're talking."

"I didn't say anything." I shoved the rest of the piece into my mouth. When was the last time I'd had bacon? Why didn't I have it more often? So damned good.

"I know. I like you better when your mouth is occupied." He winked and put most of an entire half piece of toast in his mouth.

"Gross. Did your mother teach you to eat like that?"

And now we were back to normal. I breathed a sigh of relief. Sex hadn't changed us—if anything, it made our relationship better. We were still the volatile duo with barbs ready to fly. With our priorities still intact, I tucked in to eat as much of his village-sized breakfast as I could, content in the knowledge that Atlas was still an ass and I was still the woman who would serve up the sass on a platter. Only this time, the platter had a heaping serving of bacon and eggs.

CHAPTER ELEVEN

SOLAR PLEXUS
C H A K R A

A manipura couple will value family traditions and treat each other politely. Their biggest challenge within relationships with the opposite sex is to achieve trust. They know how to act trusting, but they do not know how to truly trust, or be truly trustworthy. Wondering whether or not the other will keep their word and commitment is a constant battle they are not always willing to fight.

ATLAS

I went to work with a skip in my step and a lightness I hadn't felt in a long damn time. Not only did I find out that Mila fucked as well as she fought, but I'd also slept worry-free and sated. Waking up with her this morning had been the highlight of a tough year, second only to what happened at the club after my set, right before we went to her pad.

Silas McKnight wants a meeting with me. Knight & Day Productions. I shook my head and entered Lotus House all smiles and good vibes ready to rock a hot Vin Flow class.

Someone clapped me on my shoulder as I walked toward my assigned room. "Hey, bud, how goes it?" Dash asked, following at my pace.

I grinned, opened my arms, and looked up at the swirly ceiling of the warehouse-turned-yoga center. "Dash, today's the best day of my life. Well, technically I should say that was last night."

Dash chuckled and followed me into my room where I jogged to the riser and dropped my mat.

"You gonna share why today, excuse me, last night was the best night of your life? Something happen at the club?" His eyes widened when I beamed and gave him a thumbs-up. "No frickin' way. A scout? Who?"

The desire to prance around like a little kid was strong, but I fought it. "Knight & Day Productions."

He rubbed at his chin. "Great label." He squinted and then looked off to the side. "I read something in the paper about them. Run by a young guy now. A fella named..."

"Silas McKnight."

"Yeah, that's him. Passed down from his father. Man was the King of Soul in his day! Daddy Knight. Remember his old-school rhythm and blues? The man owned the charts for a couple decades back when our parents were our age."

I grinned. "I know."

"Man, you must be so stoked. When are you meeting him?"

"Scheduled a meeting for a couple weeks from now. He's out of town on business but caught my act last night. Stopped

Mila and me at the door before we left."

"Wait. Mila and you? You were with Mila last night?" A knowing smirk fell across his lips. "So how did that go? You two have been circling around each other for the past couple weeks."

I laid it out there. I wasn't even going to pretend to be a guy that didn't kiss and tell. "Dash, shit, she's incredible. Best lay I've ever had and sweet, too, once you get past all that spunk and sass to the soft underbelly..."

I recalled kissing down her soft stomach this morning in the shower before I lifted her leg, placed it over my shoulder, gripped her ass, and ate her through two orgasms. Straight after, she went down on her knees and returned the favor. Seeing her lips puffy from being stretched wide around my cock...best fucking view of my life. And she liked it a little rough, too. When I gripped the roots of her hair and fucked her face, she went wild, moaning and putting a hand between her legs. Far as I could tell, when I got off down her throat, she got herself off a third time. Greedy kitty.

Dash clapped a hand on my shoulder and squeezed. Dash was always the one to initiate touching. The man just had to physically *feel* the people he was near. I'd gotten used to it back in high school.

"Dude, I'm happy for you. When are you going to see her again?"

The question brought me up short. Mila and I hadn't discussed the aftermath of our choice to hook up at all. Obviously, I wanted seconds and thirds and hundredths, but did she? "I don't know. I've never wanted to actually follow up with a girl I've banged before."

"But you do now, right?" Dash's eyes held a hint of

concern.

I rubbed my hands together and sighed. "Yeah, I mean, if she's game, I'm game."

Dash smirked. "If she's game, you're game? What kind of lame ode to romance is that? Women are not toys. If you want Mila, mark my words, she's the type of girl you're going to have to chase."

"Honestly, I don't think it's going to be that hard, if you know what I mean," I leered.

Dash groaned. "You are so far out of your league. Just because you had a little fun in the sack does not mean she's all in. Hit me with your plan."

A plan. "I don't have one. What would you do?"

"I'm not you," he retorted.

"No, but you did chase after Amber, and now she's your wife."

"So you're looking for a future with Mila?"

I backed up until I hit the riser and fell on my ass. "Not exactly. We only hooked up the one night. I can't say after one night of banging her that I know she's the one. Besides, we're both knee-deep in our careers."

"You're both yoga instructors."

"Touché. But we're both reaching for something bigger. Much bigger. And I get the feeling from her that her art is something she's not going to give up for a man who wants to tour the world playing music."

Dash laid out his yoga mat and pulled off his shirt and shoes. "Guess you're going to have to find out along the way. In the meantime, if you want to keep seeing her, you're going to have to make the first move."

I hadn't made the first move in God only knew how long.

"I'll just text her."

Dash rolled his eyes and went into the yoga position downward facing dog, his body making a perfect triangular shape on the mat.

"What? No texting? How do I make my desire for a round two known, Mr. Flowers and Romance?" I goaded.

Dash shifted his weight, going up onto his toes and stretching his upper body to the sky in the upward facing dog position. "I know what I'm going to say might sound archaic to you, but have you asked the girl out on a date?"

Shit, a date? "Does pizza on the floor of my apartment count, or her coming to see me play?"

He laughed hard enough to lose his pose and come to his knees into table position where his back faced the ceiling and his hands and knees were shoulder distance apart. The pose was aptly named because when in it, the person looked like a table one could set a lamp on. "You're pathetic, you know that? Ask the girl out for goodness' sake. Really, you can't possibly be this immature."

"Don't be a dick. I'm out of practice."

"That's blatantly obvious."

"Fine, I'll ask her to Rainy Day when she has a break today."

He coughed and laughed again before giving up his stretch and turning to his side. "That's a start. You probably should do that to talk about last night, as well as where you want things to go from there. She might not even want to see you again. Maybe you suck in bed." He grinned before cackling into his fist.

"You're an ass!"

Even still, something he said struck a chord with me. What

if she didn't want to see me again? Perhaps I was a one-off for her. Hell no. No way. Not after the chemistry we'd shared last night and again this morning. Even eating breakfast together was comfortable. For me, for sure. Was it for her? Shit, now he had me questioning every last word, move, her body language, which did in fact seem standoffish when I gave her a long kiss good-bye and told her I'd see her later.

"I made her breakfast this morning," I added in a stupid attempt to sound a bit less juvenile.

Dash smiled. "That's a good start. Women love a man who can cook. Are you going to invite her out to dinner?"

Dinner. I guess I could. I didn't have a lot extra to take her somewhere extravagant. Did it have to be gourmet or would my favorite little Mexican restaurant work? Wait. Would she think I was being racist since she's Hispanic? Fuck. A sour, acidic feeling hit my gut. I had no idea how to date this woman. Not just this woman, *any* woman. I'd been out of the game for so long none of this came naturally, and she'd know it. However, Mila didn't seem the type to care about conventions.

Then an idea hit. Oh hell yes. A perfect one. Something affordable, yet thoughtful.

"I've got it. Listen to this." I went over to Dash and crouched down as the class started to fill.

When I was done telling him my plan, he smiled big, a wide, toothy grin. "If that's what she's into, it's perfect, man, absolutely perfect. Now you just have to get her to agree to go out with you."

Easy. I had that in the bag.

MILA

"No. Not happening. I don't think it's a good idea," I said to Atlas when he called me after his class. He'd asked me to lunch, and if I was being honest with myself, I needed more time.

More time to figure out what had happened.

More time to avoid the feelings I had about last night.

More time to put up the wall he'd had crashing down after our evening together.

"Wildcat, you know I'm not going to take no for an answer, so you might as well just say yes now and go out with me."

I groaned. "Look, Atlas. I'm fine. We really don't have to make more out of last night than what it was. A fun night. A lot of fun."

"And morning."

The memory of seeing his slick, wet head between my thighs this morning flashed across my vision and turned me on instantly. Thank God he wasn't here right now, because in all likelihood, I'd jump him.

"You're not playing fair," I whispered, as I entered Lotus House for my afternoon class.

He cleared his throat. "You're not playing at all. Come out and play with me, hotness. You know you want to. You can't possibly think that last night was a one and then done. There's so much more we have to experience together."

"Atlas..." I warned, clenching my teeth and grinding my molars. He was getting to me. Why the hell did I give him my phone number anyway?

"Imagine this...you naked on all fours, me naked behind you. My hand would be curled around your shoulder, my other on your hip, moving you on and off my cock while I take you from behind."

I groaned as that exact image filtered through my mind. It would be so flippin' hot. My sex clenched, and I had to lean against one of the walls in the hallway to catch my balance.

"Or I could lift you up on your counter, sit at one of your stools, spread your sexy as fuck thighs nice and wide, and put my mouth all over your pussy. I'd do it, too. Right where we ate breakfast this morning, only instead, I'd be eating you, wildcat."

"Jesus Christ..." I moaned into the phone and closed my eyes while holding myself up against the wall. The graphic visual seared my brain and sent ribbons of heat flooding the tender space between my thighs.

"That's right. You know how good it was last night. The more we get to know each other...mmm, the better it will get." His tone was sultry, sexy, and downright panty-melting.

I didn't have an ounce of will left in me.

"So how about it? You want that?" he asked.

"Mmm...yeah," I spoke, not realizing I'd just agreed to myriad sexual situations with Atlas when I was attempting, very unsuccessfully, to avoid another go with him.

I'd done well this morning after he left. Talked myself right out of anything more with Atlas Powers for a variety of reasons.

One. We worked together. Never a good idea to shit where you eat. Or in this case, fuck where you work.

Two. He was a distraction. From my teaching, from my art, from my life. Distraction. Sure, it was a weak reason, but it worked this morning.

Three. We weren't right for each other. We fought

constantly. Who fought as much as we did? Weren't couples supposed to have that honeymoon phase? Everyone talked about it. Supposedly the best time in the relationship. We'd skipped right over that and went to the turmoil phase. Then again, it made for some awesome hate sex, or was that makeup sex? I never did understand which one was right. Hate sex made sense. Makeup sex? Not so much.

Four. Moe and Lily. I was moving in with Monet and Lily. That would stop the opportunity for me to have angry, growly type sex, which was all I'd really have with Atlas anyway.

Five. Time. My ultimate enemy. I didn't have time to devote to whatever this was with him. And this date request, that proved it all together.

"Great, what time this weekend are you free?"

"I'm supposed to move in with my friend this weekend."

"What? Why?"

And here was why I didn't have men in my life. They wanted to question everything I did and said like they had some sort of right to an opinion. "Because I lost a battle with her, and she's making me move in."

"That's ridiculous. I thought you liked your little space. It's private. You've got your art setup and your living space."

He also didn't know that it cost an arm and a leg even though it wasn't the best area. The worst neighborhood in Oakland might have been more affordable, but since I didn't fancy the idea of getting burglarized or raped on my way from my car to my shithole apartment, I paid out the ass for the not-so-great tiny studio.

I sighed. "Yes, I like my space, but it's not cheap and I promised Moe I'd focus on my art, and living with her would allow me to do just that."

"Oh, I see. It's a money thing. I get it."

The fight-or-flight response grew stronger the more we talked. He didn't know my life, or that I struggled to make do. My fiery Latina side was about to make herself known. I could feel my face getting hot with embarrassment and my ire lighting up with each tick of the clock. "You don't know jack about me. You only know what I've told you. So don't act like you understand."

"Whoa, okay, what happened here? I didn't mean to piss you off. Not this time anyway."

"I have a class to teach."

"Mila, wait. Just wait. I'm sorry. Do you need help moving? I could borrow a friend's truck."

What the hell was this? He was being nice to me. After I just yelled at him and put him in his place. Either I had a golden pussy, or this man was not for real. "I'm sure I can handle it."

"But if I help you, it will go faster, and you can get it done in one day. Then I can take you out on Sunday."

Back to taking me out. He was a dog with a bone, but why? Before I could turn him down, he rushed to respond.

"I'll take that as a yes and let you get to class. And, hotness, you made my night. Blew me away, baby. Can't wait for a repeat." He hung up.

I closed my eyes and breathed slowly as the phone went dead. Atlas was a freakin' whirlwind of contradictions. At one minute he was fighting with me, the next he was being nice. Positively sweet. I didn't get what came over him. I mean sure, the sex was phenomenal, and I'd admit that, if pushed, I was not going to say no to a second round of shit-hot fucking, but this sweet side. Blech. He needed to get over that before I throat punched him.

I didn't know how to handle sweet. Usually there wasn't a problem because I never, never, ever had a man more than once. Well, more than once after the one-nighter. Sometimes with a random guy, I'd let him have me many times if the sex was good, but only until he passed out. Then it was bye-bye, so long for me, and I'd be out the door and in my bed within the hour. This with Atlas...a date. Who dated anymore? Oh hell, I'd have to talk to Moe. That in itself was going to suck, because she'd absolutely encourage me to spend more time with him, not less. I needed new friends. Mean ones who didn't give a hoot about anyone but themselves. Yeah, that was what I needed.

New plan to get shitty friends on the horizon, I unlocked my yoga room and set up for class. I opened the windows to allow some fresh air in before I got everyone all worked up sweating out their toxins. That's when I bumped into Amber Alexander, Dash's wife.

"Oh hey, Amber. How are you?"

The brunette was tall and thin, her athletic build covered in a set of workout clothes that had a cool paint-splattered pattern in the fabric. She leaned forward and folded me in her arms for a hug. Looked like her husband's touchy nature was wearing off on his bride. "I'm great! And Dash uh..."—she looked around the room to make sure nobody was paying attention to us while they set up—"he told me what you asked him."

I focused on her face while I thought about what she was referring to. I blinked and rolled around the last few conversations Dash and I'd had. "Oh! Yeah, the painting."

Her head jerked around to make sure we still had a bit of privacy.

"Sorry," I whispered, thinking it was pretty funny that she was nervous about anyone hearing what we were up to.

"No, it's okay. I just, you know, I'm going to be a doctor, and I don't want something, anything to come out about doing it. Not that it really matters or anything because Dash said it would be anonymous."

"Totally." I made the gesture of sealing my lips and tossing the key over my shoulder.

She giggled, and it sounded sugary like a young girl's.

"I just wanted to tell you that we'll do it. Dash is really interested in the concept and believes that it's an experience lovers shouldn't pass by. To be part of someone's art is such an honor."

An honor. The Alexanders thought that having me paint them was an honor. For the first time in my life, I felt proud. Proud of the path I'd chosen and that I'd stuck to my passion, giving it my all over the last several years. And now I'd get to give a gift that two very beautiful people would cherish in their lives forever.

"Thank you for that, Amber. I look forward to it. When would you both be available?"

Her face crumbled into one of worry. "Not for another couple weeks. I'm sorry. I'm dealing with my first-year finals in med school, and they are kicking my booty."

I wanted to laugh at her use of the word booty instead of ass. She was so damned sweet, I swear I could eat her up.

"Not a problem, girl. I'm moving this weekend anyway and will need time to get set up. I'll actually be closer to the center."

"Oh, cool. Okay, I'll tell Dash, and we'll check our schedules, and I'll have him relay available dates."

"Sounds perfect to me. And thank you! I promise when we set it up, I'll make you as comfortable as possible, including hiding anything you don't want to show the world."

She blushed and her arms immediately crossed over her chest.

See, so flippin' sweet, but I knew Dash pretty well, and the dude taught Tantra. I was certain he was tarnishing that squeaky clean innocence every damned day.

"Go ahead and get set up for class." I gestured to her mat before raising my voice to the patrons already set up around the room. "Everyone, let's start today in child's pose. We're going to get in the right headspace before I take you through a very rigorous Vin Flow. Set your intent and think about what your body does for you, how you want to give back to it, and remember as always...*be your strength*."

CHAPTER TWELVE

Triangle Pose (Sanskrit: Trikonasana)

A classic standing yoga pose that's designed to extend and stretch each side of the body, strengthen the legs, build flexibility and balance. Extend the legs a full leg length distance apart, slide one hand down the leg, twist the upper body horizontal and extend the opposite hand to the sky. Actively reach the arms in opposite directions and breathe through any tight or tense areas.

MILA

"I swear to God, curly, if you puncture even *one* of those paintings, you'll be walking with a limp for the rest of your life!" I hollered as Atlas and his friend Clay lifted several of my most prized possessions out of the truck.

Honestly, if I wasn't so into the messy-haired musician, I'd be drooling over his friends. It was as if a guy had to be insanely hot to be part of his man posse. Take Trent for example. Star baseball player, built, sandy-colored hair that fell just right, and a dazzling pair of hazel eyes. Even his hands were sexy. Then there was Clayton Hart. Aptly named, because he'd definitely stop a woman's heart from beating just by looking at her. Dirty blond hair, spiked on top, with a set of clear-as-day blue eyes. He was what I'd call a slice of hot apple pie, or an American man at his finest. Of course, that heaping dose of sugary goodness came in a package that included muscles upon muscles. Watching him lift my paintings as though the canvases were featherlight, I started to drool. Definitely made total sense that he was a personal fitness trainer to the stars.

I could never forget my buddy Dash. I think he'd be happy with that endearment. Buddy. I hadn't really considered Dash a friend before, more a colleague, but when I looked closer, he'd always been there for me with a kind word and a hug. He'd swapped classes with me countless times when I needed it over the years. So yeah, buddies. Throw in the fact that he was Atlas's best friend, and we had a regular brofest. Only one dude was missing.

Just as the thought took root, a deep growl of a manly exhaust rumbled through the air, announcing the fly muscle car that came careening around the corner of Moe's suburban Berkeley neighborhood. Daytona yellow Chevy Camaro Z/28 302 4-speed with a set of black racing stripes down the center and one hell of a beefed-up engine. It rolled to a stop right in front of the guys. Basically, tits on wheels.

Nicolas Salerno or "Nick" as he preferred, hopped out of his car wearing his standard garb, a black tank and a distressed pair of jeans. Taller than most Italians I knew, Nick stood at around six feet with black, perfectly slicked hair, a pair of the prettiest, palest blue eyes, a beard-goatee combo, and a wide smile. The man was always smiling. Unless, of course, a male was looking at one of his five sisters, or one of the women he'd adopted as his sisters, which pretty much included every woman who worked at Lotus House.

"Hi, Nick!" I ran down the steps and jumped at him. He caught me midair and lifted me up so that I had to wrap my legs around his waist. Then he laid a big fat smooch on my forehead. Just like a brother. I so loved Nick!

"Yo! Put her down, man. Now." Atlas's voice boomed from somewhere behind me.

The air behind my back turned icy cold. Nick's hands squeezed tighter around my form as he looked around me. I let my legs fall from around his waist, but Nick didn't let go when my feet hit the ground. Not an option when his protective brother alert screamed at full flare.

I wanted to warn Atlas, say something like, "Danger, danger, Will Robinson!" However, I was too slow. Nick used this one-armed move where he tucked me to his side and then behind him, so that he faced Atlas head on.

"I'm sorry. Who are you and why should I care?" Nick stiffened his spine, putting his large shoulders and biceps on display.

Nick had a fiery temper. More so than mine, and that was unusual. Nick had been raised in Southside Chicago where a person knew their place based solely on nationality. That meant he spent a lot of time using his fists to handle disagreements. Unfortunately for Atlas, that habit could rear its ugly head at any given moment. As far as I knew, Nick had kept his fists in the ring at the local boxing league he managed during the evenings, but that didn't mean he wouldn't use them if provoked.

Atlas crossed his arms over his chest, puffing out his goods, and I had to admit, the two were pretty equal when it came to body styles. Atlas lifted his chin toward me. "I'm seeing Mila." He said this as if it answered every question on *Jeopardy*. Um...no.

Nick looked at each guy, some of whom were trying really hard not to laugh at the outlandish rush of testosterone that, all of a sudden, was so thick it would take a chainsaw to cut that shit. "Looks like we know some of the same people."

"Including my girl," Atlas added.

Oh for crying out loud.

I laughed. "Now that's taking it a bit too far." Adjusting my position, I attempted to maneuver around the wall of Nick, but did not get past those hands of his locking me in place.

"Looks like *my girl*, Mila, doesn't see things the way you do. So the next time you want to interrupt me greeting my friend, one I've known for years and haven't seen in weeks, you can just step back...*bro*." Nick's tone brooked no argument.

I put my hands on Nick's shoulders. "Hey, Nickster, it's okay. I really am banging him," I admitted, hoping it would ease the tension.

Then the teddy bear came out. Nick lifted his head to the sky and groaned. "Now you've done it. You actually made me throw up in my mouth a little bit." He groaned again. "This guy? With the hair?" He pointed at Atlas's curly mop. "You're giving it up to him? Sweetie, we really need to talk about setting your standards higher." He sighed.

Everyone but Atlas, who had no idea what the hell was going on, laughed. Hard. The rest of the crew already knew

Nick and his protective vibe. Trent had caught on to it right away months ago and thanked the guy for looking out for his woman, Genevieve, when she was working at Lotus House. Now that Dash had innocent Amber running around the yoga studio more often, Nick even kept a lookout for her.

"Can you give the guy a chance? Look, he's the one that set up all these dudes to help me move. And...he's letting me paint him. Naked!" I grinned and waggled my eyebrows for effect.

"Oh shit, man, that sucks! You must be *into* her if she's conned you into letting her paint you. I did it once, fully clothed, and I was so bored out of my mind I fell asleep!" He chuckled and held out his hand. "Nicholas Salerno. Mila and me go way back. Like a sister to me, so you better do right by her or you'll have to deal with me. Yeah?"

Atlas blinked several times as if stunned by Nick's instant change of demeanor and friendly nature but shook his hand anyway. "Nice to meet you...I think." Atlas's tone insinuated he absolutely *did not* find it nice to meet Nick.

Nick clapped his hands and then did a round of the man-hug with the other guys. "Where's Moe?" he asked just as Monet rolled up to her three-car garage.

"Right there!" I pointed to her Lexus SUV.

Moe's sleek body exited the car looking more like a chic angel, sans the feathered wings, than a mom on the go. She wore a white ensemble of ankle-length leather pants and a shimmery white, cowl-neck sweater shirt. It had a thin gold belt cinching in at the smallest part of her waist. Man, she was stunning. The damn woman could grace any catwalk in Paris, as long as she kept her four-inch wedges on. Otherwise, she was only a few inches taller than me.

Every single man outside became dead silent, watching her strut up to the boy brigade. She walked right up to Nick and kissed his cheek.

"Hey, angel." He gave her his usual greeting. "Where's the cherub?"

"Playdate."

Out of nowhere, Clay bumped Nick aside and offered his hand. "Hey, beautiful, I'm Clayton Hart. A friend of Mila's."

I wouldn't say he was a *friend* just yet, but I wasn't about to disagree with him for fear I'd lose the extra set of hands. Moe held his hand and smiled, a pink blush staining her cheeks. Uh-oh, looked like Moe was attracted to Clay. Huh.

"Clayton," she acknowledged softly and smiled.

Clayton didn't let go of her hand, just kept shaking it and taking in all that was my friend, as if his eyes would pop out of his head and walk all over her body in a full-body caress. Totally into her.

Nick, ever the brother, put his hand on their hands and shoved them down. "Enough touching." He hooked his arm around Monet's shoulder and pointed to each man. "Trent Fox, and you know Dash Alexander, and the guy who claims to be seeing our girl. Atlas Powers."

Now *that* got her attention. She shrugged off Nick's protective hold and went right up to Atlas, grabbed both his hands, and shook them. "I'm so, so, *so* excited to meet you. I mean, you're the first guy of Mila's I've met in forever!" she gushed.

Atlas smiled wide. "Really? A dry spell, you say." He smirked, his gaze flicking to me. "Tell me all about it!" Atlas grinned and blew me a kiss.

I sighed. My best friend getting chatty with the guy I was

sleeping with...not a good idea. As a matter of fact, it was a horrible idea. They started moving toward the entrance of the house, shoulders touching conspiratorially.

"Curly, don't you dare run off. You promised to move me in today. Otherwise that date you want tomorrow is off."

He frowned, and Moe smiled, her black eyes seeming to light up at the concept of a man buying me a meal.

"You're going on a date? Like a real-life, eat-a-meal, go-to-the-movies date?" she quipped, a note of excitement accenting her words.

I slumped over at the waist and rested my hands on my thighs. "Why do I have to deal with this?" I mumbled to my feet.

"We are not going to the movies." Atlas leaned closer to my best friend and whispered something into her ear. It must have been a mouthful because it took several moments for him to finish. All I could see was Moe's eyes widening and her smile getting larger. That had to be good. Right?

While I was watching Atlas and Moe warily, Clayton came over to me. "Hey, so is your friend, uh, taken?"

It took me a moment to comprehend what he asked. "Oh, you mean by a man?"

"No, I mean by an alien. Of course I mean by a man. Stop worrying about what Atlas is telling her, and hook me up. Is she free?"

"Free of a man...yes. But, Clay, she's the relationship type, not the one-night-stand type. And she's divorced, so she's rather picky."

His face turned hard. "I'm sure she's gotta eat, though. Why not do it with someone of the opposite sex?"

I sighed and shrugged. "Honestly, I don't know. There

was definitely a spark between you two. Couldn't hurt to ask her out. But I warned you. She's relationship material, and she's got some, uh, baggage." I hated, absolutely *hated* to refer to my sweet niece as baggage, but to a guy like Clay, successful and on the prowl, who probably hadn't had a real relationship in years, that's exactly what a single divorcée with a kid would be considered.

"What does she do?" He ignored the baggage comment altogether and kept up with me as I walked back to the truck. We both grabbed another box to bring in.

I loved seeing how men responded when I told them my BFF was a shrink. A lot of men were intimidated by it. Others were afraid she'd spend all the time analyzing him. "Psychologist and court mediator."

"Damn. Professional and intelligent. I like it." He bit into his lip and kept his eyes on Moe's ass as we moved along the walkway.

I could have been nice and warned him that there was a step, but...what would be the fun in that?

Clay's foot hit the step and he went flying. "Whoa!" he called out but, the graceful fuck that he is, caught himself right away. He didn't even hit the ground or drop the box.

Moe, hearing someone scream, came running. She caught up to him and held him by the biceps. She grabbed the box he had and set it down at her feet. "Are you okay? Everything all right? Did you get hurt?"

He smiled and rubbed at his chest. "Just my pride, beautiful."

Smooth. He could not have planned that better. Moe was a natural mothering type. Suited her. And by the looks of the way he was playing it up, it suited Mr. Muscle, too.

Just as I was about to move around them, Atlas caught me at the waist and tugged me sharply, his hard chest hitting my back. I tried not to lean back into his warmth but couldn't help it. Traitorous body.

"That little scene with your friendly yogi is going to cost you," he warned, whispering in my ear and then biting down lightly on the bit of cartilage.

I scoffed. "In what?"

"I'll think of something diabolical and pleasurable." He kissed me behind my ear, and my body lit up like a stick of dynamite.

"Which has a higher weight? Diabolical or pleasurable?" I grinned, liking this naughty game. Maybe seeing a guy a second time did have some advantages.

Atlas ran his lips down the side of my neck and bit down on the sensitive spot where shoulder and neck met. "I haven't yet decided."

Definite advantages. I bit back a moan. "Kinky," I said, urging him to play more.

"Oh, you have no idea how kinky I can be, wildcat."

ATLAS

"Looking forward to it. Now, can we finish?" She bumped her booty backward, rubbing right into my crotch. A tingle started at my balls, and my dick stirred with renewed hunger for the sexy wildcat.

"I need to call in some pizzas for the boy brigade." Mila turned and hustled into the house, swaying her delectable hips with each step.

I watched her until I couldn't see her anymore. The view

of her righteous bubble butt was too much to miss, especially as she hopped up each step. I took a deep breath, turned, and went back to the truck.

Clay was standing with another set of large canvases. "Let's do these together, eh?"

"Yeah, man. Just be careful. Her art is her life," I cautioned.

Clay nodded and lifted one end, and we worked our way out of the back of the truck, making sure to keep the canvases high. They were covered in heavy tarp and tied off with rope. I knew these things took weeks to complete sometimes, and I didn't want to risk even a pea-sized dent in her work. It would be the same as someone dropping my guitar. Devastating.

We maneuvered through the really large house. For one story, it was spacious, like all the homes in the area. I could see now why her friend would offer to let her move in. The place seemed rather massive for just her and a kid. Not as big as a mansion or the Richie-rich areas of Berkeley proper, but it had to have cost Monet some serious coin.

Clay and I followed the sound of Mila's voice down a long hallway to the right side of the house. I glanced inside each door along the way to see what was near her room. Looked like an office, a guest bedroom, and a bathroom. Nice. That meant her friend's room had to be on the other side of the house. Like a schmuck, that had me grinning because it proved that Mila would have plenty of space between her and her roomie. Excellent for overnight stays by me. Not that she'd agreed to another round of sex, but I'd wear her down eventually. Two people could not have banged the way we did, with the chemistry we shared, to leave it as a one off. No way. No how.

"Coming through," Clay announced as he backed into the

room that would be Mila's.

"Oh no, guys, those are canvases. They go out in the garage," Moe said, her voice laced with apology.

"No biggie. Just lead the way."

Monet clapped her hands. "Oh goodie! I'm so excited to show you this surprise, Mila!" She opened a set of French doors that led down a small path toward the back side of the garage.

A personal entrance to her bedroom. My day just got even better.

Clay and I followed the two women. Mila's eyes were shining, and she kept running her hand through her hair. Odd.

"Guys, can you hold off right there for a moment?" Monet pouted and held her hands up into a prayer position at her chest. "I really want to show Mila this first. If you wouldn't mind?"

Clay responded before I could. "Of course, beautiful. Whatever you need." He smiled and winked. Dude was packing on the charm.

The two of us waited near a door to the back of the garage. Monet used a key and opened it with a flourish, bringing her arms up and out, saying, "Ta-da! Your new art studio!"

Mila opened her mouth and touched her chest above her heart on entering the space.

"I wanna see." I gestured over to the wall where we could lean the canvases. Once we leaned them gently along the side, we followed the ladies in.

Mila stood in the center of a space that was around twenty feet by twenty feet. Along one wall stood blank canvases in varying shapes and sizes. Another wall boasted myriad paints and brushes. An easel sat in the center of the room next to a workspace that had a sink in the center where Mila could wash her brushes and supplies as needed.

"Oh my God, Moe, what did you do?"

Monet grinned from ear to ear, and damn if that didn't make the already pretty woman a knockout. Her glossy black hair swung from side to side as she showed Mila each new feature. "For your supplies, paints, and on these shelves you can store your current pieces that are drying. And then here"—she went over to an area along the back wall where a single stool sat. Next to that were a lush red velvet chair and a chaise longue that could fit two people sitting easy—"some comfy places for your art subjects to sit, lie, and so forth."

Mila put her hand to her mouth and spoke through her fingers. "It's too much. I can't afford this..." she whispered.

Moe shook her head. "This is a gift, honey. Now I know you don't like people getting you gifts, but you have to know, this is a gift for me to have you here! Knowing that someone is in our home making beautiful art...I want that for my daughter. Lily needs to see beautiful things taking shape in the world."

Clay, who had been standing next to me, stiffened. I cast a glance his way and saw his jaw harden and his eyes go flat of any emotion. No longer were lust and excitement for the lithe Asian showing in his eyes. Then as if he just remembered he had somewhere to be, he just spun around and left, without a word.

What the heck was that? I mean, the guy had been so sweet on Monet not fifteen minutes ago. Now he went straight icy? Strange.

I walked over to the stool, moved it into the center, closer to the easel, and sat down. I crossed my arms over one another, mimicking the pose she'd had me in before. Only then, I'd been hard for her. Literally. Although my mini-me was not far off at the moment.

"Looks pretty sweet, wildcat. What's the problem?"

"Yeah, what's the problem?"

Mila glared at me, and I chuckled.

"The problem is that none of this was here last week. Moe, you did all this for me? Where's all your home supplies? This extended portion used to have all your gardening stuff, mower..." Her words trailed off. "You've changed it all for me?"

Monet went over to her friend and clasped her cheeks. "Mila, I'd do anything for my best friend. I want you here. Lily wants you here. Your home is where your family is. We're your family and you're ours. Got it? We put that stuff in a new shed I had built out back. Now shut up and enjoy your new studio. I can't wait to see what you create here."

Mila's eyes glistened, and a tear fell. I figured that was my cue to head out and give them some privacy.

I patted Monet on the shoulder as I was heading out. "You're a really good friend. Mila, I'll be with the guys. Let us know when the pizza and beer arrives."

I walked out and let them have their moment. Right when I exited, I saw Clay standing by another set of canvases he must have moved himself. Instead of yelling at him for doing it alone, because I did not want to risk any of her art getting damaged, I let it go. They seemed fine, only the big guy didn't. That hard look in his eyes remained.

"What's up, man? You went cold in there. I thought you were into Mila's friend Monet?"

"*Was* being the operative word. No longer." His voice was devoid of any emotion.

"Um, okay. That's jacked. Care to tell me why?"

"Not really. Can we just do this? I've got shit to do and somewhere to be."

That was total bullshit. He'd told me before we came over that he was free all day. "Whatever, Jekyll and Hyde. Lift that side of those pieces and I'll get this side."

Together the five guys did all the heavy lifting, and Monet and Mila got the small stuff and told us where to put things. By the time we were done, the pizza had arrived. Only Clay didn't stay. He bailed with a quick nod and a wave the second the last piece was in place. I wondered what had crawled up his ass but decided I'd deal with his wishy-washiness later. I had a petite Latina to woo and confirm with for our date tomorrow.

CHAPTER THIRTEEN

SOLAR PLEXUS
C H A K R A

When the navel chakra is in healthy alignment, you will be comfortable with your own inherent power and become empowered. You will have a sense of who you are and why you are here. When you connect with your purpose, you gain a deeper understanding of how you as an individual can contribute to the collective in a beneficial way. You will let go of the things—whether it's your job or bank account balance— that you depend on to define who you are.

M I L A

I woke to something soft running down my nose and over my lips. The sensation was repeated, like a feather trailing along my skin. The feeling moved down the side of my right temple to my chin before it moved to the opposite side. A warm pressure leaned against the left side of my body. As the little pressure came back to my lips, I kissed it, which gifted me a girlie giggle.

Instead of opening my eyes, I wrapped my arms around the bundle leaning against me and cuddled the lump, which warranted much louder giggles. Now waking to this sound was something I could easily get used to.

"Auntie Mimi, wake up!" Lily patted my forehead.

I opened my eyes and stared into the loveliest blue eyes I'd ever seen. A dark, deep sapphire shade of blue mixed so beautifully with Lily's features. She had a sprinkling of freckles across her cheeks and nose and the shiniest, thickest black hair I'd ever seen on a three-year-old. Besides the blue eyes, which in itself was an anomaly, since only one out of every hundred Asians born had blue eyes, Lily was the most beautiful child I knew. It didn't matter that she was the only child I knew personally. The eye thing, though, was special. Moe and I had looked that up when Lily turned two and her eyes hadn't changed color. We agreed that it made her even more unique. Sure wish Kyle, Moe's ex, had thought so. Douchenozzle.

"Hi, baby." I lifted my head and snuggled into her sweet neck and blew a few raspberries. She loved when I did that.

Lily squealed and flopped her entire body on top of me. Then she lifted up her head and played with my hair. "I wish I had curlies," she said in that toddler tone, the one that made all human beings melt, while she fingered a few of my curls.

I was convinced that God made all children beautiful and endearing so that you didn't kill them for all the crazy shit they did, like barf all over the floor at random intervals, destroy things, and dirty up clothes with whatever they had on their hands, which might be *actual crap* at any given time. Kids were filthy, uncontrollable, hyper, destructive magnets for disgusting things. Name it, they caught it, touched it, rubbed their little hands all in it. Totally gross. Yet they were the most loving, innocent, honest, beautiful examples of kindness on the planet. Hands down, I'd rather deal with children most days than adults. At least with them, a person knew what they were getting. They never hid who they were, always said what they thought, and lived life joyfully. Adults could learn a lot from children.

"Well, I wish I had this shiny black hair like you and your mommy. It's the most beautiful hair in all the world," I assured her.

She preened, giving me her wonky, one-sided smile. "Mommy is making us pant cakes."

"Pant cakes! Do I have to tell her to stopping cooking up her pants again?" I laughed.

"No, no, pam cakes!"

"You mean pan-cakes. Pa...annnnn cakes. Pancakes." I sounded out and enunciated with emphasis so she'd hear the difference.

She crinkled up her nose as though offended. " 's what I said. Pam-cakes."

I rolled my eyes and then lifted us both up. "All right, baby, you go meet up with your mom and tell her I want two." I lifted up my hand and showed her two fingers. "Two. Can you show me two?"

She held up three fingers; I pushed one down. "Two."

Lily grinned and kept her two fingers spread wide. "Two! 'Kay, Auntie Mimi." She scrambled off in her pink footed pajamas and ran down the hall screaming, "Two, Mommy! Two, Mommy!"

I shook my head and pulled back the covers. Now that I lived with Moe and Lily, I made an effort to wear a tank top and a pair of booty shorts to bed instead of my standard sleeping naked. The last thing I wanted to do was explain to a three-year-old why her auntie didn't wear clothes to bed. Not a conversation I planned on having. Ever.

Still feeling sluggish from all the work we'd done yesterday, I tossed on a robe and shuffled into the kitchen. Moe was looking dashing as usual in a pair of capris and a silk tank. Her long black hair was pulled back into a sleek ponytail.

I hiked my butt up onto one of the bar stools to watch her mosey around the kitchen doing her thing. Lily sat in the play area off the kitchen where she was busy cooking her own play pancakes. Like mother, like daughter.

"Damn, you make me look like a slob," I grumbled into my hand and yawned.

Moe went over to the coffeepot, poured a cup, and filled it with my favorite creamer. Someone was prepared, having my favorite in the fridge even though she didn't drink it herself. She set the cup in front of me.

"Here. Looks like you need it. How late did you stay up unpacking?"

I yawned and sighed. "I think I crashed around one. You know how I hate things unsettled, but most of it is done. Have I thanked you again for pushing me to move in?"

She smirked. "No, I believe you were *bitching*"—she whispered the word so that the little ears in the other room didn't hear—"at me throughout the entire process. Thanks were not part of that."

I pouted. "Sorry." I ran my hand through my hair. "It's hard, Moe. I know I need this change and it's definitely going to help me financially, but you know, since my dad went away and my mom moved on, I've always been on my own."

Moe sipped her coffee and nodded, waiting for me continue. She was good at allowing people to say what they needed to say before injecting her response. Made her a good therapist, I'd imagine.

"It's not hard letting you in; obviously you're the only one that I've ever let in. You and Lil are my life. But I don't want to be a burden." I rubbed at my forehead with the puffy end of my sleeve, comforting myself with the soft fabric.

Moe set down her cup and put a hand on her hip. "That is the last time you will speak of yourself as a burden to me. Ever. I mean it, Mila. It pisses me off. I need you here as much as you need to be here. So is it wrong for me to need that extra security with having someone I love share my home, helping me with Lily, being here to help us through the hell that Kyle put us through? Hmm?"

Her words were like an arrow right through the heart. Perfect kill shot. "I had no idea you really felt that way."

She stiffened her spine and turned around to the skillet where four perfectly round, even-sized disks of fluffy love were browning nicely. My mouth watered as I watched her flip them with an expert twist of her wrist. Then she set the spatula down and leaned against the counter, her head falling forward.

"You being here means a lot to me. You *wanting* to be here means more because Kyle didn't want to be here. He didn't want me. He didn't want Lily. And as her mother, I have to deal with that ache. As his now ex-wife, I have to deal with the mistake that I fell deeply in love with a man who now loves my sister. So yes, having someone who loves us share our home means a lot." She turned around and faced me, her eyes sad and a frown marring her pretty face. "Okay?"

I put down my cup, rushed around the counter, and pulled her into my arms. "Yeah, it's okay. And I am happy to be here. I'm sorry for being a bitch. Thank you for making me see the light."

She nodded into my neck and then pushed back and slid a delicate hand along her hair, making sure everything was still in place. Moe was like that. All class and focused on even the smallest details.

"Pam-cakes are done!" Lily exclaimed, holding two plastic toy plates, one with a fake cookie and another with a funky-looking donut. She delivered them to the counter. "Oh for dot the milkies! Be wite back." The little love turned on a toe and bustled to her corner where she grabbed two empty plastic cups. "Here you go! Eat up. It will get cold."

Being the best auntie in the world, I pretended to munch on my plastic food, making the appropriate noises of "mmms" and "yums" to make my girl pink up in the cheeks and smile with utter glee. Yep. Moving in with these two was a good decision. I could already feel the creative juices flowing. I watched Moe plate our real breakfasts.

"Hey, Moe, would you ever let me paint the two of you? Clothed," I added.

"Of course," she agreed without even a lull in her steps to get the silverware out.

"Really?" Usually people wanted to think about it when it came to displaying a version of their likeness. Art was in the eye of the beholder and more so for the artist depicting it.

Moe crinkled her nose the exact same way her daughter had done this morning. That tiny gesture alone made me thrilled that Kyle the douchebag was not Lily's bio-dad. Stupid pig would have passed down his devil horns or a tail or something, not the cute nose crinkle that I adored on both my girls.

"Yes, really. I'd love to see something you created of me and my daughter. I'm certain it would be the most beautiful thing ever. You'd have to let me hang it on the wall, though. I'd want to display something like that because, you know, when you're a world-renowned artist, I'll have an original Mila Mercado to boast. It will be a great story for Lily when she's older, too."

God, I loved my best friend. Some people said that best friends were only another version of ourselves we wished we were. We attracted individuals who were so much like ourselves, but the subtle differences and interests were what kept us intrigued. The things that were the same that solidified the relationships for life. Perhaps that was the trick to finding a soul mate. Maybe a soul mate was a different version of one's self, the best reflection of one, only with more to love. That could be why everyone always said "their better half" when introducing their mate.

"Cool." I shoveled a huge bite of pancake and syrup into my mouth so that I didn't choke on the overwhelming wave of emotion I was feeling toward my friend.

Moe ensured Lily was set gobbling away at her real breakfast before she sat down to eat. The cook was always the last to eat, and that sucked. In that moment, I made a promise to myself that, when I saw Moe slaving over a hot stove, I'd make sure she served herself first. Then I'd help Lily and, after that, myself.

"So today's the date, eh?" she asked and smirked.

"Yes, he's picking me up at lunch time. Any idea where he's taking me?"

Moe nodded happily. "Totally, but I'm not ruining the surprise. I will say, though, that I like Atlas. He's sweet. And for him to get all those guys to help you just to make sure he could take you out, that's pretty special, don't you think?"

I scoffed. "I think he's doing that to make sure he has some 'horizontal special time' with me, if you know what I mean."

She frowned and set down her fork. "Do you really believe he did all that yesterday just to get into your pants again?"

I took a big gulp of my coffee and looked around. "Uh, yeah. You don't?"

She harrumphed and then pushed her pancake around her plate. "No. I don't. He seems really into you, Mila. I hope you will take his overtures as they are. A male who is obviously smitten with a woman and attempting to please her."

I grinned. "Oh, he pleases me in multiple ways!" I winked.

She groaned. "You're impossible."

"What?"

"You don't even see what's right in front of you." She stabbed a piece of fruit and pancake and then shoved it into her mouth.

"Why are you so pissy about this guy? It's not that big of a deal. We're just having fun."

She wiped her mouth with a napkin. I swear, everything she did had a delicate nature to it. Even the way she sat properly, feet tucked under the stool, hands in her lap when she wasn't actually eating.

"I just want you to give him a chance. A real chance at something more...long-lasting."

Moe, forever in love with love. "Hon, I'm not sure

anything is long-lasting, most definitely not love. You witness that every day in your job counseling failing marriages and mediating custody battles."

"And yet, I'd kill to have it for myself."

I rubbed her back. "I know. I know." Fucking Kyle the bastard did such a number on her. Now she believed that everyone else could have true love but her. She genuinely believed that Kyle was it for her, and somehow, she ruined it.

"Just promise me you'll give this guy a real chance. I mean it. A real one."

I looked into my best friend's coal-black eyes and melted into a puddle of goo. "Okay, I promise. I promise. Can we eat our breakfast now without being all deep and shit?"

"Shit. Shit. Shit," Lily repeated several times.

Moe squinted. "Auntie Mimi! That was not a nice word." She waved her finger at me.

"Yikes! I'm sorry. I won't say it again. I promise!"

Moe pouted prettily. "Just remember your other promise and we'll call it even."

ATLAS

I was losing my shit. My palms were so sweaty I kept having to run them down the sides of my jeans. I curled a hand around the handle of the picnic basket I'd packed making sure it was secure behind the seat. I'd made a specific run to the grocery store and picked up the contents of what I'd hoped would be a very special lunch. Fresh strawberries, grapes, small circles of cheese. I didn't even know they made that shit, but I cornered a woman working the deli counter. She was all too willing to help me pack what she guaranteed would be a romantic lunch.

I even had a couple small, half-sized bottles of champagne she called a split. The only thing I'd ever split when it came to booze was the bill, with a friend at the pub. And I'd definitely never packed a picnic nor bought champagne for a girl.

That damn woman had better appreciate the effort. The miniscule-sized sandwiches I packed were a total joke. I mean, who ate that shit and didn't leave hungry? Then again, I'd bought enough of the tiny things and tossed in a bag of chips just in case. I mean, a man had to eat, and that genuinely meant meat and something filling like a hunk of bread not a wafer cracker. Be that as it may, the girl who was helping me also encouraged a small bouquet of flowers, so I'd gotten the cheapest I could find. It's not that I was cheap by nature, I just didn't have a lot to blow on wooing a woman. Now if I scored a record deal, then I'd definitely have no problem dropping hundreds on a beautiful, enchanting woman like Mila. Hopefully, that type of life would be in my near future, but now, I had to make do with what I had.

I thought about Mila and her tiny studio and how moving into her friend's place had already changed her style of living. Definite upgrade. Made me wonder if the woman would change. She didn't seem the type to care about material things. More than anything, she cared about art and yoga. Also her friends. Like Nick Salerno. A ribbon of irritation swirled around my mind and set up shop through a kink in my neck.

What the hell was that with the dude yesterday anyway? I mean, she flew into his arms like she hadn't seen the guy in a year, and it had only been weeks.

Relax, Atlas. You're just jealous.

And damn it all to hell, I was jealous. Jealous of a man who claimed he cared for Mila as a sister. But it was her reaction to him that took the cake. When I'd arrived yesterday, I had to snuggle her, kiss her, and even then, she barely returned the gesture. Muscle car Nick rolls up, and she ran into his arms like one of those sappy movies where the couples are running toward one another on a beach, just like long lost lovers. Did she secretly have a hang-up on the guy, or was it platonic? He did only kiss her forehead, but maybe he wasn't that into her, and she was into him and just taking any scraps she could get?

Argh! No way. There was no way on God's green earth a man could look at Mila Mercado and not want to put his hands all over her sexy body or kiss those plump lips and squeeze that smokin' hot ass. I'd have to ask her more about him. Just the thought that she had that type of affection for another man grated on my last nerve. And therein lay the biggest problem. This woman was getting under my skin. She'd scraped her claws down my skin and burrowed in, and no amount of attempting to convince myself that she was just a hot babe worked. Mila was more. More than a girl I'd bang and bolt on. However, I wasn't so sure she felt the same. Her natural inclination had been to back off, whereas I'd been pushing forward. At least she'd agreed to the date. After today, and hopefully tonight, there would be no question as to where I saw us going.

I rolled up to her house in my old ass Jeep Cherokee, not sex on wheels like Nick's car. Back in 2002, my Jeep would have been a slammin' car. I'd scored it off a guy selling it on Craigslist a few years ago. The dude was moving and offering it at a great deal. Now almost fifteen years old, the thing had seen better days, but even with over a hundred and fifty thousand miles, it still ran well, and I was able to put down the back seats and store my musical equipment safely. It worked and got me from point A to B. I couldn't complain. Only now that I was picking up Mila in it did I question whether it was good enough.

Before I could even get out of my car, Mila was pulling open the passenger side door.

"Hey, nice Jeep," she commented, hopping in.

"You know, I would have come to the door and picked you up properly for our date." I handed her the bouquet of wildflowers.

Mila sniffed the flowers, closed her eyes, and sighed, gifting me a sweet girlie smile before she leaned behind me and set the flowers neatly in the back seat. "Is that what this is? A proper date?" She grinned, her caramel-colored eyes reflecting the sun's light back at me.

I shrugged. "Yeah. It is."

She smacked her denim-clad legs and rubbed her hands down them. "Well, I guess there's a first time for everything."

I flicked on the blinker and moved out down the street. "This is your first date?"

She shrugged. "Yeah, I guess. I mean unless you count the guys I dated in high school."

"Huh. How old are you?"

She snickered. "Didn't your mama teach you to never ask a woman's age?" She grinned. "Twenty-six. You?"

"Twenty-eight. At least I've taken women out. Not in the past few years, since I've been so focused on my music, but damn. I think maybe you are more of a workaholic than I am."

She quirked her head to the side. "Is it weird that I don't take offense to that?"

I laughed and grabbed her hand, interlacing our fingers so that our palms were flat against one another's. The zap of energy jolted through our hands and up my arm. I glanced at her. She, too, was staring down at our hands. I moved them so that her hand was resting on my thigh. For some reason, I just needed to feel her in every way that I could. It was as though I needed to solidify that this was real.

"So, where are you taking me?" Her voice was low and raspy and sent another thrill through me, which got the attention of my dick instantly.

I adjusted my lower half, trying to not jostle her hand more than necessary for fear she'd spook. My girl was a bit twitchy when it came to physical displays of affection. Unless of course I'd had my cock, mouth, or fingers buried inside her. Then she was all for it.

"Can't stand not knowing? Just relax. I got this. You, hotness, are not in control." I lifted our hands and laid a few kisses on the top of her palm.

While I was tending to her hand, she'd unbuckled her seatbelt, scooched as close to my side as she could get with the console in the center, and put her other hand over my cock and squeezed.

I groaned in pleasure. "Fuck."

She nuzzled against my neck, her hand rubbing my cock over and over making me hard as stone. My jeans became far too tight and my heart raced. I held the steering wheel with a viselike grip, taking turns breathing and focusing on the road and my cock in her hot little hand.

"Jesus. You're going to cut off the circulation in my dick," I growled in a loving way.

She chuckled. "Oh, poor baby. Let me fix that," she cooed, unbuttoning and unzipping my pants before pulling out my hardened shaft in record time. "All better?"

"Fuck yes!" I grated through my teeth the second my erection hit cool air. Relief the size of my car rushed over my groin when she wrapped her hand around my length and gave it a little tug. I jerked my hips but kept my hands firmly on the wheel, knuckles whitening with the effort.

Chills of pleasure started at my dick and roared up my spine. Mila jacked me with the perfect amount of grip and fluidity. She used her thumb to smear the pre-cum leaking from the top all over the shaft, lubricating her movements. Her thumb shifted down from the crown where she tickled the underside all while kissing, licking my neck and jaw, basically, driving me out of my mind with lust. I tried to focus as much of my attention on the car moving forward, making the right turns, following the speed limit all the while being jacked by a fucking goddess.

"Where are we going, curly?" She stroked my length and then cupped my balls exactly the way I liked best—firm and with intent.

I grunted. "Not telling," came out as a growl as I tried to kiss her, keep my eyes on the road, and not move my dick even a centimeter from her talented hand. I sucked in a huge lungful of air and ground my teeth to stave off the impending orgasm that wanted to fight its way up my cock and pour out the tip like fucking Niagara Falls. Goddamned wildcat.

She hummed in my ear. "Do you want to come?"

I moaned and lost all ability to play her game, so focused on my own pleasure rather than keeping the control. "You know I do." My voice came out ragged and strained. Every tug made it harder to speak at all.

Mila bit down on the sensitive space on my shoulder at the same time she dragged her hand up my cock, gripping hard.

"Mmm. Do you want me to jack you and then lean forward and suck you down my throat until you spill inside of me?"

My hips jerked on autopilot as I fucked her hand, thrusting up, her sexy words spurring me into a furious need to come, imagining her lips wrapped around my cock...shit. The crown was so sensitive I swore if she touched it again, I'd lose it all in one go.

I slid my right hand up behind her and into her hair, where I laced my fingers through her locks so I could grip the roots with enough pressure to cause pain if I wanted to, but mostly to ensure the wildcat wouldn't back off at the last possible second. I wouldn't survive it if she did.

I shouldn't have worried. Mila jacked me like an expert. "Tell me where we're going, and I'll make you come so hard down my throat you'll be struggling not to pass out," she promised and slid that hand up and down in four quick strokes.

My body started to quake from the strain of holding out. "Do it!" I tried to push her head down toward my cock. I'd never been so hard, my penis so ready to blow in all my life. I felt as though my cock would explode if she didn't put the wet, hot cavern of her mouth on me right then.

She whispered in my ear, "Tell me where we're going?" She let go of my cock. Fucking let go. My cock and balls throbbed in painful need, and I could have shed a fucking tear at the loss of her grip.

"God damn it!" I slammed my left hand on the wheel, and the car swerved a bit. Up ahead there was a soft shoulder. The cars would still fly by, but at the moment, I did not fucking care. All I could think about was coming. Pushing my hard dick up into her mouth while she sucked me dry.

"Tell me and I'll give you what you want," she cooed and

nibbled on my jaw, wrapping her hand back around my dick. Oh sweet heaven, relief. The top of my dick was weeping a copious amount of pre-cum, which she again used to lubricate her strokes.

I pulled over onto the shoulder, put the car in park, and fucked into her hand. Ripples of excitement roared through me, my synapses firing and ready to ignite at any time. "To the museum for a picnic."

As if by magic, her head swooped down and her mouth engulfed my cock right in time. Four pitiful strokes and I was coming, my hand holding her head, forcing her to take more, my hips jerking up as she gagged but didn't stop. A pleasure so strong soared through my body, and I squeezed my eyes shut tight. Air pushed out my lungs as I worked my hips, jackknifing up to get more, go deeper into her wet heat.

"Fuck, Mila, so good, baby. Yeah, take it all. All of it. Fuck yes," I growled, pumping every last drop into her mouth.

Once I had nothing left to give, she gave my dick one last lingering suck, which tickled as much as it tingled, and let it flop back onto my open pants. She licked her lips and then wiped them with the back of her hand. Every breath left my lungs in heavy pants as I attempted to come back to earth.

She grinned a devil-made-me-do-it, sexy-as-hell smile. I could look at the smile for the rest of my life and know it would be like winning the lottery being able to be the one to see it every day.

"Now that wasn't so hard. Well, it was, but not anymore." She puffed out her bottom lip, pressed off me, and buckled back up. "I'm excited about the museum. Let's go," she said as I tucked in my junk and shook my head.

"There is no woman like you on earth. I'm not sure if I'm

lucky or cursed."

She grinned and grabbed my hand. Actually initiated something intimate and affectionate, and not because of the sexual tension or a need to fuck. "Probably a little bit of both. You better watch out."

I chuckled. "Well, if getting jacked and then blown in my car while driving down the highway is what I have to look forward to in my future...marry me."

Her face took on a look of horror. "You're a dumbass!" She socked me in the shoulder.

"Ouch! That actually hurt." I rubbed at the new tender spot. Girl could pack a punch.

"You'd do well to remember that." She bit down on her lip.

"Oh, baby, I'll never forget today. It's already one of the most memorable experiences of my life. Now I need to make it one of yours."

CHAPTER FOURTEEN

Extended Puppy Pose (Sanskrit: Uttana shishosana)
An excellent pose for stretching the spine and releasing
tension in the lower back. A basic level pose, ideal for most
body types, provided you are not dealing with any injuries.
Spread the knees hip distance apart, stretch the arms out on
the mat, push your hips back and up. Rest your forehead on
the mat. Make sure big toes are touching so that your body's
energy can circulate through you.

MILA

Atlas forced me to stay in the car when we arrived at the museum. He was dead set on making this an official date. Not that it mattered.

He ran around the car and opened my door, holding out his hand to help me exit.

"You know, I'm a sure thing," I offered, wanting him to understand he didn't have to put all this effort into getting me into the sack.

He frowned and let go of my hand. "Is that what you think this is? Me wanting to get laid?"

I pushed both of my hands into my back pockets and assessed him. He wore a dark pair of jeans, a cool as hell concert T-shirt, and a fitted leather jacket. He had several leather and silver chain necklaces on, including the ever-present key dangling at his sternum. I still didn't know much about it, other than the fact that he didn't take it off, and it had sentimental value because of his dad. A pair of leather boots adorned his feet, and he completed the look with his I-don't-give-a-flip curly mop of hair that actually was dead sexy, even though I loved giving him crap about it.

Atlas looked at me as if I'd just stepped on his guitar case. His eyes were harsh and his eyebrows a defined slash across his brow, adding to the intensity of his frown.

"Hey, I just wanted you to know you didn't have to work so hard. I'm not the type of girl you need to impress." I shrugged.

He squinted. "Maybe I want to impress you." He stepped closer and wrapped an arm around my waist, bringing me flush against his chest. "Maybe it's time a man put some effort into you." He rubbed his nose against mine. "Maybe I want to be that man." That's when he softly pecked my lips. Over and over, he brushed my lips with his, never taking it deeper, just a simple caress of lip on lip. I'd not been kissed so softly before. Every time I tried to take it further, he backed off.

"Are you teasing me?" I whispered against his lips.

"Maybe."

"Is that all you can say? Maybe?"

"Maybe." He chuckled, pulled back, and let me go. He went to the back seat and pulled out a full-on picnic basket.

I was certain my eyes were about to pop out of my head. "You were not kidding. You really did make a picnic lunch."

He smiled before looping his arm around my shoulder. "Yep. Now come on, hotness, let's check out some art. Time for you to teach the musician what you know about fancy paintings."

I grinned and paired our steps as we walked toward the de Young Legion of Honor Fine Arts Museum. "I've always loved this museum," I said, appreciating the odd V-shaped structure of the front of the building.

"Why?"

"The building itself is art. Where better to showcase beautiful work than in an architecturally artistic building?" I pointed at the dramatic copper face that had a punched, bumpy look. "See, it's designed to show light streaming through the trees. Over time, the copper will oxidize the same way the Statue of Liberty has and change color to a natural green that will coexists well with the surroundings. Is that why you chose it for our date?" I poked him between the ribs.

He jerked back, laughing. Oh. Someone was ticklish. I stored that bit of information to use against him when the time was just right.

Atlas focused on the building. "It is cool, but no. I researched the websites, and this one had a bunch of nudes on display. Figured with what you were working on, your muse might get inspired."

I stopped in place. My heart pounded erratically, and my fingers started to tingle. "Atlas, that is so sweet." And just as the side of his mouth quirked up into a smile, I laid a fat kiss on him. A ninja-kiss. A deep, full tongue, wet kiss, where I gripped his hair, delved my tongue in until my thirst for this man was quelled. At least for the time being. Once I couldn't breathe, I ripped my mouth away.

"Holy shit. We're going to the museum every weekend." He gasped and wiped his mouth with the back of his hand.

"Hey, you do sweet things, you get ninja-kisses."

He chuckled. "It was like...like a ninja attack. I'll have to keep my eye on you."

I grinned and grabbed his hand, appreciating the weight of him holding mine. An entirely new sensation, but not an unwelcome one. With Atlas, for reasons unbeknownst to me, it just felt right, like the thing to do. Plus, the way he swung our hands back and forth like Lily did with Moe made me happy. Making him happy was making me happy. Such a novel concept. I couldn't describe it, nor did I want to. I decided, for the day, I'd throw caution to the wind and just let myself feel.

Turned out today was a special free day at the museum, so the ticket agent just waved us through. I'd been to this museum countless times and knew right where to go. I led the way, pointing out pieces of art that were of particular interest to me. Atlas observed quietly, seeming to take in everything I said. He asked thoughtful questions about contemporary art and the different eras that were displayed. He seemed to enjoy the sculptures more than the paintings, which had me feeling a little bummed.

"Is there somewhere outside we can eat? The website boasted thousands of feet of a garden landscape." The second the question was out of his mouth, his stomach grumbled.

I laughed out loud, looped my thumb into his belt loop leading him to the perfect place. Since I noticed he'd taken a liking to the sculptures, the de Young had an amazing sculpture garden where people were always setting up a picnic lunch. "Yeah, come on. Wouldn't want you wasting away. Besides, I'm dying to see what you packed."

He grinned. "Any guesses?"

Knowing he was a bachelor who lived with another bachelor, I went with the obvious. "Peanut butter and jelly?"

He shook his head. "Nope. Try again."

I led him through the beautiful gardens to a space where giant apples were scattered around. "Uh, apples?" He laughed as I let his hand go and ran over to a big apple that was as high as my hip. "Voilà!"

"Nice Vanna, but no." He scanned the place and found a beautiful shady tree. He set down the basket and pulled out a big beach towel he'd rolled and tied to the side of the basket. He laid it out and then gestured for me to sit.

Once we were settled, he opened the basket and handed me two plastic champagne flutes. Then he plucked out strawberries and set them between us. He took two and put one in each glass. "Wow. You're really doing this up."

He didn't say anything, just continued lining up his items. With a patience I didn't know he had, he meticulously laid out a couple different fruits, cheeses, crackers, little gherkin pickles, olives, and some triangle-shaped sandwiches.

"And for the *pièce de résistance*..." he said, butchering a French accent, "we have a sparkling wine for the lady." He popped the cork effortlessly and filled our glasses.

I smiled. "We're probably not supposed to have alcohol here," I warned.

"Wildcat, I've learned in life that it can be easier to ask for forgiveness than permission. Cheers." He tapped my glass.

"To us and whatever the hell we've gotten ourselves into."

"Atlas, you often say the exact right thing." I clinked his glass, and we both took a sip. The dry champagne hit my tongue with a sharpness and crisp sensation I rather appreciated in my champagne.

"Let's hope you remember this moment then when I've screwed something up in the future. It will be like my 'get out of jail free' card."

I snickered and popped a grape into my mouth. He took out the plastic cutlery and served me three sandwiches, a handful of grapes, two Babybel cheese circles, a couple pickles, and six crackers.

"I have more food, so eat up," he said while layering up his own plate.

"Are you trying to fatten me up? My goodness. The way you eat blows my mind." One by one, I put half of the stuff he piled onto my plate back into its container. I may have a voracious appetite on a good day but this was way overboard.

"You blow my mind, Mila," he blurted and then sucked back all of his champagne in one gulp. It was as if he surprised himself with his own outburst.

I lifted my hand and brushed his hair out of his eyes. Then I leaned forward and kissed him. Just one, simple kiss. "Thank you for this. It's really amazing and so thoughtful." We stared into one another's eyes, and while we did, something flickered in his. A deepness he'd not shown me before, as if I was seeing the real Atlas for the first time. I now saw the broken boy who'd been abandoned by his dad, the aspiring musician who wanted nothing more than to make music, and the man who was trying desperately to impress a woman.

He cupped both my cheeks in his warm hands. I couldn't

help but nuzzle into them.

"You scare me, Mila."

"How so?" I whispered, holding myself up by leaning on his thighs, keeping our close proximity. Our faces were only an inch or two away from one another in this position. I felt like I could hold the pose all night if it meant I could be this close to his essence.

"I think about you all the time," he admitted breathlessly.

"Me too." I swallowed the lump forming in my throat.

"I want to be where you are. Be near you constantly." He whispered the words as if they were a secret he was confiding.

"Yeah." I closed my eyes.

"Look at me," he urged, a desperate tone to his voice.

I wanted to keep my eyes closed, because I knew with my entire being that something important was happening. Something I might not understand and possibly wasn't ready for.

"Mila, baby..." he begged, kissing my lips, "stay with me."

I opened my eyes. "I'm with you."

"Be with me. Be mine." His voice cracked. "Let this thing we have going be... I don't... Can we just let it be us?"

I smiled against his lips and nodded. As much as I was afraid of making this type of leap, everything he said was a mirror of what I was thinking, feeling, and desiring. He'd just been able to voice it.

"Okay. So we're an us? Whatever that is. You and me?" he reiterated, almost as though he needed to hear it, too.

"You and me, curly."

He grinned. "Damn, wildcat. See, now you've got me all hot and bothered and wanting to fuck you, when I really need to take you to see the nudes."

I kissed his lips. "I've seen the nudes many, many times. I'd rather see you nude many, many times."

He snort-laughed and nibbled on my lips. "You are wicked."

"No, just committed." I looped my arm around his neck and pressed my forehead to his.

"Committed to me. Right? To being an us." Even though I'd agreed, he'd needed to hear my words.

"Yeah, curly. Now let's finish this picnic so I can show you some art, then we can go to your pad and fuck like rabbits." I pulled back and slammed my entire glass of champagne. "More please." I held out the glass.

He shook his head. "You're something else."

"Tell me something I don't already know." I grinned and bit into my champagne-infused strawberry. The flavor exploded across my tongue, tart and sweet in one go. Kind of like us. Only I was the tart, he was quite obviously the sweet.

ATLAS

"God, yes. Fuck me! Harder!" she screamed out, her head falling forward toward my bed. I was behind her small body, slamming my cock into her pussy from behind. Her curvy ass felt like heaven against my groin and pelvis.

"I love your ass, wildcat. So fucking juicy." I squeezed both cheeks while stirring my cock. I spread those cheeks so that I could watch her little pucker wink with every thrust into her wet center. My dick pulsated as her pussy clenched around it. Excitement and lust filled the air with its heady scent as I plunged in and out of her.

Mila moaned as I palmed her ass. One of her hands

curled around the front of my low headboard while the other flattened against the wall. She was up on her knees spread wide for me, just the way I wanted. Her hair was a wild mane of messy curls. I leaned over her and thrust deep while gripping the roots of her hair and pulling her head back enough so that I could lay my mouth on hers. So dirty, so sexy, so every-fucking-wet-dream.

Her tongue tangled with mine as I fucked her, using the grip on her hair and her ass to grind my cock deep. Ribbons of lust coiled around the base of my cock making me twitch and moan in bliss.

Mila lost her breath, panting. "I'm going to come. Fuck." Her pussy locked down tight around my cock. A searing pleasure-pain weaved from my cock around my back to settle at the base of my spine.

I gritted my teeth, leaned over her farther, so I could pluck at her clit. It was wet, coated with my saliva and her juicy cunt. "Yeah, you are, wildcat. I'm going to fuck you so many times you can't remember how many times you came. Now let me hear my kitty scream!" I growled, sinking my teeth into her shoulder, tasting salt and sweet while rubbing her hot button in furious circles.

She screamed. Loud and deep like a full-body groan. I fucked her through it, waiting for the spasms to subside, my own gripping every sensation with the claws of ecstasy. I lifted back up and ran my hands up and down her silky spine. My cock throbbed hard, my balls pulled up tight to my taint, but I wanted to commemorate today somehow and fucking the daylights out of her sounded like a good plan. She definitely hadn't complained, the greedy girl and her tasty body always up for more pleasure.

Christ, and I was the lucky bastard who got to give it to her over and over. The thought rammed home with a hit of emotion I had to swallow down and manage later. Instead, I put all the warring emotions I couldn't deal with now into my lovemaking.

"Get up on your hands and knees. Gonna fuck you harder, baby," I demanded, knowing how she loved the dirty talk.

She moaned, wiggling her ass in small circles that drove me wild. I lifted my hand back and brought it down on her ass with a hard whack.

"Oh! Shit!" She popped up onto her hands.

"Listen next time and maybe you won't get punished," I goaded and smiled at her reaction.

"It's not my fault that you..." she started with her back talking.

Not happening. I lifted my other hand and brought it down on her left cheek. The flesh bounced, and both sides had matching pink handprints. Seeing that pink skin, I knew was hot and throbbing because of my hand made me harder than iron.

"Fuck!" we both exclaimed at the same time for different reasons.

"Curly!" she yelled at the same time I brought down my hand on the sensitive curve where her curvy ass met her thigh. "Oh!" she screamed and then moaned.

I grinned checking out my handiwork and loving it. "You gonna keep being a bad girl with a greedy pussy?"

She hummed in pleasure as I smacked the other side in the same spot. That time her body jerked, but she didn't call out. She just mewled and swirled her delectable ass in the air.

I palmed both ass cheeks again, thrusting my cock deep

as I spread her cheeks wide. Her asshole spread apart and my mouth watered. I licked one of my thumbs and rubbed a circle around that small rosette. Every touch felt like I was touching myself, I was so damned connected to this woman.

"Atlas...I've never..." She moaned and then stiffened when I pressed my thumb into her forbidden hole. "Oh God, I don't know..."

Her ass was tighter than I'd imagined. My mind splintered at the thought of taking her there. That possessive streak I tried to tamp down roared, making me want to pound my chest and take every inch of her, but I knew she wasn't ready for that step just yet. Instead, I settled for leaning forward and placing small kisses around her neck, nibbling her ear, and stirring my hips so she'd remember I was balls deep in her pussy, as much as my thumb was encroaching on her tight ass.

"Relax. Baby, I'm going to make you feel so good. And I will have *every inch* of this body one day. Your pretty asshole is part of that." I pushed my entire thumb in and started moving it in and out. As that tight ring of muscle loosened up, she picked up my pace and moved with me. "That's it, Mila, nice and easy. Fuck yourself on my hand."

"Atlas..." she sighed, moving her hips.

I reached my left hand around and tugged and twisted her erect nipple. Her mewls and sighs encouraged me, made me feel strong and desired. When her body got into the movement, I lifted back up and watched while I powered into her pussy with my cock and finessed her little hole with my thumb.

Sweat misted on both of us as I got lost in her body, in the sensation of mating with the most beautiful woman alive. Sex had been good before, but never like this. An overall pleasure that rippled through every limb. My cock pulsed and throbbed as I plowed into my woman. I couldn't get close enough, fuck her hard enough. Everything felt so good, so right, so complete.

"Baby, I'm gonna come. Want to coat your insides." Just the thought of blowing my load into her pussy made my head spin and my world tilt on its axis. I held on to her hip, keeping my balance waiting for her answer, hoping and praying I could go off inside her bareback.

"Go ahead. On...the...pill." Oh, fuck yes! Her body started to tremble.

"You trust me, wildcat?" Her trust was more important than my pleasure, but I wanted her to be absolutely sure before I did what I'd never done before.

Her head fell forward. "Yes, just fuck me!"

I pulled out, quickly slid the condom off, and slammed back into her. Bare. There weren't words to describe this intense feeling of complete nirvana. Taking Mila without anything between was beyond sacred. It was angelic. It was fucking divinity incarnate wrapped around my cock. I'd never had better.

"God!" she roared.

"Fucking tight! Fuckin' A!" I held my thumb deep, gripped her hip, and went to town fucking my woman bare. Her tight sheath locked down on me, her back arched, and she went into a full-body quiver. I fucked her through every shudder, every shake, until I couldn't anymore. I pulled out and twisted her body around where she flopped into place, her legs automatically going wide in invitation.

"Curly?" she gasped.

"Want to see your face when I come in you. Kiss your mouth," I said like a heathen and plunged into her perfect heat in one go. There was no finesse, just straight rutting. Again her sex sheathed my cock like dipping your toe into a hot tub that first time. Splendid right to the core.

Her legs came up and wrapped around my body, her heels digging into my ass. I cringed with the burning prick of that tender flesh. Then she offered up her throat, and I licked and sucked her taste until my balls were ready to erupt.

"Shit, gonna come again," she moaned.

"Greedy fucking pussy!" I growled and took her mouth. She bit down on my lips, and a searing fire hit my muscles as I convulsed and exploded inside of her. Long spurts poured into her while I kept thrusting. Mila encased me in a full-body hold as I let go, her pussy squeezing every last drop until nothing remained but a throbbing, sated man.

I wrapped the clean hand around her chin and held her face while I kissed her. It was my best kiss yet. Messy, sopping wet, no finesse whatsoever as I took her mouth. I needed that connection with her in every way. With my filthy hand, I held the back of her head, forcing her to take my kiss. She took it all willingly and gave even more. Wet, drugging plunges of her tongue as if she also wanted to devour me.

Once my breathing resembled something more even, I softened my kisses. I tasted her slowly, sipping from her lips, licking across the swollen bits of flesh, wanting to soothe and mend my harshness. "Mila..." My voice broke.

I expected her to pull away from the emotion that scored through my body. I felt like weeping, crying all over her, and I'd never felt that way in my life. Not with any woman, not even when my dad walked out on me and my mom. But this woman, this feisty wildcat had my number. She brought out a side in me I myself didn't recognize.

"I know, me, too." Her voice was rough, and I couldn't tell if it was the fucking or if she was feeling something hard to define.

I held her face and forced her eyes to meet mine, my heart pounding out a steady anxious beat. Her eyes were glassy, sated, and...more. So much more. "Curly." She ran her hand through my hair, scoring her nails along my scalp the way I loved.

My entire body responded with a shiver. "You're making me fall..." I spoke so low I could barely hear it.

"Don't fall..." Her eyes got more wet, and a single tear slipped down the side. I captured it with my lips, tasting her salty tears.

"What if I can't help it?"

She croaked, "Try?" Her words held a note of panic, of concern I knew I'd heard but wanted so badly to change.

"Maybe I want to fall," I admitted, playing my cards wildly, emotionally, and all for this woman who had shocked me to no end with what I could feel for her.

She shook her head and ran her nails down my scalp again. "I don't know how to be what you need."

I knew my girl was scared. Hell, I was cross-eyed with fright, but no one fucked the way we did and it meant nothing.

This time I ran my hand through her hair. "Have you ever been in love?" I asked.

Her eyes went sad. "No. Not that I know of."

I smiled. So Mila.

"Have you?" Her voice was a whisper.

"No, but I'm starting to think I now know what it should feel like." Because I was falling ass over dick for a mocha-colored wildcat with a mean streak a mile long, a feistiness I wanted nothing more than to tame for myself, and a pussy that tasted like the sweetest nectar.

"You think?" She swallowed and frowned.

I kissed her frown away until she smiled softly.

"It's a definite possibility." I'd give her that at the very least after all we'd experienced.

She hummed and continued to play with my hair. Chills made the hair on my arms stand up. Her touch lit me up.

"Since we both don't really know what that specific feeling is, how's about we make up something of our own?" I offered in compromise.

That statement garnered me a wide smile and a leg clench. "I like that."

I thought about it for a second, taking in her caramel eyes, her high cheekbones, her fantastic body, the way she made me feel...dazzled.

"I've got it." I leaned forward and kissed her full, wet, and so deep her pussy clenched down on my dick, making it perk back up. I shifted my hips and started to move around in her heat. She was much wetter with the combination of my release coating her. That alone made my dick go from limp to rock hard.

Her eyes widened at the feeling of my hard shaft filling her again.

"Mila Mercado...wildcat, you dazzle me."

She chuckled, lifted her head, and kissed me so sweetly my heart figuratively stopped. "Atlas Powers...curly, you dazzle me, too."

Then we dazzled each other, repeatedly, all night long.

CHAPTER FIFTEEN

SOLAR PLEXUS CHAKRA

As you work on managing this chakra, try to gain insight into your understanding of power, individuality, and how you identify yourself. Maybe there are areas of your life where you feel powerless? Why? What brought those feelings on? In some individuals, a misaligned third chakra can make thoughtful self-expression challenging. Negatively, it can manifest as aggressive, overly rigid, or controlling behavior, or on the flip side, it could breed a victim mentality, neediness, and lack of direction or self-esteem to stand up and take positive action. Aligning this chakra will help obliterate those feelings of lack of self-worth.

MILA

For the next few weeks, Atlas and I became an us. We didn't define it, definitely didn't discuss it, somehow, we just worked. On the nights we spent together, we fucked like animals and cuddled like lovers. I painted a new canvas of him each week in various poses, detailing his godlike naked body. While I worked, it seemed as though we laughed more, spoke more deeply of our desires, figured out that both of us were up to our eyeballs in making our dreams happen.

At some point in the last month, Atlas had a very brief meeting with Knight & Day Productions. Apparently, they asked him to write two or three new songs to add to the originals he'd already written. If they liked what he brought to the table, further discussions would be held. So while I painted him naked, he toiled away at his songs. It worked famously. He had another couple weeks to write, and I had a willing, gorgeous subject. Win-win.

"What about this?" Atlas's head was hanging down, shoulders curved forward while he strummed out a clever acoustic tune.

He had his guitar resting across his naked thighs, and his hair was a wild mane since only minutes ago, I'd been riding his cock and tugging it incessantly. He didn't mind. He loved when I pulled and tugged his hair, but more when I scraped my nails down his scalp. I swear it was a direct line to his dick. The second my nails touched his head, he was hard as stone. Today, I'd taken advantage. We were in my studio at Moe's. She was at work and Lily was at preschool.

As much as I enjoyed living with Moe and Lily, the best times were when I was home alone in my studio doing what I did best...creating art. Being a yoga teacher by day definitely had its perks. However, I'd given up some of my hours at Lotus House so that Atlas and I would have some one-on-one time together, and I had additional painting hours to focus on the intense details. So far, the changes I'd made this past month by moving in with Monet and giving Atlas a go had been the best of my life.

My art had never been better. I had several new pieces to show the gallery, and I wasn't in the poor house. I actually bought a dress to wear to Atlas's show next weekend. A sexy little number that he would want to rip off the second he saw me in it. Only he wouldn't be able to because he would be on stage. I couldn't lie, the concept was a little evil. I wanted him insane with lust for me while all the groupies danced around him with their bloated boobs bouncing around. At least my new dress showcased my ass. It dropped all the way down in the back, leaving the dimples at my lower spine visible.

Those twin indents were like candy-coated lollipops to Atlas. Any time they were on display, his lips were touching them. Seeing as I had a ridiculously hot man in my life, I went a long way toward making sure he had reasons to touch the places on me that gave him a stiffy. Just meant more pleasure for me.

I focused on his tune while I thought about how much my life had changed. I hadn't even had the desire to blow off Atlas and go find a one-nighter. Being in his company was truly awesome. Maybe Moe was right. Relationships weren't all bad. I honestly couldn't complain. I had a beautiful subject to paint any time I wanted, a hard cock ready to go, and a jokester who played me lullabies. Yeah, my life was definitely better than it had been. More fulfilled.

Atlas finished the lick he'd been working on.

I shook my head. "Curly, it sounds like 'Foolish Games' by Jewel."

He stared at me for a long time and then played the song in question.

"Shit! You're right. Dammit! What am I going to do?" He set the guitar on the couch cushion next to him, leaned back, and rubbed his hands over his eyes.

If I were a lesser woman, I'd jump his bones again, but since we had committed to giving this relationship a go, I couldn't distract him with sex. I needed to be there for him, or try to be.

Once I set down my brush, I went over to him and sat on his lap sideways, looping an arm around his neck. "What's really the problem? You've played me countless ditties that were amazing and I hadn't heard them before."

"Ditties?" He peered through a couple of his fingers.

I nuzzled his side and pulled his hand away from his eyes. "Talk to me."

He sighed and rubbed at his chin and then started to pet me. Interesting thing about Atlas. When he was trying to figure out what he wanted to say, he'd run his hands all over me, as if the simple act of touching me provided him the time he needed to gather his thoughts.

His fingers trailed along my collarbone. "I'm not sure anything I've written is good enough for Silas McKnight."

I frowned, and with thumb and forefinger, forced his chin toward me so that I could see into his eyes. One brown, one blue, so extraordinary, so Atlas. A fierce sense of protectiveness washed over me, a sensation I hadn't felt since my dad went away.

"Atlas, your songs are you. They are filled with heart, hope, and a depth you don't hear nowadays. If Silas Mc-Fancypants-Song-Producer doesn't like them, then you don't want him producing them."

He closed his eyes and inhaled deeply. "I just feel like this is my last chance to make something of my music."

"You've already made something of your music. You have beautiful originals that definitely speak to the audience. You should be proud of what you've already accomplished."

"And you're proud of what you've accomplished with your paintings?"

I scowled. "Well no, they're not done."

"And neither are these. In addition, technically, you have a ton of them complete. When are you going to show them to the gallery?"

I shrugged. "Not sure. When it feels like it's time."

He tipped his head back and laughed. "Baby, we are a pair. Two artists who work their asses off but are afraid to share their work for fear of failure."

"Failure is not an option," I whispered.

"Exactly my point."

I sighed. "No, I get it. You don't get anywhere in life by keeping your talents bottled up. How about this—you give yourself a break on trying to make the exact perfect songs, and I'll talk to the gallery about showing them what I've got in the hopper?"

He smiled and wrapped his arms around me. "Deal."

Before I could get up, Atlas kissed me. His lips were warm and wet, tasting of the lemonade I'd served him after we'd made love the first time. It tasted even better mixed with his unique flavor. I sucked on his tongue and rubbed my crotch against his hardened cock. The man was so damned virile. We'd just had sex twenty or so minutes ago, and he was ready to go again.

"Round two?" he offered, nibbling down my chest where he stopped to suck on my nipple.

I ran my hands back into his hair. "Oh yeah, round two."

He grinned around my tip and bit down. "God, you dazzle me, baby."

Instead of responding, I centered my slit over his cock and impaled myself. "How's that for a little dazzle?"

He gritted his teeth and gripped my hips hard. "Just the right amount."

ATLAS

"Haven't seen you around much." Clay scratched the back of his neck as he poured a cup of coffee for himself. "Mila still here?"

I grinned, thinking about the wildcat. I gave her the nickname because on the whole, she was wild and catlike with a sharp tongue I couldn't get enough of. But lately, the acrobatics in the bedroom had been fitting the endearment far better than I'd ever anticipated. "Mila just left. Had an early class to teach."

"Good, means you can hit the gym with me," Clay said.

I groaned, shuffled over to the fridge, and pulled out some eggs and the English muffins. "Egg sami?" I held out the loot and set it on the counter.

"Sure. Thanks." Clay leaned against the counter as I cracked six eggs into a bowl and beat them with a whisk. "So you and Mila seem to be hitting it off."

I crouched down, got the pan going, and poured my mix in. While I stirred, I thought about his question, *really* thought about it. "Can't complain. I mean look at her."

Clay smirked. "She definitely has it going on. And that ass..."

I pursed my lips and kissed the tips of my fingers like an Italian would. "Perfection. I know, man. Blows my mind and my load pretty spectacularly."

He laughed and then shuffled his bare feet. He wore a simple pair of pajama pants and nothing else. I had on a pair of running shorts, figuring I'd run later, but I'd hit the gym with Clay since he offered. I don't pay for the gym when I go because I only ever go if I'm attending as Clay's guest. Then it doesn't cost me a dime, and he enjoys the company as much as I do.

"How's, uh, her friend doing?" he mumbled, looking down into his coffee.

I shook my head and pushed the eggs around while they cooked. "Moe?"

"Monet. Yes."

I rolled my eyes. "Dude, you kind of blew that whole deal by bailing last month. The two of you seemed into one another and then just...nothing."

He frowned. "I didn't blow anything. I was just making conversation. Wondering how you and your girl were getting along while having to share space with a woman and her...uh... kid." His voice lowered when he mentioned Lily.

"It's totally fine. They do their thing; we do ours. Mila spends a lot of time painting, and Moe works a lot. When she's not working, she's spending time with Lily. And, man...that kid. She's a riot!" I laughed, remembering last week when Lily came storming into Mila's room unannounced.

"How so?"

I pushed down the toaster and lowered the heat on the eggs so the muffins had a chance to catch up. While talking, I hit the fridge for the cheese. "The little one caught us kissing, right?"

He snorted and sipped his coffee. "Bound to happen."

I stopped and lifted my chin. "Totally. But the funny thing was, she felt left out and then got positively angry when I wouldn't kiss her. Went screaming down the hallway telling her mom that PowPow wouldn't kiss her." I chuckled and buttered the bread.

"PowPow?"

"Yeah. Little thing is only three. Atlas was way too hard to say, and when her mom first introduced me as Atlas Powers, she chose PowPow. Apparently, she has this double word preference. Calls Mila Auntie Mimi."

Clay sighed, turned around, and rested his hands on the counter. "Yeah, kids are unexpected that way." His words had an underlying hint of sadness that I couldn't quite place.

"You, uh, ever think of having kids one day?" I threw that out there.

His shoulders tightened, all that muscle bunching. "Once. Thought I was going to be a dad. Didn't work out."

I plated the egg sandwiches and handed him one.

"Uh, thanks."

"Yeah, sure. So what happened with the kid thing?"

He inhaled sharply and then looked away. "It's history. Let's just say I don't have any children at this time, and I'm damn sure not likely to have any in the future, either."

I nodded and bit into my egg and cheese. Fuck, it was

good. My stomach was so empty it practically reached out a hidden arm to suck the sandwich straight into my gullet like one of those alien movies.

While the two of us ate in silence, I thought about kids and the fact that I was nearing my twenty-ninth year of life. I'd always thought I'd have a child one day. I knew my ma would be in heaven if I gave her a grandchild. Heck, seeing Mila rounded out with my progeny in her...fuck yeah. A shiver rippled through me, and gooseflesh rose on my skin. My heart started pumping hard, and my hands went a touch clammy at the single thought of Mila having my baby. A little boy or girl with crazy curls from us, a set of deep brown eyes, both the same color like his or her mom, only tall like me. I could teach the little guy or girl some music, and Mila could teach painting. A beautiful life.

The song I'd written had just then taken on new breath. *Maybe never, probably someday* seemed more about my future than the last words my father had said to me over two decades ago.

"You ever think about it?" Clay's words broke me out of my revelation.

I huffed. "No, man, but I did just now, and I gotta say, if Mila was my forever, having a kid or two with her would not suck."

He smiled and rubbed at his spikey hair. "Nor would it from her roommate."

"Excuse me?" I shot back, catching him off guard.

"Uh, nothin'."

I laughed. "No, you just put yourself in that same scenario with Monet. Admit it. You like her."

His attitude was nonchalant when he strode over to the

coffeepot. "You're reading too much into it. She's my type, all right."

"Dude, she's every man's type. She's hot, got great hair, a nice body, and a killer smile. Plus, she's not a bitch. And of course, her kid is funny. Oh, and she's rich. Doesn't need money."

"Her kid. Yeah," he murmured grumpily.

"What was that?"

"Just agreeing with you," he lied. "Besides, I've got my own money. I'd never go after a wealthy woman because of her bank account." The chip firmly on Clay's shoulder got pointier.

Something was up with Clay and kids or Clay and Monet, period. I didn't think it had anything to do with Monet's kid specifically because he hadn't even met Lily, and from first-hand experience, anyone who met that kid was going to fall in love with her. I did, and I'd only spent a short amount of time getting to know her.

I finished up my breakfast and went about cleaning the plates, letting Clay stew in his thoughts.

"What's the deal with her ex? How often does he come around?" Clay asked.

"I fucking knew it!" I turned around, pointing a wet soapy finger and flinging soap suds across Clay's chest. "You like her more than you're letting on, but something is putting you off. Spill it."

"What are we having...a love fest now, bro? Want to braid each other's hair?" He shook his head. "All you guys are all alike. You fall in love with a woman and decide it's time to hook up all your friends. I get enough of that shit from Trent and Dash; I don't need it from you, too."

I dried off my hands and lifted the towel in the air where

I waved it in a peace offering. "Not trying to hook you up. Just wondering why you won't go after a woman who very clearly seemed taken with all that is your studliness." I gestured at his very obvious bulk and brawn. "And I'm not in love."

At that comment, Clay laughed so hard he sprayed coffee all along the sink and counter I just cleaned.

"What the fuck, man! You're cleaning that up!" I tossed the towel at him. He caught it midair.

"You are so full of shit. You're not in love with Mila? You're going to tell me she's just your fuck-buddy?" He harrumphed.

A slither of anger shredded through my pores, and I clenched my teeth. "Not a fuck-buddy. Not even close."

"Then she's your lover?"

"Yes," I growled, still a little tweaked by the fuck-buddy comment.

"And you spend almost all of your time not working... together?"

"What are you getting at?"

He shook his head, wiped at the counter, and rinsed the sink. "Hate to blow the roof off your house of denial, but you're balls-to-the-wall in love with the girl, and everyone but you knows it." He finished and tossed the towel on the counter.

I scoffed. "Whatever. You have no idea what you're talking about. Mila and me, we're just doing our thing and enjoying ourselves."

"Do you fuck other women?" he asked crudely.

I cringed. "No, man."

"Does she fuck other guys?"

At the mere mention of Mila anywhere near another man's dick, a rage so strong fired through me I felt positively violent. "Fuck no!" I ground out between my teeth.

"You think about her all the time? Wonder what she's doing? Think of ways you can make her happy the next time you see her?"

I squinted and focused on my friend's pretty boy face. His California surfer boy look, complete with blond spiked hair, blue eyes, and tanned skinned made him a perfect candidate for a Hawaiian Tropic campaign.

"Your point?" I was finally able to mutter.

"If it walks like a duck, quacks like a duck, looks like a duck...man, it's a fucking duck."

I pushed off the counter and walked around him, ignoring his comment. "We hitting the gym or what? I find I have a renewed need to punch something really hard over and over."

He snickered and followed me from behind. "You wanna spar today? Bring it, boy. I'll take you so far down you won't even know what hit you."

"Looking forward to it, asswipe," I called out from my room, digging through the basket of clean clothes Mila had washed for me and delivered last night folded and freshly laundered.

Clean clothes.

Fuck.

I sat on my bed holding the clean tee and looked at the subtle changes that had already taken place in my life. Clean clothes. A couple sets of her yoga clothing in the top right drawer along with some of her toiletries, brush, hairspray, that kind of shit sitting on my dresser. On the mirror over the dresser were a couple of pictures of us being silly and several of her doing yoga randomly. She called it, "Stop. Drop. Yoga." She'd literally just rocked a complicated yoga pose in the middle of the sidewalk, another in front of a cool wall sprayed with wild graffiti markings in bright neon colors and others I couldn't forget. I tugged on the faithful key hanging around my neck and ran the key over the beads, allowing the comforting sound to tick with each metal bead it ran past.

Since Mila and I'd been exclusively seeing one another, we'd never used the word love or even the string of three words that are so often said to express that feeling when you know that the other person is your one. For Mila and me, we'd just been dazzled. And since that night, we'd used that phrase more often than not..."you dazzle me." Was it really just a way for us to deny stronger feelings toward one another?

I gripped my hair and remembered a conversation not long ago that I'd had with my mom about Mila. She'd been afraid I wouldn't let a woman in because I'd been abandoned by my dad. Apparently, it was a real source of worry for her. My mother believed wholeheartedly in love and loved my dad with her entire heart and still, to this day, hadn't been in another relationship. She said my dad was it for her. Had that been the reason I'd never followed through on a longer relationship? Fear of abandonment?

Was I afraid Mila would walk away? Hell yes. It was all she knew, too. Her dad went to prison, and her mother up and left her, moving three thousand miles away to make a new family. Did I believe that Mila could be capable of doing the same to me? I honestly didn't think so. She might not have allowed herself to have much, make too many long-lasting relationships, but the ones she did have were intense. Her connection to Monet was steadfast and reciprocated. Perhaps that was the answer to Mila. Reciprocate her commitment and she was yours for life.

A knock blasted me out of my thoughts. "We hitting the

gym or did you think more about the fact that there's no way in hell you're going to beat me sparring and you decided to wimp out?"

I chuckled and picked up my gym bag. "I'm not wimping out, but dude. Don't wound me in there today. I've got plans with my girl later."

"You mean the one you're denying you love?"

"I'm not going to do that."

"Do what?" He opened the door to our apartment, and I walked through.

"Not going to deny it anymore."

He smiled huge and smacked my back, hard. "Good man. You gonna drop this bomb on the wee one?"

I shrugged off his arm and spun around. "Man, you better stop making jokes about her height. I like her petite. She's fucking perfect."

He shook his head and hooked me around the neck. "Of course she is, man, but I love grinding your gears."

"Asshole," I mumbled.

"Takes one to know one." He grinned.

"Ain't that the truth?"

CHAPTER SIXTEEN

Bow Pose (Sanskrit: Dhanurasana)

Bow pose is an asana often used in intermediate to advanced level yoga classes. If you are suffering a back injury, do not attempt this pose. However, in retrospect, it can be used for strengthening the back, core, glutes, and thighs. To move into this pose, start by lying flat on your belly. Press into your arms slowly stretching your upper body, bend your knees into ninety-degree angles. If this is comfortable, slowly grab one ankle and then the other. Make sure to attempt this pose first under the watchful guidance of a registered yoga instructor.

MILA

La Luz Gallery was a large building in a high-traffic area. I put on the hazard lights of Moe's SUV and ran around to the back. Moe had let me switch cars with her so that I could bring several of my newest pieces for a pre-viewing by the art director for the gallery. Typically, the director viewed the pieces and evaluated whether or not they would fit in with their other works or justify a dedicated showing. The individual showing was my goal, and I finally had enough pieces to have one. With the addition of the ten nudes, seven of which were of Atlas, I was solid at about twenty-five pieces. The director had already seen the other fifteen and loved them. However, those paintings had been of buildings and architecture from an abstract perspective. These were straight-up nudes.

I pushed my palms down the tank dress I was wearing to remove any oils and grime I might have picked up. I'd paired the teal dress with my gold gladiator sandals. Two metal, homemade, leaf-shaped earrings hung from my ears, adding a bit of chunkiness to the outfit. Nerves were making me shaky. The energy around me felt thick and laden with anxiety. The paintings I'd brought to show were not my norm. I just hoped he'd see the uniqueness and inspiration behind them.

One by one, I brought each of the five paintings I'd chosen into the viewing room off the front. The sales associate helped me in and let me do my thing while she assisted the few customers who were perusing art.

After about a twenty-minute wait, the director, a tall, thin man with pointed features, entered. His hair was coiffed into a bouffant on top, and his suit was pristine. I'd never seen Steven Schilling in anything other than the finest threads, making my cheapo sundress look like a dirty dishrag alongside him.

"Mila, daaah-ling..." He drew out the endearment, making it sound like it had ten vowels. "It is magnificent to see you." Steven embraced me and air-kissed both of my cheeks. "You look lovely and boho chic as always. I trust you are doing well?"

Polite conversation would typically last between two and five minutes depending on how much time he had.

"So...let's see the precious, my dear. I'm positively *dying* while I stand here breathless in anticipation." He punctuated his request with a dramatic flip of his hand.

I laughed nervously and started uncovering my pieces.

Atlas leaning on the stool, hard as a rock and looking like a god.

Atlas lounging on the chase, ankles crossed, manhood tucked, eyes closed taking a snooze.

Atlas with a guitar over his thighs, strumming me a melody.

Atlas arched in a good-morning stretch. Now that one had been hard to get him to repeat over and over, but I'd given him a nice blow job before and promised sexual favors after. The man was a glutton for my mouth.

The last was my favorite. Atlas in bed, the sheets pulled just above his soft erection. We'd just dazzled one another. His hair was messy, and he was leaning against the headboard with a sated smile and a come-hither look as he was crooking his finger at me. The. Best. Ever. I swooned every time I looked at the canvas, remembering just the moment when he'd done it.

Steven walked to each painting and spent several minutes inspecting them.

"These are nothing like the others," he mused.

I answered anyway. "No, they are a new concept and side to my art. I figured at the show we could have one area that had my architectural canvases and then slice it down the middle where we could then show my nudes. I have another five already completed."

He scoffed. "You have *more* of these?"

Steven shook his head again and again while he continued to inspect my blood, sweat, and tears with a critical eye. "I'm astounded."

I frowned. "Um...thank you?"

Steven glanced up from where he was crouched next to the one of Atlas on the stool. The first painting that started this craze for my muse.

"That was not a compliment, I'm afraid."

My heart sank. Literally, the weight of his words wrapped around the muscle and drowned it in despair, so much so that it probably didn't even beat anymore. A chill whispered across my skin as if the air was also against me, freezing my skin from the outside as the inside was caving in on itself.

"I honestly don't know what to say." He stood and crossed one arm over his chest while he rested his chin on his hand, still taking in my work.

I blinked and licked my suddenly Sahara desert dry lips. "You don't like them."

"Like them?" He squinted. "Darling...I *loathe* them."

Bullet right to the chest. I stepped back, the need to be farther away from this heartache a physical imperative.

"Uh...I don't...um...what?"

"Is this your boyfriend?" he asked flippantly.

"I'm not sure why that matters."

He snorted. "Because, darling Mila, these paintings are clearly created by a woman in love. There's no tortured nude, no disgusting, rotting flesh. They simply won't do."

I'm pretty sure I lost my voice. Not only did he hit me with the L-word, but he also mentioned tortured and rotting flesh.

"Huh? What are you talking about? I wasn't trying to

paint those disgusting images."

He sighed. "It's all the rage right now. Perhaps if you made the man bleed, put a couple holes in him, made him a little uglier, they'd be something I could show the public."

A wave of nausea and dizziness pummeled through me. I ran my hand through my hair and leaned over, taking a few deep breaths until I felt a bit more under control. Steven didn't even try to assist me. He just stood there silent while I physically and mentally had a meltdown. The guy was probably used to artists losing their minds during his critiques.

I inhaled deeply and righted myself. "You're telling me that you don't like my paintings because they are what? Too..."

"Pretty. Beautiful. Stunning." He nodded. "Awful, really. Such a shame. I had high hopes for what you were going to bring me today."

"Steven, you can't possibly mean that."

His eyes widened, and then a flicker of shame crossed his face. "I'm sorry, darling. I know it's hard to hear a tough critique, but these paintings will not sell."

I looked at each image of Atlas in all his glory. His beautiful eyes the only part on his body besides the shadows that I'd actually painted colors into. I'd wanted something to be unique to him specifically, except for the nakedness. "But I thought graphic nudes sold pretty well."

He nodded. "Yeah, but those were women, not men, and the male ones were all dark and had a thrilling edge of danger. And of course, the bleeding ones were practically sold before I ever placed them up for a showing. A perfect male, even a godlike one, is unrealistic. There has to be something wrong with him. I just see no flaws."

At that point, I had no idea what to say. I'd spent the last several weeks painting what I thought were riveting pieces that would truly resonate with the masses, and Steven was telling me that I needed to gore them up. "I don't do blood and violence, Steven."

He pouted. "I know. We can show the architectural pieces with two other artists in two months' time. I cannot, however, show these. Until you come up with something that actually speaks to the masses, we, La Luz Gallery, will not be giving a Mila Mercado solo showing. Sorry."

I closed my eyes and let his words sink in. "Fine. Yes, thank you, Steven."

He walked over to me and patted my shoulder. "I look forward to seeing you in a couple months. Perhaps by then you'll have something magical to show me."

Yeah, like actual dead, rotting bodies tacked to canvases. The flies will really give it that au natural effect.

With my heart broken, my mind destroyed, I packed up my canvases carefully, though I didn't know why, since Steven had basically informed me that they were unsalable. Shit. What was I going to do? This was the direction I'd chosen to go, and I believed in my work. Maybe I'd just been distracted.

"Are all of these of your boyfriend?"

"These paintings are clearly created by a woman in love."

"There has to be something wrong with him."

"I just see no flaws."

He couldn't see any flaws because the flaws were in me. My stupidity. I let myself get carried away with a man and look what happened. Disaster. All my work...worthless. How the hell did I let this happen, and better yet, how did I get my edge back? Failure was not an option.

Then the truth smacked me upside the head like a shovel

to the face. The only way to fix this was to get rid of the one thing that had my muse working in the wrong direction.

Atlas.

ATLAS

Mila was not right. She avoided eye contact all through dinner. Moe had invited me over for her famous Mediterranean chicken, which of course, I jumped at the chance. Mila's best friend was a damn fine cook, and I was a man who liked to eat hearty. Any opportunity that a woman wanted to fill my belly of something homemade and hot out of the oven, I was right there, fork in hand, and a willingness to clean up after.

"You okay, wildcat?"

"Hmm?" Mila glanced up, letting the rice she'd barely touched fall off the fork and back onto her plate. She'd mostly moved the food around, and that in itself had me wanting to call out the National Guard. My girl liked to eat and had a hearty appetite most days.

"I asked if you were okay."

Lily, who was sitting next to me, which she always did when I stayed over, got out of her chair and ran around the table.

She crawled into Mila's lap and put her hand on her forehead. Then she put her lips to it. "You not hot."

Mila's first smile of the night crept across her lips. "No, baby, I'm not hot. Thank you for checking though. Mimi is fine."

Apparently, that was not explanation enough. "You wanna me to kiss it better?"

She smiled and presented her cheek. "Yes, please."

The little girl kissed her cheek and then popped off of her. "Now your turn." She pointed at me. "Kiss her better."

I leaned over my chair toward Mila. As I got closer, she frowned. That would not do. Not even. I grabbed Mila's hand and squeezed her fingers.

"Hey, uh, Moe, leave the dishes. I'll clean them later, yeah?"

She waved a hand as she pulled out a hot apple pie from the oven. "Got it!"

"Come on, hotness. We need to talk."

Mila licked her lips and sighed. "Yeah, I think we do."

I led her down the hall toward her room. When I got there, she entered behind me, and I shut and locked the door.

"What's going on?"

She bit her thumbnail and started pacing. Mila pacing was a shit sign of potential bad news.

"I just don't know what to do anymore. This thing..." She wrung her hands together as she walked.

"Thing? What thing?"

"Us."

"What about us?" Dread clawed its way up my chest to poke at my heart with a pointed, curved talon.

She shook her head and continued pacing. "It's not working."

I jerked my head back. "Fuck if it's not. What the hell happened?"

She slapped her hands to her sides. "Nothing happened. I'm just telling you that we need to cool it. Take a break or something."

"Really? And for how long would that break be?" I sneered.

She ran a hand through her hair and blew on her forehead. "I don't know. A while."

"Sorry, wildcat. You need to reevaluate, get some sleep or something because we"—I pointed to her and pointed to me—"are not breaking up. Period."

Mila put her hands on her hips. "Oh yes, we are."

I shook my head. "Babe. We're not."

I swear she stomped her foot or, at the very least, tapped her toe. "I'm sorry, Atlas, to have to do this to you. I didn't want to..." she started as if I hadn't just told her what was going down.

"To have to tell me this. Why do you have to tell me anything?"

"Because it's not working," she screeched, running a hand through her hair, making a mess of it.

"What exactly isn't working between us?" I held out my hand and counted off each finger. "We have a great time together. We are dynamite in the bedroom. Time spent with friends and family so far has been stellar. Our work schedules aren't perfect, but we've worked it out. And I'm in love with you. So tell me what's not working between us because I've failed to see a problem." My voice had risen to almost a yell.

"Atlas...you love me?" She choked out a sob.

Oh no. "What the fuck, babe! This is not you. This is not us. What happened?"

"My work is suffering," she muttered through her tears.

"Lotus House is fine. They were okay with your reduction in hours. They know you want to be an artist one day and need the time to work on that. It's all good. Now come here." I went to embrace her, and she shoved me away.

"No! My art is suffering. Don't you get it! My muse is all

jacked up."

I crossed my arms. "Says the woman who has painted more pieces in the past month than she has in the better part of a year."

She groaned. "You don't get it. That's just it. I'm painting, but the paintings suck! They hated them." Another sob tore through her as she clutched at her chest. "Hated them!" She fell to the bed face first.

I landed right next to her, curled her against me. At first, she struggled, but then the tears took over and she cried. Deep, gut-wrenching, throat-shredding sobs tore through her. I just held on and let her cry it out until, after about twenty minutes, she calmed enough that only a sniffle could be heard. Her head was burrowed into my neck, her breath hot and wet against my skin.

"Baby, tell me what happened."

Her chest shuddered and shook as she spoke. "I went to La Luz Gallery. To my viewing."

"Viewing? But I thought you had to plan those way in advance."

She nodded into my neck. "Yeah, but they have a review in advance. To determine whether or not the gallery wants to show your work. They don't."

"They don't what?" I asked, running my hand down her back in soothing, methodical sweeps.

"Want my work," she croaked.

I frowned and shifted our weight until we were on our sides face-to-face. "They didn't like the paintings?"

"No. Steven, the art director, hated them. Said they were too pretty. That the new rage was tortured and bloody."

"Tortured and bloody?" I couldn't believe what I'd heard.

She nodded.

I laughed. I couldn't hold it back. "Babe, that's ridiculous!" The guffaws came harder as I watched her face twist from an expression of horror, and then recognition, and then finally to humor. And then my girl was laughing right along with me.

"Do you honestly want to paint ugly shit? Besides, who hangs disgusting paintings in their home? I can already see it. Come sit at my table for dinner but don't look too hard at the murdered man on the wall. Just swallow down that beef Wellington while looking at a woman's throat cut."

Mila started laughing in earnest.

Just when I thought I had her back, and cuddling into me fully, the laughing switched around and the tears fell again. "But they still didn't want my paintings."

"So?"

Her head popped back a few inches. "So? It's my life. It's my work. If my muse is broken, I have to remove the elements that are making it that way."

"Which would be me." I stated matter-of-factly.

Mila bit down on her bottom lip and nodded.

"I can't believe you'd do that. Well, I can. I get the need to put your dream above anything else, but that's not how you deal in the real world. There are going to be times when someone doesn't like your art, just like there are people who don't like my music. Do I want people who don't like my music listening? Not really. There're plenty of music-loving ears around to share. Just like there are plenty of buyers in the world who are going to want to see, love, and purchase your work. Trust me on this."

Mila's face crumbled again. "I'm sorry."

I pulled her closer and hugged her hard. "Don't give up on

us so easily. Don't abandon me. I couldn't stand it."

Mila lifted up her face, now a mask of regret. "I'm sorry." She kissed my lips. "I'm sorry." Kiss to my forehead. "I'm sorry." Kiss down the side of my face. "I'm sorry." My shirt lifted up as if by magic and her lips were on my abdomen. "I'm sorry." Her hand covered my hardening shaft where she worked my jeans open like an expert. "I'm sorry." She covered my hard cock with the warm heaven of her mouth.

I gripped her hair and tugged until she looked up at me. Her eyes were still glassy from her crying jag, and remorse floated across those chocolaty depths. She sucked hard, hollowing out her cheeks and giving it her all...but her eyes, they stayed on me.

"Fuck, baby. You're forgiven."

CHAPTER SEVENTEEN

SOLAR PLEXUS
C H A K R A

*In order for a couple to achieve harmony when driven by the
Manipura chakra, they need to work very hard on themselves
to overcome their high expectations of the future. Both
parties must communicate and commit to one another's goals
and ambitions evenly to find mutual success in life and love.*

ATLAS

Mila lay spent on my chest, her breathing labored pants
against my skin, warming my nipple. We'd just had the best
makeup sex...well, the first makeup sex I'd ever had.

I nudged her arm. "Hey, have you ever had makeup sex?"
I asked, twirling my fingers through her hair.

She shook her head and then licked my nipple. It hardened
instantly. I groaned in reply. Damn wildcat was going to make
me hard again, even after the wild romp where I'd given her

my all. Rest was needed, badly.

"No, never been in a relationship long enough to fight."

That comment had me cracking up. My chest rumbled as I held her close and laughed into her hair. "We've been fighting since day one."

She tilted her head. "Then maybe all we've ever had is makeup sex."

I played with her hair and then leaned forward and kissed her forehead. "Then what was it that we just had?"

Mila worried her bottom lip. "Normal relationship sex?" She grinned.

"If that was normal, we are so going to last forever, wildcat."

She snickered and kissed my chest. "I really am sorry about earlier. What I did..."

"You mean what you were trying to do?"

"Yeah, that. I was being foolish. But you're right in the end. I don't want to paint what they want me to paint or whatever everyone else is painting. I want to paint what's in my head and you, curly, are definitely in my head." She straddled my hips more fully and leaned up enough to grace me with a long, tongue-tangling, wet kiss.

I moaned and curled a hand around the back of her head, delving my tongue deep, enjoying her humming at the back of her throat when I sucked on her tongue. "I told you, I forgive you."

She picked up the key around my neck and moved it back and forth, the beads clacking with every move, kind of like unzipping a pair of pants. "Yeah, but it wasn't cool. I love being with you. This relationship, it's the best thing that's happened to me in a long, long time. I can't believe that meeting today had me so fucked up I almost ruined it."

I ran my hands up and down her thighs. "You couldn't ruin it. Remember, you dazzle me, baby."

She grinned. "Oh, do I? I thought before it was love."

Instead of saying what I knew she wanted to hear, I hedged around it. "That too," I offered.

She chuckled but didn't push me, nor did she say it back. I didn't request that of her, either. The last thing I'd want was for someone to say they loved me just because I'd said it first. I wanted her to say those words to me when she couldn't *not* say them. I'd not been with a woman long enough to hear those words said to me. I planned on being fully in the moment when it occurred, but I definitely wouldn't urge her to say it when she didn't feel it. I had a sneaking suspicion she did feel it, just as deeply as I did, but was too afraid to go there. That was fine. We had lots of time to solidify what we had with one another.

While my mind wandered off, I came to, realizing Mila's concentration wasn't on me. She kept flipping the key that I'd worn for two decades, over and back, lifting it to the light. She squinted and got really close to the metal surface.

"I know what this opens," she remarked nonchalantly as if she'd just said it was raining outside while looking out the window.

Five words. Five words that had the power to knock me on my ass. I'd been wearing this key for twenty years, and I had absolutely no idea what it opened, nor had I ever found the lock that it went to.

I tightened my grip on her thighs. Mila squinted and looked at me.

She set the key over my heart and then gripped my hands where they dug into her cinnamon-colored flesh. "Let go." She petted my fingers until I loosened my hold. The room kept going from color to black around the edges. My heart pounded so hard and so loud within my chest, it obliterated all other sound. Before I knew it, I was gasping for air.

Mila hopped off me and ran to the bathroom where she grabbed a glass of water.

"Here, Atlas, drink this." She ran her hands through my hair as I pushed up, leaned against the headboard, and drank the water. "Now breathe in for five beats, good...now slowly out for five." She breathed with me as the tightness I felt in my chest started to dissipate. I focused on her eyes and her chest moving in my periphery. She'd tossed on my T-shirt when she went to get the water, and just in my tee I wanted to throw her down and have her again. At least when my heart wasn't about to pop out of my chest.

"You okay?" she asked, and I nodded, still caught in the clutches of my anxiety.

She nodded and then got up. I grabbed hold of her wrist, stopping her from moving. "Don't leave me," I muttered, not recognizing my own frightened voice.

Mila ran another hand through my hair and then cupped my cheek. "I'm not. I wouldn't. I'm just going to get something in that box on my dresser, okay?"

I glanced at the jewelry box she pointed at and nodded.

She rushed across the room, her bare ass peeking through the bottom of the shirt when she bent over to rummage through the jewelry box. "Ah-ha! Got it."

Now at the end of the bed, she crawled up it and straddled my hips. "This okay?" She settled her bare ass on my thighs.

I locked my arm around her waist and pressed her even closer, rubbing my hardening shaft against her moist center.

"Very okay. Sorry about that. I don't know what happened. It's just that you mentioned the key, and you don't know what it means."

"Tell me then."

I inhaled slowly and pushed her curls away from her pretty face. "It's the last thing my dad gave me. He told me that it would change my life. Only he was so far gone on drugs and his leaving that he neglected to tell his eight-year-old son what it opened. I figured I'd either find out one day or not, but honestly, I hadn't thought about finding out what it opened in a long time. Then you said what you did... Uh, did you mean it?"

She smiled and looped her hands around my neck. "Yeah. I know what it opens. It just dawned on me now when I was looking at it."

"Why?"

"Because I have a key just like it." She opened her palm, and in it was a similarly shaped key, the same color, with the same two letters but three different numbers etched into its side.

I held the key and looked at it as if it were not a simple key, but the answer to all that ailed the world. "What does it open?"

She smiled huge and looked me right in the eye. "A safe-deposit box, baby!"

A safe-deposit box. I jerked my head back and bumped against the headboard. What the hell?

"What the heck was my father doing with a key to a safe-deposit box, and how am I going to find out what bank and what box?"

Again, my girl grinned, only this time it came with a little bounce in her booty. She was getting excited, and along with her, my cock took notice every time she bumped her pussy against it. I held her thighs in lockdown. "Wildcat. Seriously. I want to know what you have to say, but can you do it while not bouncing on my dick, unless you're properly going to bounce on my dick?"

She laughed and lifted the key that was around my neck, putting the letters directly in front of my face. "See that SF and the three digits?"

"Yeah."

"They're the same as mine."

"Okay, so?"

"That means the SF means San Francisco and more specifically, if it's the same as mine, it's San Francisco International Bank."

"And the three digits?"

"The box number, silly!" She once again rubbed all over my cock, still not being able to contain her excitement. "Let's go open it tomorrow!" she squealed in straight-up glee.

I didn't know how to respond. Of course, I wanted to know what was in the box, if this key did, in fact, open a box, but I wasn't sure I was ready. Instead of telling her all the thoughts running through my head, I lifted her up and planted her on her back with me hovering between her thighs. "We'll see, hotness. We'll see. For now...I fuck you."

She made a point of pursing her lips in thought but then breaking into a gaggle of giggles when she couldn't pretend anymore. "Okay!" she said and wrapped her arms and legs around me, both of us getting lost in the other's body once more.

Only I still had the key on my mind, never too far away. Tomorrow I'd know what it meant. Twenty years of waiting and I'd finally know what my father left me that would change my life.

MILA

"I'll have to verify your identification. May I have your ID and social security number?" the banker in a bad suit requested of Atlas as we sat in front of a boring oak desk in a really old bank.

Atlas handed over his social security card and his California driver's license. The bank manager left us and entered a room off to the side, presumably verifying his information.

I rubbed my hand down Atlas's thigh. "You okay, curly?" I was trying to lighten the heavy nature of what could possibly be in a safe-deposit box that his father left him over twenty years ago.

He looked at me, his one blue eye looking icy, and the one brown seeming dark. "No, I'm not." He lifted my hand and kissed the back. "But I will be."

I gave him a small, sad smile. I knew this had to be killing him softly. His dad had meant a lot to him, and when he'd been abandoned, Atlas had lost faith in all people. Last night, after several rounds of lovemaking, we shared in the dark. He spoke about his dad, how much it had hurt when he left, how he and his mom had struggled to pay the bills. They'd even had to move in with his mom's sister for years until he was old enough to work himself and contribute to the homestead monetarily. That was when he and his mom got a little apartment. Now, his mom had her own place, mostly because Atlas still helped chip in for her rent. I loved him more for that.

Yes, I finally admitted to myself that I was in love with Atlas Powers. The annoying, overconfident, arrogant, combative jokester who was also an intense lover made me laugh constantly, appreciated my art, was a talented musician, and more than that...he loved me back. No man besides my dad had ever loved me.

Men had only been in my life to scratch a sexual itch, not participate in anything of value. Now though, I couldn't image not having Atlas in my day-to-day life. He had so easily interwoven himself into the very threads that were the fabric of my existence. Moe and Lily adored him and he them. The instructors and owners of the studio all knew we were an item and, believe it or not, thought we were cute. *Cute.* I was in a relationship that people thought was *cute.* Atlas's friends seemed to dig me, and he'd even gotten on a level with my buddy Nick.

The bank manager brought back something for him to sign, confirming that he was the Atlas Powers who was the only other individual approved to access this box. "There you go. I can take you in now."

I stayed seated as the two men stood up.

Atlas held out his hand. "Will you go with me?" His eyes held such hope I'd have never let him down. If he needed me, I was going to be there.

I stood up fast and grabbed his hand. "Of course. Whatever you need."

"I need you," he admitted, his voice filled with an unshed emotion.

Sometimes I wished men weren't men. A woman in this situation could cry and carry on and no one would care. Hell, they wouldn't even pay attention. A man, though, no, he had to be tough. Had to "man up" for fear that he'd be considered weak for showing any real emotion. Except, Atlas showed real emotion all the time, though I would admit, he mostly only did it with me and within the confines of one of our bedrooms. There he could let himself be free...with me.

That thought had my protective mama bear side popping to the surface. The only other time I'd ever felt like I could take down a car racing at me at fifty miles an hour was when Moe had given birth to Lily, and Kyle had left her hanging to raise what was supposed to be their daughter, alone.

While we walked, Atlas held my hand in a viselike grip. I rubbed his arm and matched my steps with his as best I could, making sure he'd feel me close at all times.

We got to the back room where all the boxes were held.

"Number five seventeen." The banker pointed to a shoebox-sized black square along the wall and unlocked the bank's lock, leaving Atlas to use his key to finish off the task. "Take as much time as you need," he said, attempting to leave.

"Wait!" Atlas stopped the guy with a hand to his elbow. "I have a question for you."

"Certainly." He turned around and clasped his hands in front of him.

Atlas licked his lips and frowned. "If this box has been here for over twenty years, that means someone had to be paying the fee on it, right?"

"You would be correct."

"Do you know how and when it was paid?" Atlas asked.

"I can look that up for you, and when you leave, I should have that information."

Atlas nodded. "Thank you, yes. I'd appreciate it."

"Of course, sir." The banker turned and left.

The room was cool, the air-conditioning pumping in the confined space. There were a couple of bright drop lights hanging from the ceiling directly over a set of high tables that ran down the center of the rectangular space. The walls were painted a dark navy, so the black shiny boxes looked ominous and foreboding, like liquid oil floating on the surface of the ocean.

Atlas closed his eyes, took a deep breath, and then walked over to box 517. He pushed the key in, turned the lock, and pulled. The sleek box pulled out with the key as if it was on rollers. He hefted the bottom with his other hand until the box was clear. In total, the thing was around fifteen inches in length, ten inches in width, and another four or five inches tall.

He set the box down on the table and then placed his hands on either side of it. His shoulders curved forward as if he was holding a heavy burden on his back.

"Do you want me to leave, give you some privacy?" I asked, not wanting to intrude.

He shook his head, his hair falling into his face. After a couple of moments spent listening to the air-conditioning and our ragged breaths, Atlas lifted a hand and popped the top up on the box. It had a hinge at the back, so the lid fell all the way at the hinge and slammed to the table.

I gasped at the sight of the first thing I saw. Neat stacks. Money. Lots of it. By my count, there were ten total stacks, and they looked to be varying amounts.

"What the fuck?" Atlas growled, lifting one of the stacks that was all one hundred dollar bills. "There has to be fifty thousand dollars in this stack alone. Where the hell did my old man get this money?"

Now that was a good question. My bet would be drugs

since Atlas had said he liked to partake.

Atlas's hands turned into fists as he stared at the cash. "Do you think he robbed something?"

I shrugged. "Honey, I don't know. This is so far out of my wheelhouse I'm swinging at foul balls left and right."

He sighed and lifted each stack, placing them outside of the box on the table. As he removed one and then two, it became clear there were several documents under the money. A five-by-seven-sized envelope sat on the top of the other full-sized pages.

"Atlas" was scrawled on top.

I pointed to the card. "Read that first. Might explain a bit more. I'll...uh...I'll count the money."

He smiled and chuckled a bit under his breath. He didn't want to laugh, but at least I'd made him momentarily come back to himself.

Atlas fingered the envelope and pulled out a single sheet of paper. I could tell from the other side of the table, where I'd finished pulling out the stacks of cash, that both sides of the page he held had writing on them. Instead of attempting to read the bits that I could see, I set about counting the money.

Stack after stack I counted and then made notes of the amounts on my phone. When I'd finished, Atlas had already moved on to the other documents and was thumbing through them.

"So?" I said noncommittally, uncertain whether or not to intrude.

"I can't talk about it yet."

"Fair enough."

"How much cash is there?"

I swallowed and focused on my phone. "Let me add it up."

When I was done, I stared at the number. "Two hundred and sixty-five thousand."

Atlas braced himself on the table. "Fuck." He scowled.

The scowl was surprising. I mean, if I'd just come into two hundred and sixty-five big ones, I'm pretty sure I wouldn't be scowling. Tossing it in the air and dancing in it like it was raindrops, sure, but definitely not scowling.

He huffed. "Fucker couldn't stay with mom and me. Had to chase his art, leave us hanging, poor and struggling. All the while, he had this money set aside for me. *For me,*" he growled.

I came around the table and put my hand on his back, rubbing it up and down. "And you're mad, because..."

"He left us with nothing, Mila. Mom made very little money. She cleaned the houses of rich people while her husband gallivanted day and night with his artsy friends, did drugs, and sometimes helped out. I remember back when he was still with us he'd randomly bring home a thousand bucks. Those nights we'd eat good, and Mom and Dad would dance in the kitchen like young lovers. Mom would be so happy because that money would catch up the bills, and he'd swear to bring more so that they weren't getting behind every month. Then we'd go months with nothing again, and whammo, more cash would appear. Until he left and didn't come back."

I sighed and snuggled under his arm and plastered myself to his side. "Was he selling drugs?"

Atlas's head jerked back. "No, wherever would you get that idea?"

I balked. "You! You said he did drugs, and when he left, he was high."

"Medicinally, and yeah, he liked to be high, but no, he didn't sell it. He never seemed that far gone."

"Then where did all this money come from?" I picked up a stack and ran my finger across all the hundreds.

Atlas looked at all the cash, grabbed it, and tossed it back into the box. He didn't even care enough to stack it up nicely again. "This? This is bribe money. It's money he made over the years from all his art selling in shows, at auctions, and galleries."

"You're kidding."

He shook his head and shuffled the papers. "Said he owed it to me. That he hoped that the cash and the other things he'd signed over into my name would make up for leaving me behind."

I knew my man. Material things were not the way to his heart. "And does it?" I asked.

"Fuck no. He can keep his money and shove it up his ass. You know where he is?" He sneered in a way that told me he now knew exactly where his father was located.

"Where?" I was almost afraid of the answer.

"Hawaii. Living on the beach attached to a successful gallery on North Shore Oahu." He choked out a wry laugh. "And you know what? It has been my mother's dream her entire life to live on the beach. Carefree and doing something she loved. And while she worked her ass to the bone cleaning up other people's shit, making their homes sparkling clean, breaking her back doing it, he was sitting in the sand, tinkering with his art, enjoying the good life."

I blinked and just stared. How could a man do that? Leave his family and just live his life on a beach somewhere doing what he loved while his family back on the mainland suffered. "Asshole," I murmured under my breath.

"Exactly!" He grabbed up the files and put the money

back into the wall with the box.

"What's in the files?"

"I don't know yet. All I know is I've learned enough for one day."

As we walked out of the deposit room, the banker bustled over to us. "Mr. Powers."

"Yeah?" Atlas stopped, frustration written all over the lines in his face.

"You asked me to research the unit fee?"

"Oh. Yes. Find anything?" Atlas asked with far less enthusiasm than he'd had before we opened the box.

The bank manager smiled and handed him a piece of paper. "Kenneth Powers has paid the box in full every year. The bill goes to his physical address in Oahu, Hawaii. I've taken the liberty of writing the address there."

Atlas looked down at the piece of paper, his body stiff as a board. "Thank you," he gritted through his teeth. "Come on, Mila. Let's go." He grabbed my hand and stuffed the paper in the top folder. He dipped his chin at the banker and led me out of the bank into the chilly San Francisco morning.

He tucked me into his car and got in. Then he just stared out the window, not moving, not doing anything.

"What are you going to do with the information?" I wasn't sure what else to say.

His shoulders fell, and his head lopped forward and hit the steering wheel where his hands rested. "I don't know. Fuck. I don't know."

CHAPTER EIGHTEEN

Tiptoe Pose - Standing (Sanskrit: Prapadasana)

I personally consider this a tiptoe pose modification. Prapadasana is typically done while crouching with the knees together and the bum hovering over the heels. However, this particular modification helps with stretching the spine, opening the chest and shoulders, as well as working on balancing. It's a beginner level pose that makes the yogi feel strong and alive.

MILA

For the next week, Atlas was like a stranger to me. He didn't smile as often, didn't hum random tunes, and did not sit for my art. Not that it mattered, since I wouldn't be showing those pieces anytime soon. Atlas taught his classes at Lotus House but canceled last weekend's show at Harmony Jack's.

He was able to reschedule to this weekend, but he didn't seem any better, and I knew he had an appointment early next week with the Knight & Day team for them to hear his new songs. However, I wasn't sure he had finished those, either. Basically, Atlas was a walking, talking zombie. He needed to snap out of his funk, but I had no idea how to get him back to himself.

I walked through the doors at Lotus House and made my way to Atlas's class. I didn't usually attend his naked yoga class because he'd said it was too distracting having me there. Said it was too hard for him to avoid getting an erection. Today, I didn't care. I wanted him to have an erection because he hadn't touched me since he'd opened the damn safe-deposit box. I almost wished I'd never have seen the correlation to the stupid key in the first place. Then none of this would have happened, and I'd be sexually satisfied instead of grouchy and horned up. Well, that was going to end today. My man was going to fuck me six ways from Sunday if it was the last thing I did in this world.

As I entered, he was setting up at the riser. Without bringing attention to myself, I sneaked all the way to the far right corner. The same corner that I'd been in when I first took this class. Atlas continued to do his thing, prep his area, set the music, light candles, and close the blinds. Right at the strike of three, he closed and locked the door. I'd already shed my clothes and sat down among the other patrons.

He still hadn't noticed me, which, truth be told, actually hurt more than I wanted to believe. We'd always been in tune with one another, ever since the first day a couple months ago. Now that he'd found out about his dad and knew where he was living high on the hog while his mom was struggling, he hadn't been the same. From this experience, I learned my guy felt things deep, and I had to find a way to break through it.

I watched as Atlas stood on the platform and dropped his yoga pants. My mouth watered at the sight of his cock, free of hair, hanging down along with a nice set of balls. His thighs were solid muscle and corded beautifully to the knee where his large calves showed off the hunk of toned flesh down to his slim ankles and bare feet. My God, he was everything a man should be, and all mine. I had to bite back a groan at seeing my guy naked for the first time in a week. Every day since the bank run, he'd blown off staying with me and found reasons to not have me stay with him. I knew he was hurting and needed time to think, but from what I've read, when you're a couple you needed to lean on the one you loved, not push them away.

"Thank you for coming, everyone. Now, I want you to close your eyes and set your intention for today's practice. Think about what you want to get out of freeing yourself from your clothes and your inhibitions, and leave anything that doesn't serve you at the door. This time is for you." He scanned the entire room. His eyes flashed in recognition when they landed on me, and the first smile I'd seen on him in a week spread across his face. He walked over to me slowly. I blatantly admired his body in all its sculpted glory. When he got to me, he kneeled down on one knee, grasped my chin between thumb and forefinger, and leaned close enough to speak directly to me without anyone else being able to hear.

"Hey, baby." He smiled, and my heart did a straight-up pitter-patter.

"Hi, curly." I offered him my own cheesy grin.

He leaned in and slanted his lips over my mouth. His spicy, earthy scent filled the air around us as he delved his tongue just enough to tease. I sighed, opening up for him instantly. He pulled back and sucked on my bottom lip.

"You know I don't like it when you come to this class," he said, all the while leering at my tits.

They peaked instantly at his gaze. He reached out one hand and cupped my left breast, swiping over the nipple with his thumb. I bit my lip hard enough to bruise.

"Yeah, but it's the only way I thought I could see you naked."

He hummed, still playing with my nipple. "Are you feeling neglected?" He plumped my tit perfectly in his giant hand.

I nodded, unable to speak.

"Class, I want you to keep your eyes closed and sway from left to right, like you're flowing in the current, just like seaweed under the water. Loosening that spine, let the neck tip and flow with it." He addressed the class but didn't take his hands off me.

"Atlas..." I mewled and grabbed him by the back of the neck and forced his lips to mine. I kissed him with everything I had. My fear, my strength, the divine desire split me in half, but more than that, I kissed him with all the love I had within me.

He took what I had to give and growled his need in return. Before long, we were kissing like horny teenagers right in the middle of a naked yoga class. His dick was rock hard, my center was slick as hell, and we needed to fuck. Straight up, we needed to mate.

He pulled back and rested his forehead against mine, breathing roughly.

"I love you, please come back to me," I whispered the three little words I'd never once said to him before but meant them with the enormity of this moment. I needed him. I wanted him. I loved him, and he needed to shake off this funk and come back to me.

He curled a hand around my nape. "Baby, I never left."

"But you did," I choked out, tears filling my eyes.

With that, he pulled up and then walked away. I almost bawled right then and there, until I realized he was tapping someone on the shoulder. Dash's dark blond head lifted up. In my haste to pop in unannounced, I hadn't realized that Dash and Amber were sitting in the class next to one another. *Way to go, Amber!* When I'd painted them a few weeks ago, she started out shy, but before too long, they were totally comfortable being naked in front of me. During that session, Amber had complained that Dash wouldn't let her take the naked yoga class, and she wanted to try it, to set herself free. Apparently, she'd worn him down because there she was, pert boobies and athletic body on display. Good for her!

I sniffed my own emotion back and noticed that Dash nodded, glanced over at me, and grinned. Then he stood up and took to the riser. Before he turned around, I noticed Dash had a fine ass. Rock hard and svelte to go with the rest of him.

"Change of plan, folks, I'll be teaching this class today, but don't worry, I've studied with Atlas and I'm happy to fill in. Now let's stretch those arms up and above your head reaching for the sky..." Dash continued the class, but I stopped hearing him.

All I could focus on was the alpha male looming over to me. "Time to go, hotness." He grabbed my bicep with one hand and my things in the other. He took the time to put the simple maxi dress I'd worn over my head. He was only wearing his yoga pants. Then, without a word, he led me out of the room, down the hall to one of the private rooms. We entered, and within seconds, the door was shut and I was against it.

Atlas pulled my dress up and over my head again, baring my body to his desire. His lips went straight for my breast, and he wrapped that hot mouth around one erect bud and sucked... hard. I called out, arching into his succulent kiss. "Missed you." I raked my nails along his scalp.

With that, he growled and sucked even harder. He ripped his mouth away from my breast as if it were a serious hardship. His expression was a scowl. "Need you. Need everything about you. Can't get enough."

Atlas suddenly dropped to his knees, and his lips hit my clit so fast I barely had time to hold myself up. He curled his hands around my ass and pushed me onto his face, forcing my legs to a wider stance.

He growled and hummed as he ate me with a wild abandon. His licks were fierce, his suction deep, and his tongue unrelenting against my clit until I came hard against the door. Shaking, knees buckling in the most divine pleasure. In seconds, Atlas had his pants down and lifted me up until I'd wrapped my legs around his waist.

"Sorry," he said, notching the wide crown of his penis against my entrance. "So fucking sorry." He thrust inside, all the way to the hilt. I inhaled hard as the pressure struck deep. There was absolutely no space between us.

"Mila, baby..." Atlas whispered against my face, kissing anything his lips came into contact with.

I gripped his hair and pulled his head back. "Don't do that to me again. Don't abandon me," I growled, my heart pounding in my chest. Tears filled my eyes and fell down my cheeks. "I don't like it. So don't. Do. It. Again," I ground out between my teeth.

He rested his forehead against mine, shifted his hips back until his cock barely clung to the lips of my pussy, and then he rammed forward as he covered my mouth with his.

I cried as he fucked me. Cried for the loss of his dad, for the little boy who'd been abandoned, for the hell he'd been put through, and for the fact that I'd gone an entire week without this connection. When we were together, everything seemed right. Nothing could break us as long as we stayed glued to one another.

"I love you. I won't abandon you again, Mila. Never again," he promised and lied.

ATLAS

The lights above blinded me as I went into my second original song, but the last of the second set for the evening. Bodies swayed and gyrated all around the stage, but I only had eyes for one crazy-beautiful woman. Every time she turned around and presented me with her bare back and the ass-hugging, barely there dress, I groaned internally. My girl was going to get a massive spanking for rocking that dress when I couldn't be there to touch and tease. I'd have to make her wear it again, only to a proper dinner. Even though we'd been officially a couple for closing on two months now, we didn't spend much time dining out. Frankly, neither of us had the money. But we found ways to make up for that. Like tonight. I was rocking out at Harmony Jack's, and my woman was dancing the night away.

I couldn't wait to sing the song I'd written for her especially after I had avoided her for a week. The shit we found in the safe-deposit box had taken its toll on me. I had been treading water, drowning in a sea of heartache over what my dad had done. Leaving me that money and the gallery my grandfather had owned. Another thing I still hadn't discussed with Mila but would much later tonight after I'd made love to her. And it would be making love. We'd both said the words, however randomly, but they were there; the feelings were mutual, and we didn't have to repeat them all the time to know it lived between us.

When she showed up at my class a few days ago and put me in my place after leaving her hanging all week, that meant more to me than she'd ever know. It meant she'd fought for us, for what was between us. I'd never had a woman besides my mom fight for me. An entirely new but not unwelcome sensation. Since that day, I'd gotten inside Mila as much as humanly possible. I wouldn't have been surprised if the girl was bowlegged for how many times I'd fucked her the past few days. I just couldn't get enough. She didn't complain and now she was here, supporting me in my dream even if it was just a pub in San Francisco.

Standing away from the stool, I shimmied my hips in a silly Elvis-esque move and shredded on the guitar to get her attention. The crowd went wild, clapping and screaming when I belted out the last word. Mila had been dancing and clapping along with the rest of them. The lights blinked out right at the end of my song. Once they slowly came back on, though lower than normal, I knew it was break time.

"Thanks so much! I'll be back for another couple sets in about thirty minutes."

After I addressed the crowd, I hopped down and went looking for my girl. I found her waiting dead center of the dance floor, as usual, arms ready for me.

She surrounded me with her flower-and-cinnamon scent

as I put my arms around her. I pushed my hands right into the open back of her dress and palmed her ass. I felt a pathetic scrap of lace going straight between her butt cheeks covering absolutely nothing of the goods that lay under it. "You're wearing underwear?" I growled into her ear, nibbling on the bit of flesh.

Mila jerked her hips against my denim-covered hardening cock. "Yeah, I didn't think you'd be happy with me going commando in a dress this short."

"Dead right." I squeezed her ass and teased the fabric with my finger. "Yet, you still chose to rock my world with this sexy as fuck scrap of fabric. Are you trying to taunt me?"

She pulled back and grinned. "No, but anticipation is half the fun, right? Just think how great it will be to take it off of me later."

I ran my nose along the thin column of her neck, inhaling deeply of her scent, imprinting it on me. I kissed her once, then twice. "Come on. I need a drink before my next set."

Mila threaded her thumb through my belt loop, a comforting weight I'd become accustomed to.

Just as we hit the bar, Jack was there.

"Sounding killer, Powers! Your fans are doubling the nights you're here. Need to get you on the schedule for the next couple months." She laid out a frosty cold beer for me and what looked like a gin and tonic for Mila. I never knew what the girl was drinking because it always changed based on what she was in the mood for that evening.

"Thanks, Jack!" I dipped my chin and then sucked back a long pull of the pale ale. The hops flavor instantly quenched my parched palate.

"She is not wrong," came a voice from behind me. I half

expected one of my bros, since I'd told the guys I'd be playing tonight, and usually on a weekend, the gang would come. So far, it had been crickets. I turned around and stopped short at a man in a suit. Now, I wasn't talking about a suit you'd get at Macy's. No, this suit cost more than my rent—for the year. He wore a pair of black wire-rimmed glasses and a satin tie that said, "I can buy whatever I damn well want and will look damn good doing it."

"Uh, thanks." I looped my arm around Mila's neck. "Can I help you?"

The man smirked. "No, because I'm here to help you." His tone was overconfident and rather smug.

"Is that so?"

"It is." He rolled back and then forward from his heels to his toes.

"Care to elaborate?"

He pursed his lips and put his hands into his pockets. "Name's James Pinkerton and I'm going to make you a very rich man."

Pinkerton. Pinkerton. Pinkerton. Where the hell did I know that name?

I knew I'd heard it before, but for the life of me, I couldn't remember where. Mila chuckled next to me.

"Guy is pretty sure of himself, babe," she said dryly, looking him up and down.

Mila and I didn't exactly have an easy go of trusting others. We were trying our damndest just to trust one another in this relationship we'd agreed upon. Daily, I had to press down the desire to second-guess every decision either of us made because I wanted us to work. So far, I'd never been happier, but having two driven individuals, both used to being alone and so set in their ways, trying to be one half of a whole wasn't easy. It took hard work, and the results to date had far outweighed any of the downsides.

The man pulled out a shiny black card with raised metallic blue lettering. Blue Lake Entertainment. James Pinkerton, Executive Producer.

Holy shit.

"Uh..."

"I see you now understand who I am and where I come from. I've been watching you. Three times now. You have a great voice, an interesting grunge look, and you play well. You're a bit old to be entering the industry this late in the game, but I'm good at my job. I can make you everything you want to be and more."

My heart stopped. Just stopped beating. Everything I'd ever hoped for had happened. Blue Lake Entertainment was the biggest record label in music today. Everything they touched turned to gold and every artist they took on went platinum. They were the dream makers.

"I'm, uh, gonna dance while you talk okay?" Mila said, patting my arm.

"Yeah, sure, okay." I watched her go and then turned so that I could keep my eye on her and speak to the executive.

"Hot piece of ass. You share that tail?" Pinkerton's smarmy tone made my hackles rise in spite of my excitement.

I shook it off and held my hands in front of me. "No, man. That's my woman."

"Oh, well..." he huffed, "not for long. You're about to get so much tail on the road you'll be up to your eyeballs in pussy every day of the week."

I cringed. "Not likely. I'm happy with what's mine."

He laughed and watched Mila shake her ass on the dance floor.

"So, what is it that you're interested in?"

Pinkerton rubbed his palms together, his eyes still on my girl and not on me, nor was his attention focused on the conversation we were having, though he still answered. "Everything. You'll work for Blue Lake Entertainment exclusively. Go where we want you to go. Sing what we want you to sing. Wear what we want you to wear, and together we'll make millions." Eventually his eyes flicked back to me. "You dig?"

A sour taste hit my mouth. "Not really. Sing what you want me to sing? I have my own music."

He laughed hard. "Nobody writes their own music anymore. Besides, your songs are alternative. I'm going to make you into a pop star. By the way, can you dance?"

I cringed. "Dance?"

His eyes once more were not on me but glued to Mila's ass. Admittedly, it was a mighty fine ass, but he also knew she was mine. Typically, when a guy knew a girl was off limits, he reacted by not continuing to eye-fuck her. This suit-wearing, needle-dick had not apparently learned that social grace.

I clenched my jaw, trying to breathe through the anger boiling just under the surface when I saw a man approach Mila on the dance floor. His hands went to her hips in a proprietary way, and she pulled away and turned around. I took a step toward her, but Mr. Pinkerton's arm came out and stopped me from progressing.

"Last thing you need for your image is a bar brawl. Wouldn't look good for my newly *signed* talent." He emphasized the signed part even though nothing had gotten that far.

I ground my teeth so hard I could hear them inside my head. I grabbed his arm and pushed it down. "Not everything ends in a fight. Excuse me while I tend to my woman."

Mila was struggling with the guy grabbing at her waist, attempting to rub up her body. I rushed to him and shoved him away from her. "Dude, get your fucking hands off her."

The dude laughed. "Don't worry, guy. It's okay. I've had my hands and mouth all over this woman. Just a couple of months ago, right, sweetie? You sucked me off so good."

Mila frowned and looked away.

Another man wearing a cowboy hat standing near the dance floor stepped in. "This your woman or yours? Because I've had her, too. Yeah, what's your name? Chelsi or something."

"Mila," I said, looking at her with my hand still out to the handsy fucker at my right.

"Mila?" the other guy said, shaking his head no. "That was not her name when I was fucking her the month before last, either. Actually had her a couple times, months in between, but she couldn't remember my name the first time, so I figured why bring it up. Shit, I'll bet every guy in here has had a go. Definitely hot in the sack and sucks dick like a Hoover!" the big cowboy-looking man said.

That was all it took for me to lose my mind. I pulled my arm back and crashed my fist into cowboy hat's face.

His head jerked back unnaturally before he fell back a few steps.

"Atlas, no!" Mila screamed.

That's when the handsy fucker came at me, shoving me to the ground. I popped up and barreled into him like a linebacker knocking him into a table. By this time, cowboy hat had gotten back up and wanted his own go.

"Let's go, partner..." He gestured in a come-hither move.

"No! No! Please stop!" Mila jumped in front of me.

I growled, "Back up. No one talks about you like that. No one!"

"Even if it's true?" she screamed in my face. "I fucked both of them. I barely remember, but I did before I met you."

"Told you, man. She's a whore." The handsy guy rubbed at his jaw.

At this point, Jack, the owner, was right in the middle of our circle with her burly black security guard who could bench lift about a million pounds on each arm. "Break this shit up. Now. You and you"—she pointed to the cowboy and handsy—"out. And don't come back. You're blacklisted."

She then turned to me. "Atlas, I don't even know what to say," Jack whispered, her face set in a grimace. "You of all people know better. No fighting in my bar. It's a hard-and-fast rule. The one rule you don't fucking break! Now get out of here. Both of you."

"What about my set?" I grated through my teeth.

"I think you've given the crowd enough entertainment for the night, don't you? I'll call you if, IF I'm going to have you back. You know better." She shook her head again as if she was more depressed about kicking me out than I possibly could be. "Fuckin' best gig I had. Christ!" she finished, threw a towel over her shoulder, and went back to the bar.

I turned around and walked toward the stage. James Pinkerton stood there with a scowl. "Lose my card. Told you not to interfere. Blue Lake Entertainment doesn't hire losers with control issues. We're in control."

Then he walked off, my dreams of working with the

biggest label of all time a whisper in the wind.

Mila didn't say anything to me, but followed me silently as I gathered my things and headed for the exit.

The car ride was excruciating. All I could think about was how fucking stupid I had been to think I was special to her. She'd had two guys in her bed not long before we got together. What kind of woman does that? Shit!

When we arrived at her house, I pulled up to the curb. I had no intention of coming in. I hadn't said a word to her because I didn't know what to say. In one single night, I'd gotten in a bar fight, ruined my chances of ever working for Blue Lake Entertainment, my dream label, and probably lost my highest paying gig, all because I'd defended a woman who fucked everything with a hard cock.

She opened the door and turned sideways to look at me before getting out.

I shook my head and put my hand up. "Go," I growled.

"I'm sorry, Atlas. Can we please talk about this? Those men, they were before you." Her voice was a broken mess of tears.

"Yeah, and you didn't even recognize two men that you opened your legs for. What's that say about me? You gonna remember down the road when you scrape me off, too?" I clenched my teeth and ground out, "I'm sorry I ever believed you loved me. I'm sorry I ever thought I could love a woman. You made me lose everything tonight. Everything! All because you couldn't keep your legs closed." I roared, "Now Get. The Fuck. Out."

I didn't even recognize my voice as she got out of the car, tears streaming down her pretty face. She was pretty even when she cried. Once the door was shut, she leaned into the open window. I gripped the wheel so hard I thought my knuckles would crack.

"You said you'd never abandon me," she whispered.

Mila's tone was so filled with remorse I had to choke down my own tears and fill my mind with the anger of what occurred that evening.

"Yeah, and I thought our relationship wouldn't ruin my life. We were both wrong," I managed through clenched teeth.

I had to go. I just had to get the fuck out of there, away from her, away from heartache, loss, and everything she represented. So I revved the engine until she removed her hands, and I sped away, leaving my heart at the curb in front of her house.

CHAPTER NINETEEN

SOLAR PLEXUS
C H A K R A

When a person's solar plexus chakra is in alignment, they are not only very ambitious, but also self-aware, and they naturally evoke an energetic strength that is desirable and magnetic. This person has a deep value to those in their life that can keep their word and fulfill responsibilities and obligations without their interference. Connecting with someone with a fully engaged manipura is like standing next to a living, breathing power source.

ATLAS

They said when a person went from a dry state such as California and enters a humid state, such as Hawaii, they acclimated quickly. I did not find that statement to be true. Every breath I'd taken felt as though I was breathing under water. And the heat, wet heat....Jesus. Nothing like back home.

In California, it was hot. In the dead of summer, it could be absolutely brutal. At least in the Valley it was. In the Bay, I appreciated the chill off the ocean, so it was never too hot and never too humid. Hawaii, though warm, made you sweat, and that sweat did not dry. Ever. I felt perpetually misty, either from the random bouts of rain that would fall, or the dewiness settling on my skin from the heat or humidity.

Hawaii was beautiful and all, but just like the song, I left my heart in San Francisco. Literally. I hadn't talked to Mila in two weeks. I'd left her at that curb and spent the last two weeks fucking off and figuring out what the hell I was going to do with my life. One thing I did was take the money my father left me and gave half of it to my mother. When I handed her a check for a hundred and thirty thousand dollars, she started crying. Big heaving sobs. She thought I'd signed a music deal and hit it big. Which I had, but not in the way she thought.

Last week, I also met with Silas McKnight. The guy in person was, by far, the coolest dude. He had just enough hair that you knew he cut it that short on purpose, not because he was bald or had a receding hair line. He rocked dark jeans with a white T-shirt and a black corduroy blazer that, on him, looked sharp and expensive yet still casual. He sat me down and made me a different offer than I'd ever expected.

★ ★ ★

"Thanks for coming, Atlas."

I nodded. "Glad to be here. Thanks for the extra week on the songs. I was in a bit of a funk that I had to work through."

Silas rubbed at his chin. "And did you work through it?"

"Yeah, by writing those songs." I gestured to the written

words I'd handed him so that he'd have a copy of what I'd worked on. Six songs in total. Three I'd had, including "Maybe Someday," "Probably Never," a couple others he'd heard at Harmony Jack's, and the three additional tunes he asked for where I'd included the most precious one I'd simply named "Wildcat."

Silas had read and heard the songs prior to my arrival. He wanted to hear them in advance of our meeting, so I'd recorded them using my acoustic guitar, singing a cappella on my cheapo player, and sent them via e-mail.

"So, I'm sure you think you know why you're here, but man, I need to be up front with you. I have a different reason than you probably imagine."

I frowned and leaned my elbows on my knees, clasped my hands in front of me, and rested my chin on them. "Okay, shoot. Why am I here?"

Silas sat back and put his ankle up on his knee. "You're a brilliant song writer."

I smiled. "Thank you."

"But I'm not going to sign you as a musical artist."

My heart plummeted. This was it. My last chance to make something of my music career. I'd already fucked up the Blue Lake Entertainment, though the more I'd thought about it, the less likely I would have wanted to truly work with them anyway. They just wanted to change me.

"Okay then, help me understand why you couldn't just deliver that news over the phone." My tone was flat and lacked any emotion. Just like my heart over the last week. Emotionless.

Silas ran a finger along his bottom lip. "I want to make you a different offer."

I pushed up and pressed my palms down my denim-clad thighs. "Such as?"

"Song writer and producer."

I blinked and then blinked again, trying to wipe away any remaining shock that blasted my vision completely. "Excuse me?"

"Atlas, bro, your songs are deep. Intense. Make people feel things. Unfortunately, you have shit for stage presence. You can't dance. And sorry to say, brother, your voice cracks and becomes pitchy after the second set."

Boom! Nothing like getting smashed between the truth and reality. I knew my shoulders sagged and all the wind left my sails. "But you want me to write for you?"

He nodded. "I know talent when I see it. Part of what makes Knight & Day Productions so good is that we know how to work with people on using their best assets to come together as a team, building greatness. I see you writing songs and honing new talent into something great, something Knight & Day could be proud of."

"Songwriter and producer. Man, I like the sound of that." I didn't even try to hide the awe in my tone.

Silas grinned wickedly. "Me, too. Also comes with your own sound room. You can work from home as much as you like, when you're not working with the talent, that is. You can help me scout out talent; you'll receive a six-figure salary with bonuses if your songs hit lists, full medical, dental, retirement, and all that jazz. We take care of people because when we've got skill like yours, we want to keep you happy."

"Holy shit. Six figures?"

"To start, you'll be making a hundred and seventy-five a year and then you've got the bonuses to look forward to. I believe in you, and I'm going to put my money where my mouth is."

"Wow, um, yeah you are."

"Take some time to think about it."

I shook my head. "Don't need it. This was my end goal, man. I planned on singing and playing music until I could get in with a company and do what I love best. Create music. The stage is great, and it's fun, but I want a family one day in the not-too-distant future. Besides, like you said, I can't dance, my voice cracks, and I'm pitchy."

Silas chuckled and held out his hand. "Too true. Welcome to the family, brother."

★ ★ ★

The gallery was yellow, and an ocean was painted on the entire back side of it where I parked my rental. As much as I wanted to dread this moment, I didn't. I hadn't seen my father in twenty years. Knowing he'd been living the good life on an island while my mom and I barely made ends meet destroyed any emotion other than anger, the anger I held onto as I walked through the gallery. The sales associate, who I found out was his current woman or *"wahine"* in Hawaiian, told me that Kenny was out soaking up the sun on the beach in the back of the gallery, which was conveniently attached to their home.

I thanked the pretty woman. She seemed younger than my mom, but still was an appropriate age for a man my dad's age. Then again, who knew? Mom had wrinkles on top of her wrinkles from having to live a harder life than she should have.

Once I'd made my way through the gallery to the sliding glass doors, I saw an umbrella plopped into the sand around a hundred or so feet out in the distance. A pair of feet stuck out from the view.

With a heavy heart bristling with anger, I tromped

through the sand toward the sunbather. When I arrived, I stood looking at my father. He'd aged a lot. Twenty years would do that to a person. Nevertheless, he was tan and thin, with a sculpted chest and arms, a salt-and-pepper beard and matching curly hair. He was me, only twenty-five years older. I could easily imagine looking exactly like him when I was in my fifties.

"Hey, brah, you're blocking my view," my father said.

I stood there unmoving, just taking in all that was my father. Then I removed my glasses and crossed my arms over my chest.

He sat up and pushed his glasses up into his hairline. The same eyes as I'd seen in the mirror every day of my life stared back at me. It was funny how you didn't remember things like that until you came face-to-face with it again.

"Well I'll be damned. You finally came," he said, awe and excitement clear in his tone.

I squinted. "I finally came? That's what you have to say to me?"

He huffed. "Took you long enough. What's it been, twenty years?" He sat back and lifted a beer to his lips and sucked a slug back. "I gave you that key forever ago."

He'd given me the key... "What? Are you for real?"

"'Course I am. I'm your old man. Now pull up a chair, son." He gestured to the lounger next to him.

He could not be for real. "You left me. Us. Mom and me. Twenty years ago, and you want me to just pull up a chair?"

My father frowned and sighed. "I'm taking it you didn't get the money until now?"

I saw red. And instead of punching his lights out, I lifted my foot and kicked sand at him. Several times actually, just like a fucking child throwing a tantrum.

He lifted his hands and hopped up. "Not cool, man."

"Not cool! *Not cool?* Abandoning your eight-year-old is not fucking cool!? Leaving a woman who loved you in the lurch is *not cool*? Disappearing for twenty years is *not cool*?" I yelled so loud I was pretty sure the folks on the connecting islands heard me. If not, they were about to get another earful.

My father pressed his hands up and down in an "easy there, fella" move. "Now just wait a minute. I left you the key. Told you it would change your life."

"You also said you'd come back." The hurt in my voice overwhelmed the anger, and I winced, not wanting him to hear what his actions really did to me.

"Well, you've got me there," he admitted.

I scoffed. "Just tell me right now. Why did you leave Mom and me?"

He ran a hand through his windblown hair and then rubbed at his beard. "Loved your mom. I did. Loved you something fierce."

I huffed. "Yeah, then why you'd leave?"

"At the time, I loved my art more than your mom. With you, felt I had nothing left to offer you. Promised myself I'd make something of myself, put it all away for your future. That's why I gave you the key. Knew when you were older, you'd figure it out. Didn't think it would take this long, though."

I gripped my hair and tugged on the strands. "You didn't think it would take this long. You're insane."

He shrugged. "Maybe. But I'm happy. I did well by you monetarily. Gave you that business so you could keep having something to live off of." He clucked his tongue. "Way I see it, me leaving was the best thing for you."

"You are certifiable. A boy needs his father, not cash or a business. I can't believe you think that's what I'd want. What I wanted was you, in my life, every day. Taking care of me, taking care of my mom." I glanced around at his beachfront gallery on the North Shore side of the island. The place must have cost a mint, yet here he was, soaking up the sun and thinking that abandoning me was a good decision.

"Now that I've seen you, I can tell you exactly what you did. You leaving...broke me. It practically killed my mother. We struggled so much and so hard, there were times I wasn't sure where we were going to get our next meal. But we kept on working hard and finally we came out of it. Without you. And you know what, *Dad*..." I spoke through my frustration. "We're going to continue doing it without you. I got your letters, I got your cash, I got the business you left for me, and you know what? I'm going to use it to do some good. So thank you for that, for that small token of kindness. Now you can live free in the knowledge that your son and wife back on the mainland are just fine without you in their lives."

"Son, please. Come on. Let's get to know one another. Share a beer. I'll introduce you to my *wahine*."

I bit down on my lip so hard it hurt, but not as much as my heart. This man, he didn't love anyone but himself. He saved up that cash and gave those things because he felt obligated and guilty. As he should have, and should continue to feel for the rest of his natural life. He abandoned me.

Briefly, I thought of Mila. I'd abandoned her, too, just like my father did me. Abandoned the only thing I knew was real in my life. I was no different than him. Abandoning the one person who loved me for me, regardless of what I could give her. Fuck. I messed up. So bad. I knew that I had to deal with my father, my life, my career, before I went back to her, but I was going back to her. After the time that had passed, though, I hoped to hell she'd take me back. Again.

"I gotta go." Suddenly, the need to hop back on an airplane headed for California was all encompassing. Getting my shit in order would take priority so I could win back Mila. "Have a nice life, Dad."

He scrambled to follow placing his hand on my bicep. "Wait, are you ever coming back?" His voice sounded rough, as though he'd actually felt a hint of emotion. Maybe even remorse, but I doubted it.

I shrugged off his hold and said the same words he said to me, only I switched them up a bit. "Maybe someday...probably never."

MILA

The last two weeks rivaled the weeks leading up to my dad getting indicted and my mom leaving for her new family. Atlas might have been abandoned when he was a little boy, but he'd still had his mom. I didn't have anyone back then. I thanked my lucky stars for Moe and Lily, though. She'd been my rock since the breakup. Of course, she'd also been hopeful that Atlas would get his head out of the sand and come groveling back. So far...nothing but crickets.

Moe handed me an omelet filled to the brim with spinach, black olives, tomatoes, and cheddar cheese. And she made it to where the insides were full and the thin layer of egg flapped over the goodies instead of scrambling it all together.

"I'm telling you, that man loves you." She flung the spatula around in a circle. "I for one am not ready to give up."

I rolled my eyes and cut the tip of the omelet. "If he loved me so much, he wouldn't have gone, and *stayed gone,* for the past two weeks."

She pursed her lips. "Yeah, but no one else has seen him, either. Even Dash mentioned that he'd fallen off the radar."

"Yeah well, I hope he fell into a hole and smashed his pretty face!"

Moe gasped. "Mila, you don't mean that."

I groaned and then let my head fall into my hand. "No, I don't mean that. Fuck, this whole loving someone sucks so bad."

"Love? You love him?" Moe's eyes sparkled with interest.

I sighed. "Honey, isn't it obvious by how miserable I am? It seems like people in love are always miserable for one reason or another."

"Uh, yeah, but you've never admitted it before." She blinked prettily.

"Probably because this is the first time it's ever happened to me, and would you look at that...I ruined it without even trying. Go figure." I cringed.

Moe's shoulders slumped, and she leaned against the counter. "Everyone has a past, and most people's aren't ever that good. Believe me. I know."

I thought about the fact that all she did was talk people through bad marriages, bad divorces, grief counseling, life counseling, child custody battles, and court mediation. She definitely knew what she was talking about. Still it didn't change the fact that two weeks had gone by with no sign of my curly-haired musician.

"Have you tried to call him?"

I shook my head. "What would I say? Sorry I'm a whore?"

Moe slapped the counter. "You are not a whore."

"But I kind of was. I had a lot of one-night hookups, girl. Too many to even count. I'd go to a bar, let a hot guy buy me drinks all night, go back to his place, scratch that sexual itch, and then, when he fell asleep, I'd slink away into my Uber and go home. One and then done."

"I'll agree that's a bit slutty, but a whore gets paid and you weren't taking their money. Besides, you are a sexually independent being and can have sex with whomever you want. You weren't doing it when you were with Atlas officially, were you?"

I shook my head hard, my hair flying against my cheek. "No. Not even since the day I met him."

"There you go. You're in the clear. Frankly, it's on him, but I do think maybe since it ended so badly with both of you saying some harsh words, maybe you could, at the very least, extend a teeny tiny olive branch?" She held up her thumb and forefinger about the size of an inch.

Right then the phone rang. Moe answered, listened for a minute, and handed it to me. "For you."

Very few people knew Moe's home number because I didn't give it out willy-nilly. She was a hot commodity and freak-nasties in the court system along with pissed off jealous exes tended to like to take out their anger out on someone, so we didn't advertise our phone and had the number blocked.

"Hello?" I said.

"Hello, Ms. Mercado?"

"Yes."

A nasally voice came through the line. "I'm Ingrid from Second Chances Gallery."

"Okay, uh, how can I help you?"

Moe narrowed her eyes and crinkled her nose. "Who is it?" she mouthed.

I shrugged.

"I was given your information by an anonymous source who has seen and shared photos of your recent work. I understand that La Luz Gallery passed on a solo showing of your work, but we'd like to offer you the opposite."

All at once, it felt like the blood had drained from my entire body. My bones turned to mush, and my heart leapt as I gripped the phone tightly to my ear. "You what?"

"Want to show your work. In two weeks' time."

"In two weeks?"

"Yes, is that going to be a problem? According to my source, you haven't sold any of the paintings, and you're not slated to show the architectural work for another month, which means we can scoop you up now. Is that not correct?" Her voice hardened.

I rubbed a hand over my face, not sure how to take what I was hearing. "No, I haven't sold them and no, La Luz wasn't going to show the architectural pieces until next month sometime. We hadn't set a date."

"Good for us. Bad for them. I'd like to come and take photos and specs of the canvases so that I can plan a layout. We'll also need to determine pricing for the art, provided you want to sell them after the six-week long showing. Will that be possible today? There simply is no time to waste."

My mind scrambled to keep up. Not only did my fondest dream call me directly, but they also were fast-tracking my career into the stratosphere, and I had no idea why. "No, that will be fine. I just...I didn't expect you to call. This is all so sudden."

"Yes, well, our owner is very interested in your work and having you show."

"I...I don't know what to say."

"Say you'll be prepared for me in two hours, Ingrid."

"I'll be prepared for you in two hours, Ingrid."

We both chuckled, though hers was a bit more forced.

"All right then. We'll see you in two hours," she continued, reading off my address. How she got that, I had no idea.

Moe sipped at her coffee. "Who was that? I thought I was going to have to take the phone away and find out who was threatening you. In the span of a five-minute call, you went white as a ghost, then red as a strawberry, and now you just look shell-shocked."

"That was Second Chances Gallery in San Francisco. They're even bigger than La Luz."

"And..." Moe rolled her hand in a move-it-along gesture.

"They want to do a showing of all my work in two weeks."

Her mouth dropped open. "Oh. My. God. A full solo show?"

I nodded, no longer capable of speaking.

She jumped up and down and did a dance, and then she ran around to me. I hopped out of my stool, and she barreled into me with a hug. Then we jumped up and down, screaming at the top of our lungs, laughing and crying.

"I knew you could do it." She wiped at her eyes. "I just knew someone special was going to see your art and know its value. We have to celebrate!"

"And we will." I wiped at the tears tracking down my cheeks, too. "But first, we get ready because Ingrid is coming over in two hours to size and price the paintings and discuss a layout plan. Oh my god! This is so awesome and crazy, and

I have to call Atlas!" I squealed and then it hit me. I couldn't call Atlas. He was no longer in my life. He didn't care about me getting my first solo showing because he left me.

"Yes, we'll tell everyone!" Moe said, not catching on to my troubling moment.

I nodded and then plastered a thin smile on my face. "Yes, yes, we will." *Except for one person, because he doesn't care anymore.* I kept that last part to myself and followed Moe into my room so we could pick out what I was going to wear for the gallery rep who was coming to the house. Then we'd pick out what I was going to wear for the actual showing. My dreams were coming true. I was getting the one thing I'd always wanted. The shitty part—I no longer had the man I loved to share it with.

Sometimes, life sucked.

CHAPTER TWENTY

Child's Pose (Sanskrit: Balasana)

Child's pose in yoga is the primary resting pose. It is used in almost every single yoga class to give the body and mind a moment of peace. Typically, the position has the arms out, lying on the mat, stretched out in front of you, but the modification of tucking the arms can also be done. Kneel with your knees wide. Lay your chest down between your bent legs resting your forehead on the mat. Stretch your arms out wide or tuck them in. Breathe.

MILA

Everything was perfectly in place. I followed Ingrid around the room, making sure each piece looked just right. The walls of the gallery were a muted gray. Red trim ran along the edge of the ceiling, giving it a very modern feel. Movable track lighting worked its magic, highlighting every single painting beautifully. I couldn't have dreamed of such a stunning setup. Along one wall, the gallery had a bar, and a variety of bite-sized desserts were set up for patrons to nibble on while they perused the art. Waiters were set to walk around hand delivering appetizers and noshes. Ingrid assured me this was standard and that the gallery was paying for it. The event fees would come out of their cut on whatever sold. Which was risky in my opinion because what if nothing sold? Totally not my problem.

I shook my head, flinging away the negative thoughts. No, someone would buy a painting and when that happened, I'd silently squeal.

"Mila, I've changed the price on *Blatant Desire* because I honestly feel as though you've priced it far under its value." Ingrid frowned.

Blatant Desire was the nude of Atlas sitting on the stool his erection strong and proud, standing at attention. I wanted that painting gone. G-O-N-E. I needed no further reminder of what that man meant to me, now or then.

"Whatever you say. I just really want it sold, so if someone seems interested and needs a price adjustment, feel free to go a few hundred lower so that it disappears."

She nodded curtly and turned in her Louis Vuittons. In the corner, I was surprised to see a gallery attendant setting up a microphone, a stool, and small amplifier. As Ingrid breezed past, I grabbed her arm.

"There's live music tonight?"

Ingrid smiled flatly as if it took her extreme effort to do so. "The new owner wanted to offer something special. It's completely unprecedented. We've had music in the past but usually just pumped through the speakers, not live." She put her hand on my shoulder. "Don't worry, I'm told he's very good. Anyway, he's the boss and what he says, goes. Do you have a problem with it?"

I blinked and shook my head. "No, not at all." I shrugged. "Whatever works." The last thing I planned on doing was rocking the boat of the man who'd given me my first big break. "Did you ever find out how the owner learned about my art? Was it Steven at La Luz?"

She pursed her lips. "Not sure. Maybe. I didn't question him since we were just recently informed he owned it. I was under the impression that there was someone out of state who owned it, but all of a sudden this young man was being introduced by the gallery lawyer as the new owner. Don't worry, dear. The plan to show your work for the next six weeks was his idea, so you haven't anything to be concerned about."

Just as I was going to tell her to thank him, she bustled off again, her face pinched and her heels clicking against the marble floor, going after someone adjusting one of my paintings. "Don't you touch that! Are you mad? That piece is worth several thousand dollars."

I spun around on my wedge heels and slimmed down my simple red dress. It clung to every inch of my body, but I worked hard and I felt good about the way I looked. Today of all days I had to put up the front that I was happy. And I was, for the most part. My dreams were coming true, my paintings were on the walls of a swank San Francisco gallery, and all my friends were coming to see the show.

God, I miss Atlas. If I could only share this with him.

No matter what I did, the curly-haired yoga hottie was never far from my thoughts. I hadn't seen him in a month, and

I still couldn't get him out of my mind. He'd left Lotus House and practically disappeared. At one point, I did break down and ask Dash if he'd seen him and whether or not he was okay. Dash said he'd gone to Hawaii to work out something. I knew that to be his father, but I didn't share that with his friend. If he wanted to tell Dash about his father and where he'd been and what he'd been up to for the last twenty years, that was on him.

Dash did, however, confide in me that Atlas had taken a position with Knight & Day Productions. Hearing that information had filled my heart with extreme joy. Knowing that he didn't lose out on all his musical options because of me made it somehow that much easier to breathe.

Slowly people started to fill the gallery. Way more people than I expected. I walked over to Ingrid and waited patiently behind her while she explained to prospective customers that the painting I'd labeled *Tantric Innocence* was the only painting hanging that was not for sale. Much to her dismay, I'd promised it to Dash and Amber and would not budge on it. She directed them over to the other painting around the corner that had a nude couple. It was actually the same couple, only they were facing one another. Amber had her legs around his waist and was sitting in his lap. Her breasts were smashed up against his chest, and they were kissing. If you didn't know the couple personally, you'd never know it was them. They were fine with me painting this one and selling it, just not the one that showed their body parts or their faces forward.

"Ingrid, there are a lot more people here than I expected," I said as the patrons kept coming through.

She nodded and glanced at the door. "Yes, the new owner spent a considerable dollar marketing this show. He's apparently very taken with your art." She grinned.

"Will I meet him?" I asked.

"Of course, although he wanted to stay anonymous until the time was right." She batted her lashes and smirked. "Guess you're special to him."

I gasped. "I just have no idea why."

She shrugged. "Secret admirer perhaps." She leaned forward, as if to share a golden nugget of gossip. "He's really good-looking and every time he mentioned your name, his entire face lit up like a Christmas Day parade. I think you've got a crush on your hands."

I laughed out loud. "I don't know anyone in the art world besides Steven, and he's gay!" I shook my head.

Right then, I felt a little tug on the bottom of my dress and looked down. My baby girl was cheesy smiling at me, her hair in perfect pigtails with little pink bows. I crouched down and scooped up Lily. "Hi, baby." I snuggled against her neck, her sweet baby lotion smell comforting my nerves.

"We are here to see art!" she said with glee and clapped her hands together. "Mommy says you a star!" She crunched up her nose and tilted her head one way and then the other. "I see no stars on you."

I laughed and snugged her again as Moe chuckled behind us. I spun around. "Hey, Moe. Thanks for coming."

She looked affronted. "As if I'd ever miss this. I saw the entire gang from your work parking cars. Oh, there they are now." She pointed to the door.

True to her word, in came Trent with his arm wrapped around Genevieve. He wore a slick suit with a pocket square and tie that were the exact hot pink of Vivvie's dress. Total class. Behind them were Dash and Amber. Dash was wearing dress slacks and an artsy button-up shirt. Amber, always prim and proper, looked like Audrey Hepburn in a cream-colored sheath, and her hair was up in a high bun. Next in line was Nicolas Salerno, who had Dara Jackson on his arm. I knew they were best friends, but together they did look like a model duo. He wore a suit with no tie, the collar of his dress shirt unbuttoned at the neck to show a bit of his golden chest. His hair was slicked back perfectly. He led Dara, who wore a navy-blue sequined, strapless cocktail dress with her dark skin seeming to glow along with the sequins and her tawny hair falling down her bare back and around her shoulders. Simple elegance.

They all made their way toward me. "Hey, guys! Thank you for coming."

I hugged each of them individually as the men went to get drinks. Clayton Hart came through the door, spotted me, and smiled as he walked over. Before I knew it, he was hugging me. "Proud of you. Atlas is, too," he whispered in my ear.

Just the mention of the man I loved and hadn't seen in a month was an icicle to the heart. I stiffened in his arms, forcing that armor around my heart to harden. "Yeah, well, I wish he were here to see this." My voice shook, but I swallowed down the emotion. This was no time for breaking down now. Not tonight. Not when everything I'd ever worked for was hanging on the walls for all the world to see.

Ingrid rushed over to me. "Excuse me. We need her." She pulled me away as I waved at my friends. Clay looked at Moe, then at Lily, and then turned and left them standing there. I had no idea what that was about, but I planned to ask him when I got a chance.

"You'll never believe this," Ingrid spoke speedily in my ear, her overwhelmingly fragrant perfume invading my senses and tickling the back of my throat.

I coughed trying to expel some of her scent. "What?"

"Every nude has already sold and several of your architectural ones as well. You may end up with a sellout show. That would be the first time that has ever happened in the two years I've worked here!" She was practically bouncing. I wanted to hold onto her wrist to make sure she didn't fall over in her shoes, but then I heard the strum of a guitar.

I attempted to listen to Ingrid, but the guitar and the murmured voice that went with it was too familiar. The notes dug through my pores, went into my bloodstream, and wrapped around my heart.

"I've got to..." I started walking away, and she grabbed my hand.

"Mila..." she said, concern coating her tone.

"No, I know that voice. It's..." The crowd cleared a path, and there he was. Sitting on a stool, his foot resting on one rung, his acoustic guitar resting on his thigh, the most beautiful smile adorning his lips. And he was looking at me. Atlas's eyes shone under the light, and in that moment, he was more stunning to me than any piece of art in the entire place.

"Aw, there's my girl. The woman of the night. The artist we are all here to see. Mila Mercado everyone. Let's give her a hand for sharing this beauty with us tonight."

Everyone around applauded as I made my way to where Atlas was sitting. I still couldn't believe he was here. I stopped about ten feet away in the semicircle that had been created around him. All my friends were there, the guys grinning and the women tearing up.

"You see everyone, a month ago, I walked away from the only woman I ever loved. Tonight, I'm here to grovel, beg, borrow, and plead to win her back. I love you, Mila, and I wrote this song for you. It's called, 'Wildcat.'"

ATLAS

Mila was a vision in red. The dress clung to every inch of her beautiful mocha-colored skin in the most delectable way possible. I wanted to run my tongue down the silky fabric and see if her natural taste and scent would bleed through the fabric. I'd bet every last dollar I had that it would.

Her hair was filled with curls, one side swept back so that I could easily see her caramel-colored eyes. Christ, I missed her. Not until that very second did it hit me how much I *ached* for her presence in my life.

I addressed the crowd but kept my eyes on the woman I loved while she stood there, as still as a statue. Not a hint of her facade cracking. Only I knew better. Inside she'd be an emotional wreck. I could see it in her eyes, the way she wanted to run to me, the way she hurt for me. It broke my heart how very much I'd screwed up what we had by not fighting for her, for us. I'd never make that mistake again. Never. My only hope was that through being here tonight, showing her work, singing this song, she'd find it in her to forgive me.

I cleared my voice, strummed the melody and then let my soul speak.

Seeing you is seeing my future
Painted brushstrokes on a picture

These days away, have broken me down
With our love we'll rebuild it now

I never meant to break your heart,
Please, please, let me start,
To find a way, to make it right
Wildcat, I'll work so hard,
all day, every night

Until you believe it's just you and me,
Us forever
It's what's meant to be

I belted out the chorus, singing only to her.

I never meant to break your heart,
Please, please, let me start,
To find a way, to make it right
Wildcat, I'll work so hard,
all day, every night

As I sang, I swear I saw her body tremble, the armor around her heart cracking and crumbling as tears made her eyes glassy.

I'll never let you go this time, I swear
Promise you forever, forever there.

My work will never be done
Until our lives are lived as one.

Please, wildcat, I need you to see,
Please believe, it's just you and me,

Us forever
It's what's meant to be
Please, baby, just dazzle me.

Mila sobbed as I sang the last note. I stood, placed my guitar on the stand behind my stool, and went to her. Her body shook and tears poured down her face. I cupped her cheeks. "I'm sorry, Mila. I'm so damn sorry. I was selfish, inconsiderate, despicable..."

She swallowed once. "Shut up." Her voice was rough and gravelly, as if she'd spent too long not speaking.

"But, baby, I was wrong, so wrong. I should never have left you. I love you."

"I said, shut up."

My heart pounded so hard I couldn't hear anything else but the whooshing inside my head and her words. "Please..."

"Shut. Up. And. Kiss. Me," she spoke between hiccoughing sobs.

For a second, I was going to continue groveling, get on my knees and beg, but then her words resonated, and I watched a small smile slip across her beautiful lips.

"Are you deaf, curly?" She had more control over her voice then.

"But I...but you...I left and..."

She nodded. "Yes, you did. You fucked up huge, and I'm going to take every opportunity to throw it in your face. But not tonight. Not after you sang me that song. Not after you said you loved me and shared that with the entire room. Now, are you going to kiss me or what?" She tipped her head coyly.

I grinned, wrapped my hands around the sexiest woman alive, the woman by which I measured all others, and kissed her. I kissed her for every day I missed kissing her. I licked and nibbled and practically fucked her mouth in front of a room full of people, and I didn't care. The best part, Mila didn't either, because she was mine. All mine, and my girl wanted to stake her claim as much as I wanted to mark her as mine.

Our tongues tangled and danced until I ran a hand down the bare back of her dress and groaned. Her skin felt like silk as I let my fingers caress her spine from nape to the swell of her ass. She shivered in my hold and then pulled back.

"Jesus." Her low, sultry tone spoke of sex and sin. Two things I wanted to explore with her right then.

"Yeah, you could say I missed you." I swallowed, my throat feeling like it was coated in wool.

She chuckled and cupped my cheek. "I missed you more."

"Really?" I croaked, my voice still not working properly.

Mila swept the hair out of my eyes. "When you drove away, you took my heart with you," she said, shyly mimicking my exact feelings that night. "Simple as that. You had to come back because otherwise I wouldn't have made it."

I ran my thumb across her bottom lip. "Never again."

"You said that last time," she warned. "Don't make promises you can't keep. I can't live through it a third time."

I lifted her hands and kissed the tops and then proceeded to kiss each knuckle. "I can't give you anything more than my word. I know that's shit after what we've gone through, but I'm different. I've learned. After meeting my dad, dealing with my career, and taking ownership of this gallery, I realized that nothing in this world was going to make me a whole person, unless I had you to share it with."

"Atlas," she whispered, her voice shaky.

"I'm prepared to take the time to win you back, to do right

by you. Tonight, this..." I gestured with one hand around the room. "It's only my first attempt."

She smiled. "Pretty good one. How did you come to own the gallery anyway? Last month you were a struggling artist like me."

"Turns out the old man was good for something. He left me Second Chances Gallery. Aptly named, don't you think?"

That made her laugh. "I would say so."

"And Ingrid tells me that your paintings are selling like wildfire."

She grinned and looked around the room. People had left our little spectacle to mill around, partake of the food and drink, and enjoy the art. "Yeah, well, most of them are of you. Who wouldn't want a sexy specimen like yourself, naked, hanging on their wall?"

I chuckled and then pulled her back into my arms. "Are we going to be okay?" I asked, hope lacing every edge of my words.

Mila ran her hands down the lapels of my jacket. "I don't know. I'd like to think we are."

"I'm never going to stop trying to make things right."

She pressed her forehead to mine. "This was a pretty great way to bridge the gap, curly."

"I love you, Mila. So fucking much, and baby, I'm sorry. I promise never to abandon you again. Please forgive me. Love me again. Be with me again. Be an us. Whatever that looks like."

She scraped her fingernails over my scalp, and I shivered, my dick perking up and taking notice.

"Okay," she whispered so low I could barely hear her.

"Okay? That's it?" I confirmed.

"That's it. I love you, and I'm not just going to stop loving you because we had a falling out. A pretty big falling out, but that doesn't change that I don't want to live my life or create art in a world that you're not in. I'm not even sure I could anymore."

I kissed her forehead so softly. "Me either. I love you." I kissed her lips hard and fast. "I love you." Kiss to her right cheek. "I'll never stop loving you." Kiss to her left cheek.

"You better not. Now come on." She laced her fingers with mine. "I've got some new paintings to show you, and I want to hear all about Second Chances Gallery and your work with Knight & Day Productions."

I looped my free arm around my girl and kissed her temple as she led me over to one side of the gallery. "You've got it, wildcat."

"No, but I do have you." She smiled and grinned up at me.

"This is true. This is definitely true."

EPILOGUE

Six months later...

"Wait, wait, don't you dare change it!" I slapped Atlas's hand away from the radio dial in his new Alfa Romeo 4C Spider. Boys and their toys...yeesh.

He groaned and changed gears and sped forward toward Second Chances. "Not again. Please God, make it stop!"

I squinted at him and turned my song up. Way up. "Wildcat" was playing on the radio. Knight & Day Productions had let Atlas pick the talent that he wanted performing his songs. The twenty-two-year-old singing my song had added an entirely new level to it. His voice was far richer than his age in years, and during the time Atlas worked with him, the love of his young life had broken up with him. That gave the guy an extra depth to the lyrics, and it showed in his rendition.

"It's on all the time. I'm tired of it." Atlas flicked the turn signal and sped around the corner as if the car was on rails.

I braced my arm on the dash and held onto the "oh-shit bar" to keep my body from slamming into the console and then the door. "Do you have to drive the damn thing like you stole it?" I growled, righting myself and pushing down my dress that had ridden up.

He grinned and waggled his eyebrows. "Yes. This car is sex on wheels."

I snorted. "I'll remember that the next time you want to take a ride in me."

Atlas moved his hand from the gearshift to my thigh where he started pulling up my dress. "You know, we haven't christened her." His voice took on a seductive tone.

I shoved his hand away. "And we're never going to, because you're going to kill us before we ever even get the chance! Keep your eyes on the road, pervert, and not on my dress."

He pursed his lips and shifted into fourth gear. The car jumped forward as if it had been given a power boost.

"Really?" I quipped.

Atlas laughed. "Wildcat, you need to relax and enjoy the ride."

"I would if you didn't act like this thing was a race car and all of San Francisco was your racetrack," I protested as he whipped around another corner.

He slowed down as traffic got thicker the closer we got to downtown San Francisco where the gallery was located. "Babe, seriously, relax."

I cringed and turned up the radio, singing along with the platinum hit that had been written for me.

"Has anyone ever told you that you're tone-deaf?"

I opened my mouth, shut it, opened my mouth again, but

no words came. I kept trying to figure out a smooth, razor-sharp comeback but was failing miserably.

He looked at me, then at the road, and then back at me. "Hotness, no, I was totally kidding."

Preferring to ignore him, I crossed my arms over my chest, then crossed my legs too and looked out the window.

He placed his hand on top of my thigh. "Mila, really. I was playing around with you. Baby, your voice is fine. No, it's great. Really great. I would totally take you on as new talent," he lied.

I huffed, working my irritation into a good little snit internally.

By the time we parked in our reserved space at Second Chances, he'd locked the car so I couldn't jump out, and then he turned to me. "You know I was kidding, right?"

I shrugged, playing it up, because truly, feigning hurt was the only ammunition I had when he was dead right. I did have a shit voice.

He curled a hand around my nape. "I'm sorry, baby."

That was when I smiled huge. "You owe me two orgasms for that." I held up two fingers, and he grinned sexily.

"I'm happy to pay up." He slid his hand back to my leg until he reached between my thighs. I wasn't wearing underwear. He growled, and I closed my legs in a lockdown, not allowing him to get in.

"But not now. I have work to do in the gallery." I clicked the lock and freed myself from my seatbelt so fast he was still trying to figure out how we went from his hands up my dress to me bailing from the car.

I ran into the gallery, leaving him in the dust and feeling super proud of myself until his arms came around me from behind, and he pushed and walked me to the back office. The staff wouldn't arrive for another hour, so we had some time to fool around, not that I planned on letting him after his wild ride through the city and the catty comment about my singing.

"Let me go, curly!" I growled through clenched teeth.

He didn't listen. Instead he bodily lifted me up so my feet no longer touched the ground, and I was kicking forward.

"Nope, we need to make up."

"We don't make up! We have normal sex!" I reiterated a long-standing joke of ours.

He chuckled all the way to the desk in the office where he sat me. "I'm fucking you, and there's nothing you can do about it." He plastered my butt to the top of the desk and locked my legs around his waist.

"Is that right? You think you can just lift me up, using all your big man muscles on the poor defenseless little woman, and get your way? No way, nuh-uh... Oh yes, fuck..." I said when his thumb rolled around my sweet spot and two fingers slipped home.

"That's right, wildcat. You were saying?" He fingered me deep while he hooked those digits up and rubbed on that spot far inside that only he had ever reached. "I'm paying up on my two orgasms starting now." He ran his tongue down the column of my neck.

I braced both of my hands on the desk behind me, leaned back, and lifted up my skirt. I wanted to watch him fuck me with his fingers. He slid them in deep, and I moaned. When he removed his fingers, I whimpered at the sight of his thick fingers coated in my essence.

"Baby..." I sighed as he picked up the pace, fucking me deep with his fingers and then swirling his thumb around my clit.

My entire body shook as we both watched his fingers disappear in and out. Suddenly, it became too much. Tendrils of pleasure rippled up my chest and through my arms where I gripped the back of the desk lip to hang on. Shock waves zipped down my legs and curled my toes as I locked my ankles around his waist while the orgasm ricocheted through every ounce of my body.

I let my head fall back as I heard his jeans being undone, and then he was there, *right there*, in one slow thrust.

"Come here, baby," he spoke softly before sweetly lifting me in a full-body embrace.

Atlas thrust deep, and I buried my face against his neck and bit down, his musk and spicy scent imprinting on me the same way his heat warmed my soul. He took me from zero to a hundred in half a dozen well-placed thrusts, his cock long and thick inside, his pelvis crushing my clit with every jolt. I held him while he fucked me and did the best I could from my position to tip my hips, taking him as deeply as I could.

When Atlas made love to me, it was everything beautiful in life rolled into one moment. The pleasure acute, the way he desired and loved me, divine.

I held tightly to him when he pounded into me, reaching for that succulent height we both needed, the sweet release. Atlas lifted his head and took my mouth in a blazing hot kiss. Then he grabbed my ass with both hands and ground me onto his cock, stirring his hips perfectly. The thick root was so hard and took me so deep I cried out, but he never let my mouth go, delving his tongue in, breathing harshly through his nose as we both came together in a mountainous rush of heat, passion, and love.

"You okay?" Atlas asked when we were done. His hands

stroked up and down my arms, clavicle and neck, his normal after-sex petting. "Was that normal enough for you?"

I chuckled against his neck and kissed him there until my own breathing came back to normal. "Yeah, we should *not* have makeup sex more often," I agreed.

He laughed and pulled out, and then handed me a couple tissues from a box sitting on the desk. I took care of business and cleaned myself up in the connecting bathroom before coming out.

Atlas was leaning on the desk with his ankles crossed, holding a piece of paper in his hand.

I nodded toward the item. "What's that?"

He smiled so sweetly I wanted to jump him all over again. "This, baby, is me promising you forever." Atlas handed me the piece of paper, which turned out to be the deed to the gallery, but it no longer had just his name on it. It had both of our names.

"You're making me a co-owner of the gallery?"

He grinned and looped me around the waist, bringing our lower halves close. "I want you to be my partner in all things. Home, music, art, and love. Our us."

I bit down on my bottom lip and focused on the paper. "You know you could have just given me a ring, it's a lot cheaper, but a gallery works."

Atlas chuckled. "Would you have said yes if I offered a ring?"

I shrugged. "Probably not, but we'll never know because I just became a gallery owner." I roped my arms around his neck and brought our foreheads to within an inch of one another.

"You're a piece of work, you know that?"

I pushed back, laid the paperwork on the desk, and signed

my name in a flourish. "Yep, and now you have to work with me forever. Sucks to be you."

He grinned, brought me back into his arms, and kissed me. "You know, one day you're going to have to legally become mine."

I pretended to think about it. "Who says? Besides, maybe I'll be the one to make a grand gesture like giving you a gallery, or a ring, or something."

"How about a baby?"

My head flew back as if it weren't connected to my body, and I had no control over it. "What?" I choked out. "You want a baby?"

He nodded. "Yep, with you."

"But..."

He shook his head. "No butts. Me, you, a gallery, a wedding, then a baby."

"Atlas, you want to knock me up?" I squinted and focused on his eyes. They were shining with happiness.

"I believe that goes gallery, which you already signed on for, wedding, then baby. So how's about a wedding?"

"I hate weddings." And that was not a lie. I absolutely abhorred weddings. No one really wanted to go to a wedding and watch two other people smooch, sit through a boring ceremony with a bunch of whacked out traditions like tossing flowers and garters, stupid dances with fathers that aren't there and mothers that would demand to be involved but had no right. "I really hate weddings."

Atlas bit his lip to prevent his laughter. "So justice of the peace then?"

I nodded and bit my nail. "Yeah, that I could do."

"Can I get you a ring?"

"We could pick out some together."

"Deal."

We kissed for long minutes as if sealing our new plan to get married.

He pulled back. "So when are we getting married?"

"Isn't it obvious?"

Atlas blinked and his hair fell into his eyes.

"When you knock me up, of course." I winked.

That time he laughed, and he laughed hard. "You know, there's absolutely nothing normal about our relationship. We're kind of a strange couple."

"I know. Don't you love it!"

He nodded. "I love you," he countered and held me close, his hand coming up to curl around my cheek. "You dazzle me, Mila."

"You dazzle me too, Atlas. Now let's go back to the part where we fight and fuck."

THE END

Want more of the Lotus House clan?
Continue on with Monet Holland and Clayton Hart's story in:

Limitless Love
Book Four in the *Lotus House Series.*
Coming Soon

EXCERPT FROM *BODY*
THE TRINITY TRILOGY (BOOK #1)

Silk whispers across my forehead, against my temples, down the side of my face. I try to stretch and realize I can't. Something prevents me from moving. The blankets are pinned on either side of me. I can't move. I can't move! I gasp for breath and scream. My heartbeat speeds, and I start to panic and struggle.

"Shhh, baby, there you are. You're finally awake."

Chase's voice penetrates the layer of fear, calming me instantly. I breathe in and out a few times. The panic eases. For a scant moment, I was back there. Back to when I'd awaken tied to the bed against my will. The room is dark, though I can still see Chase's sly smile. He's in the same suit from this morning and distractingly handsome. I take a deep breath and exhale slowly. The rest of the anxiety trickles out the edges of my pores as I inhale his woodsy scent. His fingers slide along my temple and he cups my chin. He pets the apple of my cheek, which is probably still twice its normal size.

"What time is it?"

"It's six. I'm taking you out. Get up. Get dressed."

A sigh escapes. "I told you, I was tired. I'm not going out." I stick to my guns, though Chase's nearness sends all pretense of a defense crumbling into a pile of mush. When he's close, I just want to be with him. Alone, it's easy to pretend what's happening between us isn't real.

He brings his mouth down for a slow luxurious kiss. Mmm, this man can kiss. He slowly sweeps his mouth across my lips and nibbles on the plump lower one. I groan as he deepens the pleasurable assault. His tongue enters my mouth, sweeping along mine. He tastes so good. Like a perfectly ripe strawberry. I know he's using my lack of restraint when he's touching me to get what he wants. Sneaky bastard.

I twine my fingers through his thick dark hair, scraping his scalp lightly. He groans while sliding one hand against my chin to turn my head, delving deeper. He swipes his tongue languidly against mine, and I feel that tingling down low in my belly. God, I want this man. Just as I grip at his waist to pull his shirt out of his pants, he pulls away.

"Seriously?" Frustration seeps out in a snarl.

"Gillian, as much as I'd like to take you right now, you're in no state."

I roll my eyes in disbelief. He's the only man in the universe with a conscience.

"Believe me, I want to sink so far into you, you won't know what hit you, but it would be taking advantage." He stands and tucks his shirt back into his slacks. "I'm taking you to one of my restaurants this evening. I've had a dress sent over." He grabs a box that he must have brought in because it wasn't there when I went to sleep.

"How did you get in here?"

He shrugs. "My hotel."

"Do you ever take no for an answer?"

"Rarely," he admits. "Now slip this on."

He holds the box out, but away from the bed, so I have to get out of bed to retrieve it.

Two can play at this game. I smile coyly, and his eyebrows rise into sculpted triangles. He has no idea what he's in for. I pull back the covers and stand tall in a royal blue bra and thong matching set and nothing else. The cups of the bra are see-through, leaving nothing to the imagination. His mouth opens and closes on a gasp. He takes a deep breath, and those ocean eyes scan me from head to toe before zeroing in on my chest.

I grab the box from him and delight in the knowledge that the second I turn around, he's going to see bare ass with only a tiny wisp of lace above my tailbone and a string across each hip holding the garment in place. I turn and sashay toward the bathroom.

"God, woman! You're going to be the death of me!"

Continue reading in:

Body
The Trinity Trilogy: Book One
Available Now

ALSO BY AUDREY CARLAN

The Calendar Girl Series

January (Book 1)	July (Book 7)
February (Book 2)	August (Book 8)
March (Book 3)	September (Book 9)
April (Book 4)	October (Book 10)
May (Book 5)	November (Book 11)
June (Book 6)	December (Book 12)

The Calendar Girl Anthologies

Volume One (Jan-Mar)	Volume Three (Jul-Sep)
Volume Two (Apr-Jun)	Volume Four (Oct-Dec)

The Falling Series

Angel Falling

London Falling

Justice Falling

The Trinity Novels

Body (Book 1)

Mind (Book 2)

Soul (Book 3)

Life (Book 4 - *Coming February 28th, 2017*)

Fate (Book 5 - *Coming April 18th, 2017*)

The Lotus House Series

Resisting Roots (Book 1)

Sacred Serenity (Book 2)

Divine Desire (Book 3)

ACKNOWLEDGMENTS

To my husband **Eric**, I could dedicate every book to you, because I know you think every male hero I write is a variation of you and maybe there is a hint of truth to that. In my real life, you will always be my hero.

To my editor **Ekatarina Sayanova** with **Red Quill Editing, LLC**...is it too cliché to say you complete me? Eh, who cares, it's my acknowledgements, and without you and your ability to understand me and my characters so completely, my books wouldn't be what they are today. Also give your husband my gratitude for chipping in on the male thought processes. His contributions made all the difference. Overall, though, thank you for continuing to take this journey with me. It only seems to get better with each new novel.

Roxie Sofia, the joy you add to the editing process with Waterhouse is beyond fun. Thank you for making a point to learn my style and connect with my voice. It's not an easy thing to do, but I'm so very blessed to have been assigned to you. I look forward to working with you more in the future!

To my extraordinarily talented personal assistant **Heather White (aka PA Goddess)**, I thought of you a lot while writing this book. I think there's a little of you in both Mila and Atlas. I love you, honey.

Jeananna Goodall, Ginelle Blanch, Anita Shofner

Gotta thank my super awesome, fantabulous publisher, **Waterhouse Press**. Thank you for being the nontraditional traditional publisher!

To the Audrey Carlan Street Team of wicked hot Angels, together we change the world. One book at a time. BESOS-4-LIFE, lovely ladies.

ABOUT AUDREY CARLAN

Audrey Carlan is a #1 *New York Times, USA Today,* and *Wall Street Journal* bestselling author. She writes wicked hot love stories that are designed to give the reader a romantic experience that's sexy, sweet, and so hot your ereader might melt. Some of her works include the wildly successful Calendar Girl Serial, Falling Series, and the Trinity Trilogy.

She lives in the California Valley where she enjoys her two children and the love of her life. When she's not writing, you can find her teaching yoga, sipping wine with her "soul sisters" or with her nose stuck in a wicked hot romance novel.

Any and all feedback is greatly appreciated and feeds the soul. You can contact Audrey below:

E-mail: carlan.audrey@gmail.com
Facebook: facebook.com/AudreyCarlan
Website: www.audreycarlan.com

ALSO BY AUDREY CARLAN

The Calendar Girl Series

ALSO BY AUDREY CARLAN

The Trinity Trilogy

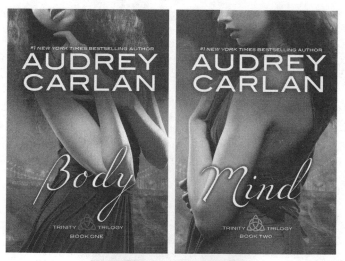

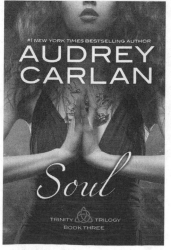

ALSO BY AUDREY CARLAN

The Falling Series

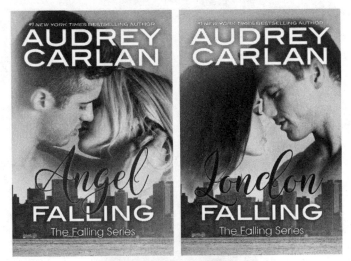

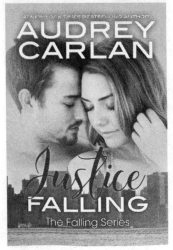